NO STRANGERS TO PAIN

No Strangers to Pain

Stories of Everyday Struggles and
People on Life's Margins

by

BONNIE E. CARLSON

Adelaide Books
New York / Lisbon
2020

NO STRANGERS TO PAIN
A collection of short stories
By Bonnie E. Carlson

Copyright © by Bonnie E. Carlson
Cover design © 2020 Adelaide Books

Published by Adelaide Books, New York / Lisbon
adelaidebooks.org

Editor-in-Chief
Stevan V. Nikolic

For any information, please address Adelaide Books
at info@adelaidebooks.org

or write to:

Adelaide Books
244 Fifth Ave. Suite D27
New York, NY, 10001

ISBN: 978-1-954351-25-7

Printed in the United States of America

Contents

Acknowledgments

Earlier versions of many of these stories were published in various literary magazines: "Children Untethered" (*Across the Margin*); "Avoiding Kevin" (*Déraciné*); "He's Come Undone" (*The Mark Literary Journal*); "No Good Deed," (*Evening Street Press*); "Not a Single Lie" (*Anti-Heroin Chic*); "Don't Talk to Strangers" (*The Normal School*); "Becoming Vice President" (*Flash Fiction Magazine*); "Too Good to Be True" and "Not Everyone Can Be Saved" (*Piker Press*); "Dog Gone" (*Mohave [He]art*); "No Stranger to Pain" (*The Mark Literary Review*); "Good Intentions" and "Tough As Nails" (*The Broadkill Review*); "Block Island" (Literary Orphans); "Looking for Solace Elsewhere" (*Crepe & Penn*); "No Choice" (*Down in the Dirt*); and "To Be Forgiven" (*Penman Review*).

Thanks to the editorial staff at these magazines for publishing my work.

Thanks as well to my husband David Duffee, critique group partners (Bob Dukelow, Judy Emerson, Stefanie Craig, Andrea Davis, JoLee Kennedy, Jan Hanson, Carolyn Weisbecker, Jim Weisbecker), and other readers who gave me feedback on these stories. And many thanks to Marylee Macdonald for her support and editorial assistance.

No Stranger to Pain

He needed to get away—away from people, from devices, from civilization. To start over in a new place where no one knew him, to develop a new persona. Joachin had spent some time researching Silverton, Colorado, convinced that for now, this old mining town was his best bet. He'd found the name of the hostel online and made a reservation. For a mere twenty-five bucks a night, a bed in the bunkhouse of the Blair Street Hostel could be yours, shared with up to six other guys.

He hoped he could outrun his past, not a very long or very bad past, but still, worth getting as far away from as possible. He yearned to be unencumbered by things of any kind. Possessions only got you into trouble after all, didn't they, even if you didn't have many? His one nod to civilization was an old iPhone 5 that still worked, sort of, as long as he changed the battery every year.

The timing was perfect. Early fall meant he could witness the leaves change into their autumn colors, something he'd only ever seen in photographs. No seasons to speak of or colorful foliage in Riverside, California, where he'd spent his whole life. Now, he longed for a glimpse of a craggy mountainside covered in bright-yellow aspens, with some evergreens thrown in for contrast. He yearned to escape civilization, to breathe crystal clear air, to fish in sparkling streams untouched by pollution, maybe see a beaver house firsthand. To gaze at cathedrals of towering, spiky fir trees and listen to the quaking of aspens—a faint rustling—all golden and occasionally flaming orange. Was that too much to ask?

So, Joachin hitchhiked from Riverside to tiny Silverton with Cleo, a sixteen-pound mongrel with long, silky fur, white and amber, the love of his life. Sure, Cleo was a bit of a frou-frou name, but she'd come to him with that name while still a puppy. He didn't have the heart to change it. After all, it was short for Cleopatra, an awesome, royal name.

On the night Joachin arrived in late September, having hitchhiked through Indian reservations with a long-distance trucker who picked him up on I40, he had to hike into town from the spot where the trucker dropped him off. The ride through Colorado had been a disappointment. The trees were not gorgeous and astonishing; this summer's drought had muted the colors. He saw plenty of faded chamisa though, its normally bright yellow flowers past prime and fluffy, the wind spreading its weightless seeds far and near.

Although Silverton had only a few streets, as soon as the trucker sped off Joachin pulled out a printed map he kept folded in his shirt pocket. In the fading light, he quickly located the hostel on Blair Street and dragged himself the few remaining blocks to a large, nondescript buff-colored building.

He walked up a single step into the hostel. The odor smacked him in the face: unwashed bodies, stale cooking smells, and piss. He smelled pretty rank himself after five days on the road with no showers. He glanced around the large lobby. To his left stood a wooden counter with a mirror behind it. A fake Tiffany lamp adorned its linoleum surface. Not a soul in sight. Next to the lamp a large bell waited to be rung.

He obliged, as he stared at his brown face in the mirror and tossed back his long, messy black hair. A young female voice yelled from the bowels of the house, "Hang on. Be right there."

While he waited, he inspected the premises. The lobby looked into what appeared to be a large parlor, with three faded old sofas pushed up against the walls. Two windows on one wall, both covered by dusty-looking drapery, looked out into the night. With few lamps, it was dark.

As he hefted a heavy pack off his back, a young woman approached him. "Howdy."

Joachin pulled Cleo out of his jacket and smiled. "Hi. I understand you allow pets."

The woman pushed her long brown hair back behind her ears. "We do, as long as you follow the rules. Who's this little cutie?"

"Cleo here won't cause any trouble. She keeps to herself and won't bark or anything. And she never does her business where she isn't supposed to." He put Cleo down on the floor. "I'm, uh . . . money's kinda tight, right now, so what's my best option?"

"Well, we have the bunkhouse—up to six guys—for twenty-five a night. And we've got three shared rooms with two to four people for thirty-five a night. Everyone shares a bathroom, and one shower a night is included with the price."

He sure could use that shower. Joachin weighed whether it was worth an extra ten bucks to spend the night with fewer guys.

"You know what? No one's in the bunkhouse now, so you could have it to yourself tonight for twenty-five bucks." Her sparkling amber eyes smiled. "We'll have to see about the next few nights."

"Sold." He pulled out his wallet and signed a form she thrust in front of him.

He paid in cash, and she took him upstairs and showed him the room. It looked clean enough. Smelled better than downstairs, like Pinesol. Triple-decker bunk beds. If it filled up, it'll be awful, he thought. But try not to get too far ahead of yourself, Joachin. Tonight, it's just you and Cleo.

He put his stuff down. "Can you recommend a cheap place for dinner?"

She suggested a hamburger place around the corner on Green Street called Golden Block Brewery. "Nothin' here's cheap, but they have excellent burgers and Mexican food. By the way, I'm Cassidy." She thrust her hand out.

"Thanks. Joachin." He shook her pale, soft hand. "Will my stuff be safe here?"

"It'll be fine. Be back by eleven."

He showered, donned clean jeans and a red plaid flannel shirt, and headed off for dinner, Cleo on her leash. Golden Block was dark inside. A long, curving wooden bar with a mirror behind it lined one wall, with booths on the other. A few beat up wooden tables and chairs littered the space in between. He sat at the bar even though he didn't drink, not that he was old enough. Seeing what drugs and alcohol had done to his mother, he decided to avoid that shit. Who knows what that crap might have done to his father, whoever the hell he was?

He perused the menu, noting the boast that the burgers were made with fresh, local —never frozen—Colorado beef. He nursed a lemonade and overheard two grizzled old guys drinking beers at the other end of the long bar.

"Know anybody who wants a dishwasher job?"

"Who's looking?"

"Whitey."

"Okay. Good boss. I'll ask around."

Joachin stared at his image in the mirror. I could do that, he thought. If it turns out I like this town well enough to stay. But first, dinner.

The bartender, an oldish guy who looked like he'd been around the block a few times, shuffled toward him. Craggy dark skin and an almost white ponytail down to his waist. "What'll you have, sonny?" When he talked his full gray beard danced.

Sonny? Had anyone ever called him that? He ordered a burger with green chili sauce and Monterey Jack cheese and sweet potato fries.

The bartender followed up with, "How about some guacamole and chips while you're waiting?"

Joachin nodded. A splurge.

"Looks like you could use it."

He hated it when strangers commented on how thin he was.

After he finished his dinner, as tasty as the hype on the menu, he walked back to the hostel. Carrying Cleo in his arms, he mounted the stairs to the bunkhouse and tossed his clothes onto an empty bunk. He fell into a deep, dreamless sleep, Cleo snoring softly at his side.

After a good night's rest and a shower, with Cleo on her leash, Joachin left Blair House the next morning to explore and find breakfast. The handful of streets formed a long, thin grid. Mountains surrounded the town. A railroad came up from the south, from Durango, bringing carloads of tourists.

By the end of his day of exploration, he liked the feel of Silverton and decided to stay for a while—if he could find a job. It was tiny all right, but somehow it felt right, with its tacky gift shops and coffee shops, and roaming, elderly tourists. No Starbucks, a good sign. Everyone knew Starbucks meant civilization.

In a little town like this, he guessed, the way you found out something was to ask around. The idea of being able to get to know everyone held appeal. Standing in the Blair House lobby, he rang the bell to find Cassidy. Maybe she could steer him toward a job.

She sent him back to Golden Block, where he'd eaten last night.

When he asked about the dishwashing job, the guy he talked to told him to take a seat in the last booth in the back. Someone would be with him shortly. Twenty minutes later the bartender from the other night came over and slid in.

Without introducing himself or asking Joachin's name he said, "So you think you want to live in Silverton for a while and wash dishes at my bar?"

Joachin stared at his tan, wrinkled face, feeling a flush rise to his ears. "I mean, yeah, I think so. My name's Joachin." He thrust his hand across the table toward the man.

The man ignored it. "You ever been around winter? Where ya from?"

"Well, we didn't really have winter in Southern Califor—"

"See, that's what I'm talkin' about. You got no idea what you're gettin' yourself into."

Unsure how to respond, Joachin squirmed in his seat. He honestly hadn't thought about winter, whether he could handle it or not. How bad could it get? As he considered how to respond, the guy thrust his hand across the table—finally— and said, "Howdy. Name's Whitey. This here's my place. What brings you to our tiny little town?"

This guy Whitey sure asked a lot of questions. Joachin hesitated. After all, he'd come to Silverton to escape his past not unload it onto a stranger. He cleared his throat. "Well, Whitey, I came to start over, to find something different from what I was used to in Southern California." He wasn't going to say more unless he had to.

Whitey fingered the end of his long, white-gray ponytail and looked up at Joachin. "How old are ya?"

Shit, he should have anticipated that. He was tempted to say he was already twenty-one, but what if Whitey asked to see his ID?

"Twenty-one next summer."

Whitey raised his eyebrows. "You look much young—"

"I get that a lot." Another thing he hated—how young everyone thought he looked. He went for his wallet in his back pocket. "I can show you my ID."

Whitey waved it away. "Don't bother. I believe you. What kind of jobs have you done before?"

Darn. He should have expected these questions. "Let's see," he said, buying time. "Um, I've had three or four jobs since I graduated from high school, like Dunkin Donuts and a hardware store—"

Whitey held his hand up in a stop motion. "Okay, here's the job. It's running the dishwasher, putting away the clean dishes, clearing and bussing tables, mopping floors. Whatever else around here the boss asks you to do. It's hard work for minimum wage."

"Benefits?"

Whitey threw back his head and roared. "You mean like retirement? You planning to retire in the next couple years?" he asked, still chuckling.

Joachin felt the hot blush spreading from his neck to his brow. When he got out of foster care, they told him to ask about benefits. Now he looked like an idiot.

"No," he stammered, "I meant, like, health insurance."

"You got some health problems I should know about?"

"No!" Joachin blurted out. "I'm healthy. I just . . . "

"Relax, kid."

Joachin felt anything but relaxed though. His mind raced as he tried to figure out how he could salvage this interview. The more elusive the job seemed, the more he wanted it.

He inhaled a big breath and let it out. Looked straight into Whitey's ice-blue eyes. "Listen, I think we got off on the wrong foot. I'm a healthy twenty-year-old who hasn't had too many jobs yet. I'm trying to make my way in the world, and I'm willing to work hard." The words rushed out. "That's me," he said, pointing to his chest, with pride. "That's who you'll get if you hire me." His voice shook and his face burned. "You won't regret it."

"Okay, kid, simmer down. The job's yours if you want it. When can you start?"

Joachin grinned and his dark eyes sparkled. "Tomorrow?"

Sure, it only paid minimum wage, but he'd get two meals on the days he worked, which made it a good deal. He couldn't afford to keep staying at the hostel though, even at only twenty-five bucks a night.

He started the next day at lunchtime and put in a full day. Golden Block bustled, so the day passed quickly, and he wasn't all lost up in his head like usual. He hoofed it back to the hostel at nine, where he'd paid for two more nights. Cassidy sat in the otherwise empty parlor.

"Hey. How are you? I got that job I was asking you about yesterday. With Whitey. Thanks for the heads up." He tipped his faded baseball cap.

"Oh sure, anytime. Glad it worked out."

"Well, I'm bushed. Heading to bed. See you tomorrow."

A couple of days later she came into the restaurant at six with her little girl in tow for dinner. Joachin noticed them as he hauled a heavy gray plastic bin of dirty dishes to the kitchen. Cassidy reached out and touched his arm. "Hi, Joachin."

"Hey, Cassidy. Hi. And who's this?" He grinned stupidly at the toddler and made a funny face, acting like clown.

"This is my two and a half-year-old, Zephyr. Say hi, Zeph."

The kid shook her head no and Joachin laughed. "Where's my respect, little one?"

"When are you off?" Cassidy asked. "Maybe we could get together."

Was she asking him out?

"Not off until ten tonight." He shifted the heavy bin of dishes to the other side, the glasses and china clinking together in the gray bin.

"Bummer. That's pretty late," Cassidy said. "I'm up early for my job with the little ones. How about the weekend, or your days off?"

"You have another job besides the hostel?"

"Yep. I work two jobs. I'm at Zephyr's day care during the day."

That surprised him. Both that she worked day and night and had a two-year-old. "Okay, so let me ask Whitey what my schedule's gonna be. I've only worked a few days so far, so I'm not sure."

That night after work, as he strolled back to the hostel, he couldn't stop thinking about Cassidy. What her long brown hair would feel like, how she would smell. How soft her skin would feel. He looked forward to seeing her at Blair Street when he got home. Her interest in him made him ridiculously happy. But when he walked through the front door the place was empty, and he didn't think he should ring the bell. His shoulders slumped as he mounted the stairs to his room.

Never having had a girlfriend, Joachin wasn't sure how to behave. He should have returned to her table before she left to tell her Whitey wasn't there tonight. He still didn't know about days off.

He asked around for a new place to live, in a rooming house maybe, if such a place existed. It only took two days to find an affordable room upstairs in somebody's attic. At six feet Joachin mostly couldn't stand up in there, and he'd have to use a mattress on the floor as his bed. He did have a comfortable chair though, where he could read. Only a shared bath and no kitchen facilities, but that was okay for now.

Two weeks later, Joachin took Cassidy on their first date, dinner at another restaurant, a little fancier than the brewery.

Cassidy looked up from the menu. "So, Joachin, how'd you end up in Silverton? You know we've only got less than seven hundred people living here?"

He grinned at her. "And it's at 9300 feet, which makes it one of highest towns in the country. I studied it before I came here." He paused to take a sip of his lemonade. "Have you lived here your whole life?" He loved her pale skin, those freckles and that upturned nose. Tonight, she wore eye makeup that accentuated her amber eyes.

"Nah, just a few years. Followed a boyfriend here. Good riddance to that asshole. That's how I got Zephyr."

He wasn't sure how to respond. Did she regret having Zephyr or was she happy about it? Must be hard to support a little kid on your own being so young. He wondered who babysat her tonight. "That sounds tough. I'm impressed with how hard you work."

Cassidy blushed. "You do what you need to do." She sipped her coffee. "You still didn't answer my question. What brought you here?"

Damn, he should have expected this. Of course, if he got a girlfriend—or any friend, probably—she was gonna want to know about you. Who you were, where you came from. He needed a minute to think, to decide how much he wanted to say.

"I hitchhiked here from Riverside—near Los Angeles—where I grew up. Big city. Lived there my whole life."

"Is your family still there?"

"I, uh, don't really have any family—"

"What do you mean? Everyone's got a family."

His face felt hot. This was a mistake. "Um, well, what I mean is . . . the family I had is kinda gone, I guess." The urge to bolt, to get out of there as fast as possible, slammed him.

"You know what, Joachin, it's none of my business. I didn't mean to pry. It's just that—"

"How 'bout you?" He'd never learned small talk and felt tongue-tied. What did people talk about on a first date? "Where'd you live before Silverton?"

She told him about growing up in a little town in New Mexico, the middle child in a big family she got lost in. "My dad was a drunk and beat my mom. I couldn't wait to get out of there. Left when I was seventeen." Her voice turned bitter. "Thought I'd be so much smarter than my stupid mom and ended up with a jerk that treated me just as bad as my dad."

The uncomfortable silence demanded to be filled. "I guess my background's not all that different. Well, it's different, but just as shitty, probably worse."

"Like, how?"

Were they going to play the game of who had the worst childhood? "Never met my dad. Spent most of my childhood in foster care, changing schools all the time 'cause Mom had some pretty bad mental issues. Plus, she was an addict—"

"Ooh, way worse. Sorry. No brothers or sisters?"

Did he really want to get into this? This ugly past he was trying to escape? He sighed. "How about if we save that for another time. Wanna take a little walk around town?"

They did walk and he took her hand. She seemed to be leading the way.

"Where are we going?"

"I thought we'd head back to my place. Visit a little longer there. I need to let the sitter go home."

"Sounds good." His heart raced with excitement. Was he finally going to get to kiss those full pink lips?

Cassidy lived in a dingy one-bedroom apartment above a coffeeshop. She handed a twenty to an older woman who said Zephyr was sound asleep and left. They sat on her lumpy brown sofa, the only place to sit. Would there be more small talk? He'd only ever had sex a few times, hookups with girls he didn't even much like. This felt different, more serious, more real.

Cassidy surprised him when she climbed on top of him straightaway, straddling her legs across his body. She weighed hardly anything. His lust awakened as he finally got to kiss her, which turned out to be as thrilling as he'd hoped. After a few minutes of smooching, Cassidy unbuttoned her blouse, revealing milky little braless breasts. He leaned in to kiss her nipples, and she led him into the bedroom where Zephyr snored softly in a tiny bed next to hers.

He wasn't prepared for this. "I . . . I . . . I didn't bring condoms or anything. You already have a kid and I don't—"

"Don't worry. I won't let you come inside me."

"Can we turn the lights off?" Discomfort made him squirmy as he realized she was more experienced than he was. Still, he loved every second of their lovemaking.

Afterwards, as they drank chamomile tea with honey, the urge arose to tell her about his past. In fact, he wanted to tell her everything, a surprising feeling he'd never had before.

Winter settled in with its snowfalls and frigid weather. The ground stayed white, which turned to brownish gray as the winter wore on. Whitey was right. It took some getting used to for a SoCal boy. His thing with Cassidy didn't unfold the way he'd hoped, not that he knew what to expect. They didn't see each other as often as he wanted to, which made him even crazier about her. He and Zephyr worshipped one another. And Zephyr adored little Cleo.

By the time they'd survived the holidays, Cassidy knew all about the past he'd run from. The father he searched for but never found. The little brother, Diego, who got sent to different foster homes because, as his social worker explained, "No one wants both a toddler and a teenager." He even told her about how he stopped trying to make friends, because losing them hurt too much.

In fifth grade, he'd had a best friend for three whole years, Connor. Until he had to move families again and change schools. Losing Connor tore his heart out. He'd vowed right then and there, no more friends. No more sharing of secrets. No more tales of the crazy mother he had, a troubled young Latina bouncing around the mental health system, in and out of the hospital. On her meds, Mom did okay. But she hated taking them and stopped. Street drugs eventually replaced prescription meds.

He told her about all of that, bared his soul. Dumped his secrets. It was all out there on the table. It left him as vulnerable as a newborn kitten and wanting to be with her every second.

In February, Zephyr's father returned—the "asshole" Cassidy had mentioned on their first date. And just like that, their relationship ended. No real explanation other than, "He's Zephyr's daddy. She deserves a father."

He knew all about not having a father. But still.

At the restaurant everyone figured out he'd been dumped. No secrets in tiny towns. He moped around wearing a glum expression and didn't eat.

One night, Whitey came up to him at the end of his shift. "Joachin, I'm worried about you. You okay?"

"I don't know. I guess." In the months he'd worked at the bar, Whitey had become the closest thing to a father he'd ever had. He couldn't look at Whitey when he was lying. Never was a good liar.

"What happened? You're not your old cheerful self." He reached out and lifted up Joachin's head, peering into his dark eyes. "Somethin's wrong. You wanna talk?'

Word around town was Whitey was a long-time recovered heroin addict. He ran a drug-free support group for locals and those passing through at one of Silverton's several churches. So, he knew a thing or two about messed-up guys. They sat down in a booth after the restaurant closed and Joachin told Whitey what had happened with Cassidy.

"I hate to tell you this, son, but I'm not surprised. Cassidy's a sweet young thing, cute as they get, but trouble. Not that it'll make it hurt any less, but you're better off without her."

Tears sprang to Joachin eyes. "She broke my heart."

"Yep, heartbreakin' is what she does best. But you'll survive. Listen, I have a suggestion. It's gonna sound weird but try to keep an open mind."

"Okay." Joachin was all ears.

Whitey told him about a Buddhist group that met every week to meditate or chant at the church where he held his support group. Joachin didn't even know what Buddhism was. Despite his skepticism, he started going. They were a ragtag group, men and women, mostly older than him. Some of them also attended the drug support group, no strangers to pain. A few of the older guys took him under their wing.

He'd heard of karma but never understood it before. It was odd to think of life as an endless cycle of suffering and rebirth. He got the suffering part, though.

The meditation was hard, and he fidgeted when he should be still. His monkey mind raced all the time, unbidden thoughts zooming around in his brain.

"Happens to everybody," a gray old codger observed. "What's important is your intention, so keep trying."

He did better with the group than he did on his own.

As spring approached with its longer and warmer days, purple and yellow crocuses poked through the ground and he began to meditate daily at home. It calmed him down some, so he could think about his future.

One sunny spring day, snow melting everywhere, daffodils blooming, he accepted a ride down to Durango. At the Durango Roasters, while ordering coffee, he overheard three people talking about their classes at a local community college. After he returned, he Googled it and found Pueblo Community College in Mancos, just south of Durango. Maybe it was time to get on with his life, to stop hiding. He thought about his high school grades, which had never been important before. Maybe this was his chance for rebirth, to start over, to move forward with his life. Wasn't that why he came to Silverton in the first place?

He spoke to an admissions counselor who suggested he might be eligible for admission. The prospect of college triggered all of his self-doubt. Unwelcome voices told him, You're not good enough for college. Not smart enough. Kids like you don't go to college.

But the guys in the meditation group encouraged him to apply. On the other hand, Whitey tried to talk him out if it. The contradiction confused him and left him feeling restless and unsettled.

Nevertheless, he got in and enrolled. In August, he made plans to move to Mancos with Cleo. He had no idea what he would study, where it would take him. He found a job at a diner waiting tables, a step up from dishwashing with the tips. He needed to find a place to live and a junker to drive.

In late August, he tried to say goodbye and thank Whitey. "Son, I think you're making a mistake," Whitey said. "There's nothing wrong with your life here."

Joachin teared up. He'd intended to hug Whitey but recoiled instead. Why couldn't Whitey be happy for him? His inner critic reared its Gorgon head. *Was* he making a mistake? His stomach did flip-flops. He wouldn't know unless he tried.

After he moved, he found out Whitey felt hurt and betrayed when Joachin decided to leave. He kind of understood that. But still, why couldn't Whitey be happy for him?

Pueblo Community College turned out to be more challenging than he anticipated. He wasn't sure what he wanted to study, so his advisor suggested he take a range of liberal arts courses to start. He found it hard to sit in classes, especially those he wasn't very interested in like biology and political science. He had trouble concentrating and felt out of practice. He had to really buckle down, work at studying, pay attention. He kept up with the meditation, which helped him focus.

He enjoyed waiting tables, and between school and work he made friends. So far, he hadn't dated anyone, cautious, not wanting a repeat of what happened with Cassidy. He couldn't afford that kind of hurt right now. This was his chance to reinvent himself.

One day, a month after school started, he got an assignment back in English class. They'd had to write a paper on some difficult aspect of their childhood. He'd chosen to write about his friendship with Connor and how hard it had been to lose his friend when he got moved to a new foster home. Writing it had been painful.

He started to sweat as the teacher began handing the papers back to each student. When she got to him, his hand trembled as he reached for the paper. Sure he'd gotten a poor grade, he felt his face get hot.

But she smiled at him. "Keep up the good work, Joachin." She'd given him a B+, and he beamed with pride. He couldn't ever remember feeling that good.

By the end of the semester he still didn't know what he wanted to do, but he'd done as well as he could. He pulled Cs in the classes he didn't like, which still felt like an accomplishment, and Bs in two others. The English teacher gave him an A-, which thrilled him.

Returning to school had been a good decision, despite what Whitey thought. In fact, leaving Long Beach for Silverton had been the right move. He'd learned so much during his brief time there, like, wherever you go, there you are. That life can be messy no matter where you are. That you can't please everyone, and you can't escape yourself. But you're not just your past. Or you don't have to be.

Avoiding Kevin

I couldn't stop obsessing about the argument I had with my older brother Kevin. I lay face down on the table. The moist, hot towels on my back and the heated table melted my insides, chilled by the snow that swirled outside, where the temperature hovered in the teens. New Age music floated from invisible speakers, the flute soothing in my ears. I inhaled deep breaths, hoping to release some of the tightness created by the detritus of my personal life.

"Is that eucalyptus, coming from the diffuser?" I asked.

"Mm-hmm." Sadie had worked on me for years. She knew every aching joint and strained muscle of my forty-year-old body. I tried to channel a woodsy California eucalyptus grove, leaves rustling in the breeze.

"Firm pressure, please."

She started as usual on my back, kneading with the palms of her hands and fingers, beginning down near my waist, working her way up toward my neck. Although her hands were magical, the trigger points were so bad she switched to using her elbows. It hurt.

"Try to relax, Vivienne. Your whole body is tense," Sadie observed.

Oftentimes at our appointments, she pointed out where I carried the tension, which I was barely aware of. But today I could feel the muscle tightness. Everywhere.

"Your elbows could be lethal weapons."

"I'll take that as a compliment."

I couldn't stop thinking about that bully Kevin. Our elderly parents now needed help, and he acted like a total pain in the ass, just like in our childhood. I hated dealing with him. It pissed me off, messed up my strategy of avoiding him.

Sadie worked on my neck now, a rat's nest of knots. It hurt like hell, all that kneading, despite the hot towels. I'd be sore tomorrow.

At the moment, my mind raced. I kept trying to shut down the obsessing, to focus instead on Sadie's hands. But I kept returning to what a jerk Kevin was to obstruct the plan the other five of us had put together. To help out our parents. He wouldn't contribute or even cooperate.

I focused on the soft piano in the background.

Sadie started on my lower body, lifting the blanket to expose my right leg. She began with my calves, as tight as guitar strings. I'd been working out at the gym and forced myself to walk outside despite the frigid temperatures. When Sadie got to my hamstrings, and especially my glutes, my whole body tensed up.

Sadie brought her face down near mine. "Vivi, what's going on? Are you okay?"

"I am." But I wasn't.

After she finished my legs, she told me to flip over so she could start on the front side. She pulled the blanket off, exposing my right leg. I worked at taking deep, cleansing breaths, still struggling to relax. After she finished my shins she started to work on my quads. As her hands moved close to the inside of my thighs I flinched, and she backed off.

"Vivienne, what's the matter?"

I couldn't talk. I'd gotten a sudden sensation of Kevin on top of me. In seventh grade, he started to sneak into my bedroom when my sisters were staying with friends. How had I forgotten this? I'd be sound asleep and would wake up with my nightgown scrunched up over my chest, Kevin humping me. When he left for college it mostly stopped. But still, when he came home, he did it a couple more times. Once, I threatened to tell my barely-keeping-it-together parents. He said, "Don't be ridiculous. I'm a jock and an A student. They'll never believe you."

I believed him. He only stopped when I left for college, when I moved away for good.

I rolled to my side and curled into a fetal position on the massage table as the memories crashed in on me. The shame the next morning. Getting drunk afterward when I was fourteen. Worrying I'd get pregnant. One time when I was sixteen and had a boyfriend, I asked my mother if I could go on the pill. I wasn't actually sleeping with Jack, but I worried about Kevin. I had this irrational fear that if I had sex with Jack, he'd magically know what Kevin was doing to me.

Mom scoffed. "Only sluts go on the pill, Vivienne."

"Vivi, can you tell me what's wrong?" Sadie brought me back to the table.

I whimpered softly.

She placed her hand on my back. "You're safe here."

Was I? Was I safe from myself?

"Do you want to talk?"

I shook my head.

"Shall I leave you alone for a few minutes?"

I whispered, "Thank you," and Sadie silently slipped out.

I lay on the table, inert, as the disturbing images flooded my brain. I felt actual, physical pain between my legs.

A soft knock. Sadie needed to use the room for another client. I unfurled myself, still feeling off-kilter, sat up slowly, and invited her back in.

"I'm okay now. A horrible memory. Anyhow, thanks for giving me the space."

"I'm glad you're all right."

Was I all right? As I dressed, I examined the space between my legs in the dim light. No evidence of damage despite the pain. Not there anyhow. Was it finally time to make an appointment with a therapist?

He's Come Undone

How much longer could he continue to brush his teeth at the kitchen sink to avoid the bathroom mirror? The prospect of facing himself after all these months filled him with a mixture of curiosity and dread. Mostly dread.

So, shirtless, in wrinkled pajama bottoms—his daily uniform—Brian spit out the toothpaste, rinsed, and brewed himself a third cup of coffee. Time to get the day started. As he lit the day's first cigarette, he glanced at the kitchen wall clock. Two p.m. He carried the mug and cig back downstairs to his man cave. Back before she got sick, his mother finished off the basement space for him after he moved back in—never mind that it violated the homeowner's association rules. As he padded downstairs, the ghost of his mother haunted him as he thought about how much she'd hate the cigarette stench of the house.

Being homeless had sucked when you had a dog and none of the shelters would allow pets. He wouldn't go any-where without Max though. Eventually, as she had in the past, his mother relented and let him move home. It took a lot of coaxing to convince her to let Max stay, that the pint-sized mixed breed wouldn't bother her cat. Little did she know how soon she would come to depend on her son.

He couldn't get rid of that nagging voice in his head. Brian, you need to get your shit together. Get a job. He kinda wanted to work, but not really. What he really wanted was money. As soon as he got his inheritance he wouldn't have to work. At least for a while.

A year and a half had passed since he'd gotten laid off from that lab job. He didn't see that one coming, and he didn't deserve it. The job paid well and had good benefits. Not having health insurance at fifty-four was a pain in the ass. Thank God he'd already moved in with Mom.

He studied the angry red rash covering his forearm and shook his head. He'd had that sucker since before his mother passed and couldn't get rid of it. Based on his EMT training, he suspected it came from changing her colostomy bag, despite how careful he'd been with the latex gloves. He needed to see a dermatologist, or at least go to one of those urgent care places but didn't have the cash.

He sat at the desk in his bedroom and opened the computer, curious to see what had happened since he'd logged off at 4 a.m. and passed out. A bunch of new emails had arrived, so he scanned through those first. Mostly junk he deleted immediately. Except for the one from Daphne. He considered deleting that one, too, but he'd been dodging her phone calls and texts for days. Or was it weeks? Hard to tell, the way the days just ran together. So, at the last second, he decided to open it.

Brian,

You can't keep avoiding my phone calls. We need to talk.

~Daphne

Short and sweet.

His mother had made his older cousin Daphne executor of her estate, because Mom hadn't trusted Brian or his sister

Linda to deal with money or anything else. It didn't surprise him, but he still felt betrayed. After all the caregiving he'd provided for the last couple of years of her life he deserved better. He'd even turned down a promotion for a job out of state to stay in Connecticut and care for her. On the other hand, what a pleasant surprise to discover Mom had left the condo to him, even though he had to split the cash assets with Linda. Like that messed up bitch even deserved a penny.

So now he had three choices. Two sucked: calling Daphne, which was bound to be unpleasant, or going out to look for a job, which would require a cleaning up. When had he last showered and shaved?

He'd probably opt for the third choice, logging back into Fortnite to play his favorite online game. Man, was it addictive. No contest, right? That way he could make contact with Cheryl, assuming she was playing. Of course, he considered Cheryl his girlfriend. His mother had thought it was outrageous he called her that, just because she lived in Washington state and Brian had never met her in person. So what? They talked all the time, and he'd eventually meet her. Once that cash came through and could fly out there.

His cell phone rang. He wondered how much longer his carrier would continue to provide service with him being so far behind on the bill. He glanced at the screen. Shit.

"Hi, Daphne—"

She wasted no time starting to hassle him. If she was going to be like that, he needed a beer, so he trotted upstairs, grabbed one from the fridge, and lit another cigarette.

"I *wasn't* deliberately avoiding you. I haven't been feeling well." Sort of true. He listened to her blab on about how he needed to stop neglecting his health. Yak, yak, yak.

"You know I don't have any money for a doctor."

Then things turned nasty. Her being in California had given him some breathing room, but she'd finally figured out he was still using his mother's ATM card and password. He'd been using it at the Mobil station, not for gas—shit, his mother's car wasn't even registered, and his driver's license had expired—but for beer and cigarettes and sundries. Like cortisone cream for his rash.

Toward the end of the conversation he asked Daphne, "When do you think I'll get my half of the cash?"

That's when she exploded and told him he already had more than his half.

"Wait, what?" She'd given him nothing.

She explained, not at all patiently, sounding annoyed, that she'd been paying a bunch of his household expenses out of his half of the assets.

"Like what?" He assumed the condo was paid for, although his mother was so secretive and uptight about her assets it was hard to tell what she had.

Like the real estate taxes, the monthly homeowner's fee, and utilities, Daphne told him. She went on to say she'd also been paying off the home-equity loan.

"But wait. Mom took that out to pay for Linda's car. Linda was supposed to be paying her back." Like that would ever happen. Something else his mother had refused to talk to him about. "That should come out of her half."

Daphne reminded him his mother had used that loan to pay for remodeling in the condo as well, specifically the finished basement where he lived.

Shit, he'd forgotten about that.

In the end, she went on, it didn't matter what his mother used it for. It was connected to the house, and therefore his responsibility. That's what the lawyer said.

This whole estate business frustrated him so much he wanted to punch something. The lawyer told Daphne the condo was his as soon as his mother died since she'd left it to him in the will. But he couldn't sell it for some legal reasons she couldn't be bothered to explain. Probate or something. He was about to ask her when the condo would be available to do with as he wished when she told him he should forget any ideas he might've had that he could continue to live there. He couldn't afford the monthly expenses, which totaled almost three grand. Even if he had a job.

What? But wasn't the condo paid for? Just as he was about to ask her to clarify what she meant, she abruptly hung up on him. God, she'd turned into such a bitch. Her parting words to him echoed in his ears: "You need to get off your ass and find a job." He assumed there would be enough cash from his mother's assets that he wouldn't have to work, at least for a while. Now he wasn't sure of anything.

He grabbed a second beer. Too bad there wasn't any whiskey around, or weed. His guts were convulsing, and he desperately needed to get high, to get the racing thoughts to stop. But he'd given up the weed a couple of months ago when it was clear he couldn't afford it anymore. The hard stuff, too.

The phone call had rattled him so badly he decided to take a shower, bite the bullet, and go look for a job. Time to take a look at himself in the mirror before he left the house, but he'd put that off as long as possible. After he showered, he wrapped the towel around his expanding waist—he had trouble getting it to stay there—and caught the first glimpse of himself in the fogged-over mirror.

He wiped off the condensation and studied his image. He expected it would be bad, but he actually flinched when he saw his face. Had he had a haircut since he buried Mom? Maybe not. His formerly brown hair now hung in gray-streaked, shaggy clumps, almost long enough to pull back into a po-nytail. Red blotches from broken capillaries covered his ashen face. He leaned in for a closer look at his eyes. A network of minuscule red veins formed a map on his eyeballs, the part that was supposed to be white instead pale yellow. His ugly, oversized nose was covered in blackheads. He shuddered. How had he let himself get this bad?

He should have been prepared for Mom's death. After all, he'd taken care of her for months while she suffered from the end stages of colon cancer. But six months ago, Daphne had lectured him to let her go.

"Jesus, Brian. Do you want your last conversation with her to be an argument because she won't drink her Ensure? She's ready. That's what she's telling you."

Easy for her to say from three thousand miles away. He was the one who stood by her side as she wasted away in the hospital bed in their living room. But somehow it still caught him off-guard. Now that he no longer needed to take her for doctor visits and cajole her to drink liquids and change her colostomy bag, his life lacked purpose. He didn't know what to do with himself and could hardly remember his life before she got sick.

Every day he wandered into Mom's bedroom and plopped down in her favorite chair. He knew he should convert it to his bedroom, to come up from the basement, but he couldn't bring himself to do it. He'd managed to get rid of her clothes though. Linda had begged him for Mom's clothes, but he donated them to a charity instead. Fuck her. But he hung onto Mom's favorite bathrobe. Sometimes he needed to inhale the lingering scent of the old-lady perfume she always wore, Chanel No. 5. Linda wanted the perfume, too. No way.

He plodded back downstairs to get dressed. He had to root around in a pile of clothes on the floor to find a semi-clean pair of jeans. They were so tight he could barely zip them under his growing gut. He donned a turquoise polo shirt he found hanging in the closet. It stunk of cigarettes. While he got dressed, he pondered a job-hunting strategy. Why not try the Starbucks in town? He loved coffee, and they always seemed to be looking for people. Plus, he'd heard it was a good place to work, with generous benefits.

So that was the plan. He left and locked the front door. High in the Norway maple trees around the condo the noisy *ch-ch-ch, ch-ch-ch* of dozens of cicadas almost drowned out the shrill voice of his old-bag neighbor.

"Brian. Haven't seen you in ages. How's it going?"

"Fine, Mrs. Ferretti, how are you?" Probably a mistake to ask. She could be gabby.

"I'm good, Brian. Sure miss your mother though. What've you been up to?"

God, was she nosey. None of your freakin' business. He couldn't afford to get sidetracked into talking to the old biddy. It was almost five. "Can't talk, Mrs. Ferretti. Got an appointment."

He hustled to the garage. By the time he started the car, microdots of sweat had bloomed on his upper lip and on the back of his neck under his still damp hair. It had been so long since he'd been outside during the day, he'd forgotten how hot and muggy southern Connecticut was in August.

As he left the complex his eyes darted left and right, looking for cops. Satisfied he was in the clear, he picked up his speed to thirty. These little shoreline towns had low speed limits. Catching people for speeding padded their puny town budgets. His mind shifted to how he would handle the interview at Starbucks. Sure, he hadn't worked in a couple of years, but explaining he'd been caring his sick mother should count for something, shouldn't it?

He made a left onto Main Street, soon reaching the tiny downtown, if you could call it that. People did. Boutiques, a coffee shop, a couple of restaurants, a barber shop, a hair salon, and a bookstore. Not a single big box or chain store. Well, except Starbucks, and the local residents had fought like ferrets to keep that out, worried about the effect on the independently owned coffee shop just steps away. Next came the CVS, beside the Starbucks, but not without another fight. Now, the sole independently owned pharmacy struggled to survive, practically empty most days. Starbucks and CVS were so busy you could hardly find a parking space. His mother had moved all her prescriptions to CVS because they were cheaper.

"I can't afford to waste money," she announced, always the frugal senior. Cheapskate was more like it.

He made a right turn into the CVS-Starbucks parking lot and caught a quick glimpse of the red flashing light in his rear-view mirror. Shit. Shit. Shit. He had to drive around to the back to find a place to park.

The cop blocked him into the spot, and in the seconds it took to turn off his car and roll down the window, the officer stood right there. Panic rose in his chest and he took a few deep breaths to calm his pounding heart. Sweat drenched his jittery, over-caffeinated body and dripped down his face. Fat lotta good that shower did. Wiping his brow, as calmly as he could, he said, "Officer, what's the problem?"

In these wealthy shoreline towns on Long Island Sound the cops had no real crime to deal with, other than the occasional break-in and teenage vandalism, so they were relentless about driving infractions. Probably something minor, Brian thought, peering up at the cop.

"Well, for starters you failed to signal when you turned in here, and then there's the broken taillight."

Whew, so nothing serious. He prayed he'd get off with a warning.

Italian-looking and fit, with black hair slicked straight back and a tan, handsome face, Officer Falcone—according to the name tag on his navy-blue shirt—said, "License and registration please."

Fuck. Now he was screwed. And probably had beer breath. At least it was almost five o'clock.

"How about if you step out of the car," continued the young officer. As if it were a suggestion.

He fished out the expired registration from the glove box, but what about his expired driver's license—was it still in his wallet? Now, sweating like someone who had something to hide, he pulled out his wallet and found the license. He got out of the car, stood next to it, and breathed a sigh of relief.

The cop took his license and registration back to his car to check things on the computer.

"Can I get back into the car and sit?" Brian yelled to the cop.

"Sure, be my guest," Officer Falcone said, like they were old buddies.

Brian's mind scrolled through the possible consequences. He sure wasn't going to get off with a warning on this one. The *ch-ch-ch* of those damned mating cicadas in the background drove him nuts. His heart beat like a hummingbird's wings, a zillion times a minute. His blood pressure must be soaring. When he tried to inhale a deep breath, he started coughing and couldn't stop. He needed to stop smoking. Well, now he'd have to, with Daphne cutting him off. While he waited, agitated, he squirmed in his seat and his mind raced, worrying about what might happen. Could they arrest him on the spot? Seize the car? The minutes plodded by. What was taking so long?

By the time the cop returned to his car, Brian was ready to jump out of his skin.

"Well, Mr. O'Connor, I'm afraid you're in some trouble here. You've got an expired license *and* registration."

Like that was news. His head dropped, and he started to hyperventilate. He was most definitely screwed.

Officer Falcone continued. "I'm afraid I'm going to have to—"

Brian's head jerked up, a pleading look in his eyes. "Please, Officer, don't arrest me," he begged. "Here's what happened." He started to sob.

The cop stood there, a shocked expression on his face. No doubt he'd probably faced weepy female drivers before, but a crying middle-aged man?

Brian got hold of himself enough to talk. "See, I've been taking care of my mother after she got cancer. Living with her. I had to give up my job to take care of her." Not true, but close, and the cop wouldn't know he was lying anyhow. "Then six months ago she—" he started to sob all over again.

The cop waited by Brian's open window, not saying anything. Several people walked by, staring, on their way into the CVS. The red lights still flashed on top of the cruiser.

"After she died, I . . . everything kind of fell apart, I guess you'd say." Brian choked back another sob. "That's why I didn't get around to . . . Maybe I'm depressed. I'm not sure. All I know is, I can't seem to get my shit together." Absolutely true. He took a deep breath and paused.

Officer Falcone waited.

"Actually, the reason I was driving here today is to apply for a job at Starbucks"—he looked up and noticed the CVS sign—"and CVS."

The cop stood there. Finally, he said, "Okay, Mr. O'Connor, here's what we're going to do. I'm going to let you off with a warning today, even though you've got three problems—ignoring your failure to signal your right turn. But you've *got* to promise me you're going to get your license and registration renewed and get your taillight fixed."

Brian nodded like one of those bobble-head dolls. "Thank you, thank you so much, Officer Falcone. I promise I will."

"You'd better, because the next time you're stopped you'll be in serious trouble."

Brian nodded solemnly. Right, except the car title wasn't his, and he didn't know what needed to happen to get it in his name. And to get his license renewed he had to pay off hundreds of dollars in traffic fines. Money he didn't have. And who knows what it would cost to fix the damned taillight?

As the cop backed away Brian used his now damp polo shirt to wipe more sweat from his face. On the one hand, he'd dodged a bullet, but on the other . . . What a fucking mess. He'd torched everything and couldn't seem to get off his ass to take care of business. He'd vowed he wasn't talking to Daphne again—especially after that last phone call. That he wouldn't ask—beg—for money, but now he'd be forced to call her and grovel, humiliate himself. Maybe it would be better to text her, or email. That way he could explain without her interrupting. Might be time to sell that used telescope he loved so much. No more stargazing at 2 a.m., but it should net a few hundred bucks on eBay. Put off the inevitable by a couple of months.

He thought about how he'd ended up here, in this parking lot. Even if he got a job, he wouldn't get paid right away. So, what was the point of going into Starbucks or CVS? Plus, that wouldn't solve the problem of the car not being in his name. He sighed. He needed a beer.

He backed out of the space, left the parking lot, and drove the speed limit home where Max would be waiting for his dinner. Maybe he'd go to bed early tonight, try again tomorrow to look for work. Or maybe not.

No Good Deed

When my Aunt Maggie received a terminal colon cancer diagnosis, I flew to Hartford from Southern California, the last time I would see her alive. I rented a car at the airport and drove an hour south to the little shoreline town where she lived. My mother had lived there, too, before she died, and I'd grown to love that little seaside town. The closer I got, the more I squirmed in my seat. I sure didn't miss the piles of crusty, dirty snow dotting the landscape even in March.

I arrived after dark, at dinnertime, pooped from my long day of traveling across three time zones. My cousin Brian, who also lived there and took care of Maggie, answered the door.

"Hey, Daphne. Come on in."

As we hugged, I could feel he'd put on weight and from the shaggy look of him hadn't had a haircut in months. The big dark circles below his eyes hinted at his exhaustion.

"Let me grab your bag for you." He returned from the rental car toting my Rollaboard.

I worried about how Maggie would look. A tiny, round woman with permed, short white hair, she didn't get up to greet me and looked like a large pale frog ensconced in her favorite comfy armchair. She wore a fluffy pink chenille bathrobe that had been my mother's. I leaned over and hugged her, kissing her pallid cheek.

"Back to the wintry Northeast from sunny California?" she asked.

When I didn't reply, she whispered, "Thanks for coming."

Brian, in a ratty sweatshirt and faded, baggy jeans, said, "We saved you some dinner. Want me to warm it up?"

"That would be great."

While he warmed my dinner in the microwave, I asked Maggie how she was feeling.

"About as crappy as you'd expect. My stomach is upset all the time. The COPD was bad enough."

It hurt me to watch her labored breathing. I loved this woman so much. "The cold weather doesn't help, does it?"

She took off her glasses and wiped them with a cloth, struggling to catch her breath. "I hate our winters. Only leave the house if I have to."

Brian brought me a plate of leftover meatloaf, mashed potatoes, and overcooked broccoli. Comfort food. "I'm going down to my room, Mom, so you guys can visit."

As I prepared to ask Maggie if he'd been taking good care of her, she said, "Is he gone yet?"

I got up and looked toward the basement stairs. "Yep."

I sat back down and ate a mouthful of Brian's tasty meatloaf.

"He's a total pain in the ass."

I raised my eyebrows. "What do you mean?"

"Can't do anything right," she huffed. "We fight all the time. All he does is hole up down in his room with his computer. Probably looking at porn."

Brian had moved into her finished basement three or four years ago after a period of unemployment and homelessness, living out of his car. On previous visits, I'd witnessed his helpfulness—cleaning, cooking, driving her to doctor's appointments. She couldn't have stayed in her condo had it not been for his help. The way he had risen to the occasion, despite always having been a major screwup, had moved me. He'd dropped out of high school and got a GED in the Army. In and out of relationships with dysfunctional women who bore his children out of wedlock. Children he never saw, supported by his garnished wages.

"I'm sorry you feel that way, Maggie." I finished my dinner. "Listen, I'm exhausted and need to turn in. We can talk more tomorrow. I think we should talk about your will."

I'd been obsessing about her will. When she'd originally drawn it up, she used a generic, small-town lawyer she met at the local senior center who offered a "bargain plan." The most important part of that plan was me agreeing to serve as the executor of Aunt Maggie's estate. She didn't think either of her children—my cousins—was up to the task. I'd offered to do it after my mother died. As Mom's health deteriorated, I saw Maggie at every visit and got to know her in a whole new way. We talked about books and movies and other things my mother and I didn't share. I adored her. She'd been very good to Mom in her last years, and very helpful to me when I was settling Mom's estate from California and selling her house. After I'd lost Mom, we'd stayed close despite the physical distance.

The next morning, the smell of bacon and eggs seduced me out of the guestroom. Brian stood in a tattered gray bathrobe at the stove, waiting for English muffins to pop in the toaster. Maggie sat in her chair in the living room, reading the paper.

"Mom, breakfast is ready."

Maggie heaved up her chunky body and trudged the twenty or so steps into the dining room, steadying herself by grabbing onto whatever she could along the way. She plopped down with a sigh.

"Brian, this is a treat, having someone make breakfast for me," I said. "I never eat bacon. Looks yummy. Thanks."

He nodded, his mouth full of scrambled eggs.

"What's the plan for the day?" I asked Maggie, sipping my orange juice.

"Somehow"—she looked at Brian—"Linda's gotten wind of your visit and will be here after lunch." She pushed food around on her plate, rarely actually putting any of it in her mouth.

Linda, my other cousin, Brian's sister, was even more dysfunctional than Brian. "Okay, what about the rest of the time? Are there things you want help with?"

As Brian stood to clean up the breakfast dishes after we ate, Maggie leaned over and whispered to me, "I want to go back to see the lawyer about the will."

I nodded, wondering what prompted that. In the original will, Maggie's assets were to be divided fifty-fifty between Brian and Linda. But that was before Brian lost his most recent job and started taking care of Maggie full time.

After Brian retreated downstairs to his room, Maggie and I settled into her sunny living room with a second cup of coffee. "So, what about the will?"

"I made an appointment to meet the lawyer this morning at eleven."

I raised my eyebrows, surprised at her announcement. Unsure how to broach the subject of the will and being executor, I said, "Listen, I've been thinking. Since Brian's been so helpful the past few years, if you wanted to make him executor, I would totally understand."

"Absolutely not! No way. For one thing, he and Linda can't get along. And I don't trust him." She fiddled with the pencil she was using to complete a crossword puzzle. "Are you saying you'd rather not do it?"

"Not at all." I put my hand on her arm to reassure her. "I'm still willing if you want me to."

Maggie looked at me. "There's something else."

I waited, listening to the wind howl outside, knowing how hard this was.

"I want to split it differently."

"What do you mean?"

"As pissed off as Brian makes me, I think he should get more than that no-good Linda."

"Okay, so . . ."

"I'm going to leave him the condo and have the two of them split the rest fifty-fifty."

Not what I would have done, but it wasn't my money.

I drove her to the lawyer's office. We left an hour later with a revised will. Easier than I expected, since they had an electronic copy on file. He asked a few questions, printed three new copies—one for Maggie, one for me, and one for the office—and we were out the door.

None of us considered the issues we should have, and if he'd been a half-decent estate attorney, instead of a small-town general lawyer, a lot of trouble down the line could have been avoided.

So, now, Brian would get Maggie's condo and its contents, and her remaining assets would be divided evenly between Linda and Brian. I had no idea what those assets consisted of. From those funds, each would get ten grand a year until the cash was gone. I had the discretion to allocate more to either of them from their half.

I drove Maggie home and made lunch. Tuna sandwiches, our favorite, with potato chips and peanut butter cookies for dessert. No sign of Brian.

I was curious about the circumstances of Brian's children. I didn't even know their ages or genders. "Have you ever gotten together with Brian's children?" I knew having grandchildren out there she never saw must be upsetting.

"I'd rather not talk about it." Head down, not looking at me, huffing. All high and mighty but also bruised, hurt.

So, I left it alone as we finished our lunch. Later, we moved into the living room to await Linda's arrival. Maggie pretended to watch TV. "At least he pays child support."

I waited for her to continue.

"Not that he has any choice." Her face was twisted. "The court takes it out of his wages when he's working. And now his unemployment. I still make him pay rent."

When I looked up, her eyes glistened. The only time I'd ever seen her cry was when my mother died. When they were kids, my strict grandmother had punished both Mom and Maggie for crying. Weeping was reserved for the weak. They'd all had it pretty tough.

Linda showed up by herself at two that afternoon. She'd put on a lot of weight since I'd last seen her, wearing a voluminous long black fleece top over elastic-waist jeans. Her mousy gray-brown hair hung in strings around her pale, acne-ridden face. She plunked down next to her mother on the worn blue sofa.

After the obligatory hug, I asked, "Where are Ashley and James?"

"Didn't Mom tell you? The State took Ashley away from me last year. She lives in a group home now. Doin' pretty good."

I wondered what had happened—finally—to warrant her removal and willed myself not to ask. "What about James?"

"Moved in with his jerk-ass father when he dropped out of high school. I don't give it more than a few months. Billy wants him to get a job. We both know that's not gonna happen."

Oh boy.

Brian came upstairs and gave Linda a frosty hello. Dressed now, wearing slippers, he took a seat in the black rocking chair, across from Linda and Maggie. "Mom, are you gonna ask her about the loan?"

I knew he was referring to the car loan, or rather home equity loan, Maggie had taken out, the only way Linda could afford a car.

Before Maggie could say anything, Linda said, "I paid you back for, like, a year and a half, Ma."

Maggie looked over at her and heaved a big sigh. "The last check I got from you was at least a year ago. I could really use that money now. I've got lots of medical expenses Medicare doesn't—"

"Oh, I know," said Linda. "As soon as I'm working, I'll start paying again."

Yet another surprise—Linda had lost her job, again.

"Well, I gotta pay the bank whether you're working or not," Maggie said.

I looked over at my chunky cousin's blank face. No response.

My aunt had never shared the details of her finances. Both she and my mother were downright secretive about money. I didn't know how much my mother had until I talked to her banker a week after she died. Maggie was no more forthcoming, even though we had agreed I would serve as executor. She fretted about money all the time, fearful of running out before she died. It came from growing up dirt poor during the Depression, their father having deserted them. Maggie had so much anxiety though, it was hard to evaluate how well-founded her financial worries were.

Brian shook his head in disgust and lumbered back downstairs. An uncomfortable silence hung between the three of us. Maggie turned on the TV, and we watched some daytime talk show I'd never heard of. How could Linda stand it, treating her mother like this?

Both Linda and Brian, adopted shortly after birth, had been difficult their whole adult lives, making one bad choice after another, always in crisis or on the verge. But, of the two, Linda had been more problematic, probably because of her two children who had, until recently, lived with her. Maggie had been bailing both of them out for as long as I could remember. For the past four years though, Brian had been living with and taking care of Maggie, despite her reluctance to acknowledge her need for help.

Finally, Linda got up and said she had to leave. "I'm glad I got to see you, Daphne. I miss you so much. Love you."

I always hated this awkward moment at the end of calls or visits with Linda. Should I say "love you" back and be a total hypocrite? Did I love this cousin who'd caused my beloved aunt so much pain?

I hugged her goodbye. "Love you, too," I mumbled. "Drive safely."

After Linda left, I wanted to better understand why Maggie seemed so disappointed in Brian. "I know you've said you and Brian fight all the time, but it seems like he's doing a pretty good job of taking care of you."

"Well, he should be," she said, her voice laced with bitterness. "Since he got laid off, I've given him a break on rent. He's supposed to be looking for work."

Not really an answer to my question. Was that her grudging acknowledgment that he took good care of her? And who would take care of her if he started working again?

Before he'd been laid off—again—he'd turned down a promotion that would have required him to move out of state, making him unavailable to care for Maggie. At the time, I'd told him I was grateful. Even before her cancer diagnosis, the COPD limited what Maggie could do. She couldn't drive anymore or walk farther than the mailbox. Despite her unwillingness to recognize it, she depended on Brian.

It filled her with resentment.

A month after I returned to California, Maggie entered the hospital for two weeks. She came home briefly, against medical advice, only to be re-hospitalized. Brian and I talked every day. I held her health-care proxy. He had a very tough few weeks before she finally let go.

I took a week off work and flew back for the funeral. I needed every second of that week to get the mess of Maggie's finances in order. A stack of mail over a foot high sat on the dining room table, including scores of unpaid bills. It looked like months had passed since any bills had been paid—ironic because Maggie had been so conscientious about paying her bills on time. On my previous visit, after we'd visited Maggie's attorney, I'd suggested adding my name to her bank accounts. Thank goodness. After presenting her death certificate to the bank, I took out the checkbook. As I got to work on that pile of bills, I learned just how expensive it was to live in her condo.

I scheduled an appointment with her lawyer to find out about getting the condo into Brian's name.

"When does the condo belong to Brian?" I asked. We sat in the lawyer's small, sparsely furnished office on a tree-lined street.

"Right now, since she left it directly to him in the will." A bald, harried looking, middle-aged man, he kept glancing at his computer screen.

"And how about the other assets, the cash and investments?"

"Well, that stuff will all have to go through probate."

"And how long will that take?"

"Not too long—six or eight months maybe."

I groaned. "But Brian can sell the condo right away?" I assumed he'd want to do that quickly, since he had no means to pay its expenses.

He shook his head. "The deed has to be transferred first. And it'll have to go to court for that to happen."

I frowned. What was he supposed to do in the meantime?

Over the next months, I came to see exactly how onerous my executor responsibilities would be. I spent hours trying to figure out Maggie's investments and annuities and how to get them converted into cash. And at the same time, I had to pay all Brian's condo expenses, constantly fending off requests from both cousins for money.

About four months into it, something happened I hadn't expected: Brian disintegrated. He'd been so functional as Maggie's health deteriorated, had taken such good care of her, I didn't see it coming. Once his reason for living was gone, he lapsed into a major depression, unable to function. He should have been job hunting, but between his grief and having a roof over his head, he just vegged, did nothing but smoke cigarettes and drink beer. I tried to prop him up without success.

It took months to figure this out from California.

A year and a half later, the estate finally got resolved, in the sense that the money got distributed, and Brian sold the condo. By the time he got his act together to sell it, its value had plummeted with the vagaries of the real estate market. As soon as he sold the condo, he went off the grid, disappeared, incommunicado.

By then, I was beyond ready to wash my hands of the whole estate business.

A week after the third anniversary of Maggie's death, I sat at home in Redondo Beach working on my laptop one afternoon. As a cool breeze wafted in from the Pacific, I heard the intercom from the lobby buzz. I wasn't expecting anyone.

"Yes?"

"Hi, it's Brian. I'm downstairs in your lobby." His voice sounded labored, raspy.

Brian? Are you kidding me? He'd responded to none of my calls, texts, or emails for a year and a half. How had he found out where I lived?

My heart took off. Hands shaking, I buzzed him in. My mind raced. What should I do? A while back, despite how badly Brian had treated her after Maggie's death and despite my admonishments, Linda let Brian move in with her for "a few days." He had blown through all the money he got from the sale of Maggie's condo. She had to call the police two months later to put an end to his freeloading and verbal abuse.

Once the estate got settled, Linda had been grateful for all I had done. But Brian had never once thanked me for the help I gave him after Maggie's death. It took me way too long to figure out that a lifetime of Maggie's well-intentioned enabling had caused their dysfunction. Bailing them out over and over hadn't done either of them a bit of good.

Any moment I would hear the *thud thud thud thud* of his feet on the stairs. A sense of panic rose in my throat. I stood at the front door, hand on the knob, trying to compose myself, buying time. I could hear him on the other side, huffing and puffing, struggling to breathe. I opened the door before he knocked.

He stood with his head bowed forward, forehead against the door frame, an enormous pack on his back, taking huge, heaving breaths. Finally, he looked up with a startled expression.

My mouth dropped open. His long hair hung in lank, greasy hunks. His face was sallow, and his eyes bloodshot, the lids red and crusty. He'd gotten way too thin. I counted three healing scabs on his face and more on his hands. He wore tattered khakis, a disintegrating red plaid shirt, and scuffed hiking boots. The tangy smells of days-old human sweat and cigarettes cloaked his body and plodded into the room with him.

I so didn't want him here, in my sanctuary, but could I actually close the door in his face given what he looked like?

"Take that heavy pack off." I watched the agonizing process of Brian, almost skeletal, removing the pack, looking as though every bone in his body hurt. Shit, was I going to get stuck with him?

"How did you get here?"

"Hitchhiked."

From Connecticut? "Are you okay? Because you don't look so good."

"Not really." He shifted from foot to foot and made some conspicuous stretching movements. "I have terminal cancer."

Oh, Jesus. Could that be true? Poor guy. "What kind?"

"I'm not sure. No money to see a doctor."

How did he know it was cancer? He certainly looked like shit, but a lot of things could cause that, like drinking way too much. Although it made me feel guilty, a big part of me didn't believe him. Both he and Linda lied even when there was nothing to be gained by stretching the truth. Why didn't he say what kind of cancer? This was part of the little dance he and Aunt Maggie used to do. Was he telling the truth? Or manipulating me?

"Here's the thing, Brian. I'm not really set up here for visitors, much less someone with a terminal illness. I don't have a guest room or even pullout couch."

"That's okay, Daphne, I can just sleep on the floor."

Then, in a brilliant flash, I remembered Brian's service to his country. "No, we can't have someone who's terminally ill sleeping on the floor. What we're gonna do instead is head right down to the VA Medical Center. Grab your knapsack." The most compassionate thing I could do. I looked at my watch. "We'll have to hurry to get there before five."

"But I don't have any ID—"

"I'm sure they're fully equipped to help with that, with so many homeless vets and everything." I grabbed my purse and car keys. "They'll be able to get you all fixed up."

"Daphne, I'd rather—"

"I'm in no position to help you, Brian. You need a lot of help. The VA will know what to do."

I suspected it would be days before the mammoth VA bureaucracy could verify Brian's status and figure out a plan for his care. But they weren't going to put him out on the street. No way I could handle him staying with me. If he had cancer, they'd know how to deal with it.

Finally, I had found a way to honor Maggie's memory. One of my father's favorite sayings echoed in my head. "No good deed shall go unpunished."

Not a Single Lie

"What was your life like growing up, Jemma?"

We were lying in my bed, having just fucked our brains out. My first hookup in like, forever. After what that last guy tried to pull, I needed to take a break. But here's the thing: I absolutely did not want to get into my so-called childhood. This was the part about sex I hated, the jagged intimacy of pillow talk. Apparently, I was supposed to feel all warm and fuzzy. But instead I felt . . . twitchy.

As I stared at the ceiling in the dark, Josh rolled to his side and gently placed his arm across my chest. His bent leg crossed my lower body.

Trapped, I tried not to squirm. "You go first." After I heard about his childhood, I'd decide whether I wanted to get into it at all. I could always make something up. Hardly anyone knew about my childhood, and I doubted I wanted to add him to that brief list. You only had to tell someone so many times and have them freak out before you learned to keep your mouth shut.

He leaned over and kissed my neck. "Not much to say, Jemma. Really kind of boring."

I wondered what a boring childhood would be like and glanced at the clock—eleven-twenty—then at the window.

The mouse-colored light of the streetlamps illuminated the heavy falling snow. "Tell me anyway," I said, buying time. "I still want to know."

"Can we turn the light on for a sec?"

"I'd rather not." My policy was hookups did not get to see my body in the light. The tats were one thing, but the scars? Not gonna happen. I wasn't prepared for that level of closeness. "You were about to tell about your—"

"Oh, yeah. Right. Well, I grew up in Denver. Jewish family, middle child. I've got an older brother and younger sister. Very normal. Very boring. My dad was a prosecutor."

Shit, the kind of guy that put Jamie away. Granted, Jamie did need to be put away after that second . . . incident. A twinge of guilt zinged through me. When had I last made contact with my younger brother, rotting away in a prison cell outside of Vegas? No way I could visit, but would it kill me to call?

"And my mom stayed home. Until I was sixteen, when she said she'd had enough of dad's being gone all the time."

Jemma jerked back into the conversation. "Meaning what?"

"Dad worked constantly. Even at home he was always on his phone with work. So, like, never available."

At least he had a dad. And a mom—who stayed at home. He'd hit the lottery. "What happened after that?" I was dying to get out from under him. Before my body imploded.

"They got divorced. On weekends my sister and I would go stay with Dad. I think we spent more time with him after the divorce than before."

Although I'd vowed to look for guys who were more normal, this guy sounded *too* normal. Give me a weed-dealing biker any day. Or maybe I should just stick with women. But they wanted to know even *more* about you than this guy did.

"Okay, now it's your turn."

Shit. "I need to pee first." Time for some mental excavation.

He removed his arm and leg and set me free. I slipped into the bathroom, perplexed about what to do. I didn't want anything more than what I'd just had with this guy, but he seemed to actually like me. And I would bump into him at work. I needed to end things so it wasn't awkward with him. I studied my face in the mirror, bleached spikes sticking out all over my head, smudged mascara. When would I learn not to hook up with people I worked with?

I climbed back into bed and sat up with my back against the headboard. I couldn't deal with Josh being all over me again.

"Okay, Jemma. Dish. Your childhood."

God, this guy didn't give up. Good thing I had my storyline all worked out. I'd tell the truth as much as possible. "Well, you know, my childhood was quite different from yours—"

"Like, how?" He lay there like a little puppy, looking up at me, all snuggly and gooey-eyed, tousled black curls.

"For one thing, I went to a lot of different schools." Gross understatement. Four in seventh grade alone, the year they carted Mom away. Okay, Jemma, wait for it. Here it comes.

Josh furrowed his brow. "Why?"

"We moved around a lot." Another understatement. Fourteen foster homes. People—foster parents, social workers, family court judges—kept labeling me "a handful." Of course, I was a handful! I hated myself. And my mother. And the whole friggin' world.

Jemma, figure out how to shut this down.

I took a deep breath. "But the important thing is, I was great at math. Math was my . . . refuge. So, I got a lot of

59

positive attention from teachers, no matter where I lived." I considered what to say next. If I didn't say something quick, Josh would hammer me with more questions.

"That's how I got to go to college even though my family was broke." Understatement number three.

"Good for you." Josh beamed a smile so bright we didn't need any lights on.

"Yeah, MIT gave me a full ride, which was, like, beyond my wildest dreams. Computer science. That's how I got into coding."

Girls Who Code. That was me.

"So that's how you got hired at Innovative Software."

"And met you." I got up and grabbed a robe. "It's getting late, and I gotta be up early tomorrow. In light of the storm, how 'bout I call you a Lyft?"

"Sure." He flicked the light on.

I was so proud of myself. Not a single lie.

The Relentless Roar of the Surf

I don't know what possessed me to go to Hawaii by myself. It didn't even make sense, given how lonely I felt.

But, desperate to get away, I made arrangements to stay at a high-end resort, an escape from winter gray and ice storms and husbands having affairs with younger women at work. What Andrew did was such a cliché it would be funny—except I still loved the bastard. It made me furious with myself for not figuring out the affair until his lawyer contacted me. No more relationships for you Larisa, I vowed. Men could be such turds.

I left Boston with a connection through LAX and arrived exhausted, having gotten up at 4 a.m. on a bitter cold, dark March morning. When we touched down in Maui's Kahului airport, six hours behind the East Coast, darkness had already descended. I picked up the shiny red convertible Mustang at Hertz and headed for the hotel, getting lost a couple of times before I even got out of the airport. Why couldn't Siri seem to get it right? I cursed not having someone—anyone—as my copilot.

An hour later I checked in at the hotel on the western coast of Maui between Lahaina and Kaanapali, found my room, and crawled into bed, savoring the comfort of the bed and the high thread-count sheets. I didn't even unpack, and immediately fell into a dreamless sleep. I awoke at four-thirty to darkness, my body thinking it was eleven-thirty at night. I tossed and turned for a half hour, finally dragging myself out of bed, desperate for coffee. I walked around the hotel, but nothing was open yet. Returning to my room, I found coffee back in my own kitchen and brewed a cup while I unpacked.

Brand new, the hotel had opened a few weeks earlier and had decadent accommodations. Weirdly though, the luxurious amenities I should have enjoyed, like a full kitchen and jetted tub, made me feel even more lonely. Somehow that big, beautiful bed made me feel horny. It felt too big, too extravagant, too romantic, for a person alone. How could I still miss that rotten philanderer?

After the sun rose, I went outside to see what Maui looked like. A cerulean sky, with a few white, cottony clouds floating by. Four sparkling pools outfitted with waterfalls, palm trees, and hot tubs, deserted at this hour. I strolled down to the beach, crossed a walking path, and listened to the soothing sound of waves crashing. The water's aquamarine color didn't even seem real. I relaxed into the breeze and started back to my room, delighted to find the hotel's Starbucks open. A second cup of coffee accompanied me back to the beach. I plopped down on the sand and closed my eyes, feeling the breeze caress the tiny hairs on my pale arms, listening to the surf crash, inhaling the tangy salt air. Maybe this wasn't such a bad idea after all . . .

I contemplated how to spend my first day. Complete freedom: I had no one else to please or negotiate with, so I could do whatever I wanted. Except I didn't know yet what the options were. Unlike the carefully planned trips Connor and I usually took, I hadn't put much thought into this one. I just knew, coming out of the lawyer's office, I had to get out of Dodge ASAP or I'd descend into an all-engulfing depression.

Back in the room, I threw on shorts, a T-shirt, and my running shoes to go for a run on the walking path. By six-thirty, plenty of others had the same idea. Lots of wild, colorful chickens, an aggressive rooster, and several cats cavorted around the path. The cats were feral, but still friendly, even affectionate, making me miss my own two kitties back home. I ran for half an hour, came back and showered, and ate breakfast at the hotel cafe on the beach. Other than being ridiculously overpriced—the cost of paradise—more than satisfactory. A trip to the concierge desk enlightened me on a host of fun things to do, ranging from snorkeling to hiking to helicopter rides. I wouldn't have trouble staying busy.

For my first day, I concluded relaxation should be my main goal, along with working on my tan. I was pasty white, so plenty of sunscreen and a big straw hat were in order. By then, the pool had gotten busy with older couples and young parents with children, so I headed down to the beach.

Time for a swim. I entered the water and not ten feet in, the shore dramatically dropped off. It was already way over my head. Very different from East Coast beaches, not only up north, where I'd spent most of my time, but also Florida and the Carolinas, where you could sometimes walk out half a mile and still be in water the temperature of a warm bath and only up to your chest.

I floated on my back, hands behind my head, eyes closed, soaking in the sun. It felt like I was more buoyant in the Pacific than the Atlantic. Could that be true? When I emerged from the water, I discovered I'd floated way down the beach, far from the spot where I'd entered the water. Must be a huge undertow, or "undertoad," as my kid sister and I called it when we were little. I must've been seven before I realized no monstrous frog lurked under the water to drag little kids beneath the surface.

I found a quiet lounge chair under a shady palapa and read until I fell asleep to the soothing sound of the wind rustling and slapping the palm fronds. The smell of grilled hamburgers woke me up. Not hungry for lunch after my big breakfast, I could hear my sporty little convertible Mustang begging me for a spin. Time to explore this end of the island. The concierge had mentioned a short hike nearby that led to an interesting blowhole among some lava rocks to the north. I got back into my running clothes and set off.

Calling the scenery spectacular didn't remotely capture it. Jaw dropping was more like it. The narrow, hilly road was empty, all hairpin curves, my favorite kind of road to drive. Lush, dense vegetation enveloped one side of the road in varying shades of green, while jagged, dark volcanic coast guarded the other. Sun glinted off the waves. Cars filled the periodic pull-offs that must access secret beaches known only to insiders.

The next day, dying to bodysurf, I went in search of big waves. But it had to be a beach with a lifeguard. On a previous trip to Mexico, I'd had a terrifying experience. I'd gotten caught in a riptide on my hotel's unguarded beach and almost drowned.

"Hi, good morning," I said to the concierge, a heavyset, dark-skinned Hawaiian woman in a voluminous, multicolored tropical-print dress. I told her what I wanted. She pulled out a map and pointed to a beach not far away.

"Fleming State Park. They've got lifeguards and a pretty good-sized parking lot."

I gathered my gear and drove to D. T. Fleming State Park, the parking lot almost full already. I locked my valuables in the trunk and headed to the beach, pleased to see a freshwater shower to wash off the sand and salt water. Signs warned about strong currents, undertow, and riptides.

I crested the ridge of the beach, gobsmacked by my first look at the water. So many different shades of blue! Were there reefs under there? And big waves, huge, foamy, powerful ones, created a deafening roar. The beach itself was not very deep, or wide for that matter. And almost empty. Where were all the people whose cars were in the lot? No matter, a deserted beach was like heaven for somebody from my neck of the woods where "beach" was synonymous with crowds. I grabbed my towel, regretting I hadn't rented a beach chair at the hotel, and strolled toward the water. There was a distinct ridge—a three-foot drop-off—where the waves ended, so it must be high tide. I put my gear down near the top of the ridge, in hopes of being able to keep an eye on it from the water.

I took off for the ocean. The water was the perfect temperature: refreshing, but warm enough to play around in for a while before getting chilly. Ideal conditions to bodysurf. The big waves would give a nice long ride if you caught them right, but not so huge you got mashed around to the point of losing your bathing suit or scraping yourself up on the sand. And no dangerous rocks in sight.

I regarded myself as a serious beach person, and body-surfing was one of my all-time favorite beach activities. My sister and I spent our summers in Connecticut along Long Island Sound, which rarely had big waves. One time when we were little my parents took us swimming in the pouring rain during an August hurricane because of the huge waves. We felt so badass.

I adored the exhilaration of catching a wave perfectly, as it crested, and riding it all the way in. Letting go of your body, completely relaxing, not fighting it when you got caught up as it crashed. Just going with it, feeling a million exploding bubbles caressing your skin, washing up on the shore. I did that over and over until I was beat and finally dragged myself out, huffing and puffing back to my gear.

Up on the shore, I dried off and spread my towel. Nearby, a man sat reading in a striped beach chair while his boys, about nine and seven, played in the waves with boogie boards. I'd never tried one of those, but they sure looked fun. Donning my straw hat and sunglasses, I read for a while. It was so windy the blowing sand stung my skin. Time for more bodysurfing.

The tide was going out, but the waves were still fantastic. I watched the boys for a bit and started to bodysurf again. After a few minutes, as I trudged through the waves to get back out to where they crested, I heard a yell. I looked up to my left and saw one of the boys, sans boogie board, out quite far. Was he yelling for his father to look at him? Yelling to his brother? Or was he in trouble? I looked back at shore. His father was doing something with the other boy, not paying attention, maybe not hearing him. I looked out again at the young boy and his head kept going under. Not good.

I gave a quick glance toward the lifeguard station to see if they had spotted him, but I couldn't tell. They certainly weren't on their way. Although it had been a long time since I'd taken a lifesaving course, I had saved a couple of kids from drowning in the past, one in a calm lake and one on the shore at Cape Cod. But not recently and never in big surf like this.

I glanced again at the dad, but he still hadn't noticed the boy. Why wasn't he paying attention?

Damn, I was going after him!

So, I plunged ahead, swimming like my life was on the line, through the crashing waves. I dove under the big ones to avoid being propelled back toward shore. It took longer than I expected to get out to him. I wasn't sure what I was going to do when I reached him. As I got close, he looked to be in bad shape, thrashing. His head was under water more often than it was above, his eyes full of panic when he surfaced.

"Hang on," I yelled. "I'm here to help." I tried to touch bottom and didn't get anywhere near it. Way over my head. He went under again. Huge swells buffeted both of us, up and down like some kind of wild carnival ride.

"Grab my arm!"

His arm flailed toward me, but he sank under again. When I got right on top of him, he freaked, both arms floundering. I tried to grab him. We both went under. I gasped for air and struggled hard to stay on top of the water. Where were the damn lifeguards?

"Stop fighting me," I yelled. I finally grabbed his hand. Had the surf gotten rougher? I fought to remember my decades-old lifesaving instructions. Yeah, that's right, grab him diagonally across his chest. Thank God he was a kid. But could I get back to shore with one arm across his chest and only using my left arm to swim, keeping both of our heads above water? In this surf? Only if he stopped struggling and trusted me.

"Listen," I yelled. "I need you to stop struggling. I'm gonna put my arm across your chest and swim us into shore. My name's Larisa. What's your name?" I grabbed his tan body with both hands around his waist and held his head above the water, using my running-strong legs to scissor-kick us up. He gulped huge breaths, his chest heaving, his long brown hair plastered over his face as I treaded water.

I don't know why I asked him his name, but it seemed to do the trick.

"Zach," he said.

Poor kid was exhausted. He still resisted, fear disfiguring his face, reminding me how terrified I'd been that time in Mexico.

"Zach, try to relax. I'm gonna put my arm across your chest and swim us in," I said again.

"Okay," he gasped, swallowing water, then coughing.

I could feel his body loosen, but it was harder than I envisioned. He was slippery. I grabbed hold of him, kind of doing a side stroke, and started back toward the shore, fighting the strong current. We must be caught in a riptide that was dragging us out. I couldn't remember what type of kick I was supposed to use, scissor or flutter. Scissor seemed better. But we weren't making much progress toward shore, only being able to use one arm. My muscles already felt fatigued.

Panicked, I looked up toward the shore. Shit, it looked like we had drifted further out! At least Zach's dad had finally figured out what was going on and was running toward the lifeguard station. The guards were already on it, getting into some kind of rescue boat I had noticed on the way in. Would they to get to us in time?

Then it dawned on me—all I had to do now was keep us both afloat! Real help was on the way. "Zach, we're going to be okay. Look, the lifeguards are on the way."

He looked up and I could feel his body slacken. "Please don't let me go," he pleaded.

"No way. I won't let go no matter what. Just hang on a bit longer. We're gonna be okay. I promise." Did I believe that?

Pummeled by the waves, we watched that orange plastic Skidoo-type thing launch into the water. Soon, two tan, buff-looking guys zoomed toward us. They came up alongside and grabbed Zach first, hoisting him up into the thing. After they got him inside, they helped me in.

So winded I couldn't even talk, chest heaving, I lay on the floor, knees bent, sucking in air. Finally, I said, "It's a good thing you guys finally noticed, 'cause we never would have made it into shore. Damn, these currents are strong!"

Zach started to whimper. I considered putting my arm around him but decided against it.

"You got that right. You guys got caught in a riptide. You his mom?" asked the one with the long blond hair.

"No, I spotted him out there and saw he was in trouble. I thought I could rescue him, and I kinda did, but I don't think I'm strong enough to have gotten us back in. This is Zach."

The other lifeguard, who had dark, cocoa brown skin and looked Asian, said, "Zach, are you okay?"

Zach's voice shook. "Yeah, I guess so. That was so scary."

The blond guard nodded. "You bet. Riptides can be very dangerous. You're lucky this lady saw you and got to you faster than we could." He turned to me. "We didn't realize until we saw you swimming out to him that he was in trouble. You did a great job out there. As good as anyone could do by themselves. Are you okay?"

"Just winded. I haven't had to swim like that in a l-o-o-ng time. And the lifesaving training I had was years ago. Gonna be sore tomorrow."

When we reached the shore, Zach's dad and brother were waiting and a small crowd had gathered. After we got out of the rescue boat, Zach ran to his dad, who hugged him. I suspected he might feel embarrassed at this point. Why hadn't the father been keeping tabs on Zach?

As Zach and his brother grabbed their towels, his father came over to me.

He thrust his hand out. "Hi, I'm Gavin Hunter. I can't tell you how grateful I am. I'm embarrassed I didn't see Zach

was in trouble." His words rushed out. "My other son, Luke
. . . The wind had blown sand in his eyes, and I was trying to
help him get it out."

His hand shook when I took it. Tears glistened in his eyes.
"I don't know why it took the lifeguards so long to figure out
you guys were in trouble."

Gavin appeared to be in his mid-forties. Looked like he
worked out, tan, like his boys. He must have been here a few
days already or lived in some warm place where the sun shone
all year.

He continued to hold my hand with both of his.

"Hi, I'm Larisa Sanderson. Yeah, I don't know why either.
It took me awhile to figure out Zach was in trouble, too. At
first, I thought he was yelling because he was playing. But he
was awfully far out. When I finally realized he needed help, I
just took off—"

"Thank God. You saved Zach's life."

"Actually, the lifeguards get credit for that. Took me a
while to figure out we were caught in a riptide."

My lungs still burned. An awkward moment passed, neither of us knowing what else to say. Finally, I said, "Well, I'll
let you get back to Zach."

I lay down on my belly to recover, feeling the warmth
and roughness of my towel. I must have fallen asleep. I heard
a voice in the distance, but then it was right beside me. When
I looked up, Zach sat on the sand next to my head.

"Hi, Larisa. My dad sent me over to say thank you. What
you did was so brave. I got out too far. And the waves kept
pulling me out farther."

I got up and sat cross-legged on my towel, the sun so
bright I could barely see him. I held my hand up to shield my
eyes and grabbed my straw hat. "You know, that happened to

me once, but there was no lifeguard. I was so scared! I absolutely know what that feels like. I'm not sure how brave it was, but I'm relieved we both made it back in okay."

Brave or foolish? Brave, in the sense I went charging through the waves to save him. Foolish, in the sense I should have realized the odds against me making it back in with that kid, on my own. I should have gotten the lifeguards right away. I finally remembered that fundamental lifesaving principle: only enter the water as a last resort.

Zach left. Several minutes later, his father returned. "I just wanted to thank you again. You're a real hero."

I noticed Gavin's eyes, soft and light blue, with long dark lashes. When he first introduced himself, he wore aviator sunglasses, so I couldn't see them. I couldn't tell much about his hair, because he wore a big straw hat that covered his whole head.

Embarrassed, I started to laugh.

"No, seriously. You were courageous to go out after my son. I should have been paying closer attention. I didn't realize how dangerous the currents here could be. I talked to the lifeguards afterwards, and apparently, they rescue people here all the time. Anyhow, I'd like to invite you to dinner to thank you properly. I assume you're here with someone?"

"Actually, no." My faced reddened. "I came by myself. Kind of a crazy thing to do, I guess."

"No, not at all. I'm here by myself, too. Well, not *totally* by myself, 'cause I'm with my sons. So, can I persuade you to join us for dinner?"

Was this a weird thing or a nice thing? I felt unsure how to respond.

He seemed to sense my hesitation. "Don't feel obligated or anything. I just wanted to do something nice to express our gratitude."

Now I felt stupid for hesitating. "Of course, I'd love to join you for dinner. Just tell me where and when."

"We're at the Aston Kaanapali Shores hotel. I could come by and pick you up, say, around six-thirty? Where're you staying?"

I gave him the name of my hotel.

"Is tonight convenient?"

"Sure, tonight would be fine. See you out front."

Hmm, I thought. What this would be like?

Back at the hotel I took a leisurely soak in the jetted bathtub. Afterwards I read outside on my balcony, listening to the relentless roar of the surf. Being unfamiliar with the restaurant, I wasn't sure how to dress. I had the impression nothing was very dressy here, so I decided on white skinny jeans and a bright pink linen shirt.

Gavin and the boys arrived right on time. As I approached the white Infinity SUV, Luke got out of the front seat and moved to the back with Zach. This was unlike any situation I'd ever experienced before. Dinner with a stranger and his two sons, one of whose lives I just saved. My stomach felt a little unsettled.

Gavin got out and opened the door for me.

Dark hair, going gray and thinning.

He wore a flowered Hawaiian shirt, crisply pressed blue linen shorts, and expensive brown Italian leather sandals. "Thanks for coming. We're headed to the Lahaina Grill just up the road. Supposed to be one of the best restaurants on Maui. I had to promise my firstborn son to get us in tonight."

From the backseat Luke said, "Dad, what does that mean?"

I laughed as we exited the hotel and started down the Honoapiilani highway.

Gavin looked back over the seat. "Just kidding. It's an expression that means it was hard to get the reservation." He looked over and said quietly, "You look nice. And smell good, too."

I blushed. "Thank you."

To disguise my discomfort, I shifted into my professional interrogation mode to get the conversational ball rolling. I turned to the boys in the back. "Where're you guys from?"

Luke answered. "Santa Barbara."

"I thought you might be from California or Florida."

"How come?" Gavin asked.

"Because it's the dead of winter and you're so tan."

"Ah. Well, winter is mild where we live, and the weather doesn't change all that much from season to season. How about you, where're you from?"

"Boston."

From the backseat Zach asked, "How did you learn to swim so good?"

"Well . . ." Gavin said. "Swim so well."

"I grew up along the shore in Connecticut and learned to swim as a kid. And I have strong legs 'cause I'm a runner."

An awkward silence settled in. Would the rest of the evening be uncomfortable? Was it my responsibility to keep the conversation going? I always had trouble tolerating silences. Why doesn't Gavin say something? After all, this is his gig. So, I asked the boys their ages. Zach was seven, while Luke was ten.

Shortly, we arrived at the restaurant in bustling Lahaina town. People carried ice cream cones and shave ice and filled the sidewalks, gaping into store after store of surfer gear and tacky Maui souvenirs. Gavin valet-parked the car. A hostess

Bonnie E. Carlson

showed us to our table where we spent a clumsy moment figuring out who should sit where. In the end, I sat across from Gavin, and Luke sat beside me.

Menus and water arrived. Reading the menu, I wondered what these young boys would find to eat in this expensive, sophisticated restaurant. They began by placing their napkins in their laps. Impressive. Zach needed a little help with the menu, but these boys felt at home in a classy restaurant.

We all ordered seafood of some kind with salads. By the time the food arrived, I had learned the boys' mother—Gavin's wife—had died four years earlier from cancer. And that Gavin was a software engineer.

By dessert, I felt comfortable and admired how skillfully Gavin included his boys in the conversation. Not having children, I was mindful of the boys and worked hard to engage them as well.

"What else are you doing while you're here, besides bodysurfing and saving young boys?" Gavin asked.

"Dad!" Zach exclaimed.

"Sorry, Zach. I didn't mean to embarrass you."

As we waited for the valet to get the car, Zach stuck his tongue out at Gavin, which Gavin missed because he was looking at me.

"Let's see," I said. "Snorkeling. Maybe a helicopter ride. Whale watching, if they're still around—"

"We can see whales off the coast at home sometimes," Luke said.

"Awesome—" I started to say.

"And we went snorkeling yesterday," Zack added.

"See anything good?"

What nice kids. This guy must be doing a great job as a parent. Must be tough being a widower, I thought.

74

"Not really," Luke said. "We're going to try again, on a boat this time. Tomorrow, right Dad?"

"Yep, tomorrow. They said there might be sea turtles, too. Would you like to join us?"

"Yeah," Luke said. "Why don't you come with us?"

I was caught off guard. "Uh . . . sure . . . I could do that." I looked up at Gavin. "Are you sure?"

"Absolutely. It's a several-hour trip. Snorkeling, food, drinks. Should be a great day."

"Hey, Dad. Can we take a helicopter ride?" Luke asked. "That sounds totally awesome!"

"Well, let's see what Zach thinks of that idea. How about it, Zachy? Does a helicopter ride sound like fun?"

"Maybe," he said, sounding doubtful.

We pulled into the driveway at my hotel. "So, about to-morrow," Gavin said, as I reached for the door handle. "It takes about forty-five minutes to get to the harbor where the snor-keling boat docks. I'll need to make sure I can get you a ticket from the concierge at my hotel. Let me walk you to the door."

He got out and walked me into the breezy, open lobby. "I'll leave a message on the hotel phone for you to confirm. We'll need to get on the road about eleven or eleven-thirty."

"Do you want my cellphone number?" Immediately, I re-gretted offering it. I didn't even know this guy.

"Sure." He took his phone and keyed it in. I thanked him for dinner and walked up to my room.

As I got ready for bed, I pondered the evening. By the time we arrived back at my hotel, it almost felt like a date, not that I could remember what a date felt like after being married almost twenty years. I climbed into bed to read. There was no doubt I found Gavin attractive . . .

Then I crashed.

The next day brought more beautiful weather for our snorkeling trip. A text on my phone confirmed that Gavin and the boys would pick me up at eleven. After a leisurely run and breakfast at the beach café, I donned shorts and a T-shirt over my bathing suit.

Gavin showed up right on time. On the drive to the harbor, I made small talk with the boys, leaning over the back seat, discussing school and their various activities, like soccer. Despite being curious about Gavin, I felt more comfortable talking to these young boys. We loaded our gear onto the boat, along with the other tourists. As we headed out of the harbor, a naturalist lectured about whales and dolphins and the fragility and importance of coral reefs. Finally, we got instruction about how to snorkel.

I turned to Luke. "But you guys are already experts, right?" They both laughed. Soon, we were in the protected harbor where we would grab our snorkeling equipment and jump overboard. The last bit of instruction mentioned the available life preservers.

Zach's eyes narrowed. "Dad, are we gonna be able to touch bottom?" After his brush with drowning, he was understandably wary about jumping back into water over his head, even without waves.

Gavin reassured him, telling him he needed to use a life preserver.

"But Luke says those are only for wussies."

Gavin gave Luke a dirty look. Luke, abashed, put his head down then turned to Zach. "I'm sorry I said that. I forgot about what happened yesterday."

Gavin gently pulled Luke aside and whispered into his ear.

Luke nodded. "I tell you what, Zach, I'll wear one, too."

I looked at Luke and whispered, "That was really nice of you." Turning to Zach I said, "I'm gonna wear one, too. Just to be on the safe side."

So, the three of us grabbed this kind of floatation device I'd never seen before, thick, neon yellow, neoprene belts that strapped around our waists.

As we climbed down the ladder into the water Zach said to Gavin, "I'm glad Larisa came today."

We'd had a ball snorkeling. In the car on the way back to the hotel the boys talked nonstop about the different undersea creatures they'd seen. My favorites were the colorful fish and corals. For the boys, the highlight was the sea turtles, which I'd never seen before in person either. Although the guides cautioned us not to get close, one had approached Luke, terrifying and delighting him in equal measure.

He couldn't stop talking about it, still ecstatic about how amazing it had been. I had to agree the word "awesome" was not hyperbole in this instance. They were gigantic! What a thrill to witness these gentle, lumbering, prehistoric-looking creatures propel themselves around under water.

As we approached the hotel, I started to feel a little twitchy. Would I be invited to dinner again? If so, should I go? Where was this headed? What was "this?" If you had asked me before this trip what I expected from it, falling in love with an entire family after a single day wouldn't have made it onto my list.

Gavin pulled up in front of the hotel and stopped. I wished my heart would stop fluttering. He got out of the car and hustled over to open my door for me. My heart melted.

As I got out both boys jumped out of the backseat and ran around, too. What would happen next? Weren't hugs supposed to happen at a moment like this? All four of us stood there awkwardly. I felt an overwhelming compulsion to hug both boys, and not just because I had saved Zack's life.

What was happening to me? I had arrived in Maui with an angry heart tightened like a clenched fist. And now it was mushy, soft and almost open, like a flower ready to bloom. Next, in a move totally incompatible with my self-contained New England character, I grabbed each boy and hugged them fiercely. Would I see either one of them ever again? "Zack, Luke"—I had to say their names—"I had such a great time today. Thanks so much for inviting me along."

I closed the car door and looked at Gavin. He removed his sunglasses. Simultaneously I said, "thank you" and he said "Larissa." We both laughed.

He leaned over and whispered into my ear, "I'll call you later." The spicy scent of his expensive cologne lingered behind him in the breezy, humid air.

As the boys piled into the backseat, Zach asked, "Dad, how come you didn't invite Larisa to dinner?" I couldn't hear Gavin's response as they drove off.

I wandered back to my room, my skin tight with crusty sea salt. I couldn't wait to get out of my uncomfortable, still-damp bathing suit underneath my shorts and T-shirt. For the zillionth time, I asked myself what was happening.

I showered and dressed for dinner. I went down to the outdoor café overlooking the beach. Although the food was excellent, loneliness settled over me like a heavy gray woolen blanket. I couldn't believe how much I missed Gavin and those kids. I ordered a second chardonnay and had them put it into a to-go cup so I could take it down to the beach. I needed to listen to the waves.

No chickens or stray cats tonight. Although I knew I shouldn't, I kept hoping Gavin would call. I finished the wine and, despite my sweater, shivered in the chilly breeze. A crowd had gathered behind me to watch the sunset. They oohed and ahhed as the big red flaming ball slipped through clouds into the ocean, whose blue it had tinted orange and yellow and fuchsia.

I had given up hope Gavin would call and started to walk back to my room when my phone buzzed in my hand. I waited until the fourth ring, wondering what he would say and what I would say.

My hands shook as I answered. "Hi, Gavin."

"Hi, Larisa. Glad I caught you. I wanted to talk to you because there're some things I need to explain. Wish it could've been in person, but I can't leave the boys alone. We were supposed to stay a few more days, but I just got a call from my business about a work crisis I need to attend to, so we're leaving tomorrow—"

"Oh, Gavin, I'm so sorry —"

"Yeah, I know. The boys are really bummed. I'm disappointed, too." His voice dropped to a whisper. "Zach is crying right now. And, despite him nearly drowning, this is been a great vacation. Larisa, you had a lot to do with that."

The gerbils in my brain were sprinting around that wheel, my thoughts racing so fast I couldn't speak.

Gavin continued. "They like you so much. I guess you remind them of their mom, what they remember of her. They really miss her—I do, too. They've been doing really well, but I haven't felt up to dating yet, so they haven't really been around women. Anyhow, I just wanted to say thank you again, for everything. I hope the rest of your trip goes well."

Rarely speechless, I struggled to put a coherent sentence together. "Gavin, I . . . I don't know what to say. I had a wonderful time with you and the boys . . . I admire what a great dad you are. Thanks . . . thanks for thawing my heart."

We left things on a positive note, so how come tears rolled down my cheeks as I dragged myself through the waning light back to my room? My rational brain knew a relationship between Gavin and me was not possible. We lived on opposite coasts, and I'd just gotten divorced. Still, I felt . . . disappointed, when I should have felt relieved.

My room felt empty. I had several days left by myself. How would I fill them?

Don't Talk to Strangers

If someone had asked Jake O'Malley if he was lonely, he'd probably have said no, loneliness being such an unmanly emotion. He just had a lot of time on his hands. After all, his dog, Milo, a little gray mutt with curly, wiry hair, was his constant companion. No, he never thought he was lonely until he met Zoe in the park.

Pushing seventy, Jake hadn't had hair on the top of his head for some time. The fringe that remained was that faded gray that blond hair leaves behind. His Irish skin, which freckled in his youth, sunburned easily so he wore a baseball cap and used the sunscreen his doctor recommended.

Years after a California vacation, Jake moved out to San Diego from Utica, New York—snow country, where he had worked a lifetime as a letter carrier. San Diego was an expensive area on Jake's fixed income. Social Security and his pension only went so far. But he fell in love with the temperate weather and sunny days, such a contrast from upstate New York. No one had told him about "May gray" or "June gloom," but, no matter, most of the year San Diego had perfect weather. Never cold and almost never hot. And, of course, it rarely rained, so he could get outside to walk—he hated the paunch he'd developed—appreciating the weather every day.

Jake and Milo led a comfortable life. Some might find it boring, but it satisfied them. He'd found a one-bedroom apartment where he still lived in a faded-yellow stucco building in the Clairemont neighborhood. It gave him easy access to Interstate 5, the main north-south freeway along the coast. Not that he really went anywhere, but if he wanted to, he could. The ground floor suited him. He didn't have to climb stairs too often, which bothered the arthritis in his knees left behind by many years of delivering mail.

He walked from the cozy living room into his compact kitchen to fix Milo's dinner. He didn't need any of the fancy amenities younger people wanted these days—stainless steel appliances, granite countertops, and the like. Jake grabbed some leftovers from the old white fridge. Should he heat them in the ancient microwave? He opted for the reliable gas stove instead, placing Milo's warmed-up chicken in his metal bowl on the floor.

"Maybe it's time for new carpeting," he said, as Milo chowed down. "After all, we've been here ten years. Let's see what the landlord says." He liked to keep the apartment nice and tidy.

Fox News wafted through the window from the neighboring apartment of his friends Joe and Sandy, older folks like himself. Sometimes he got together with them for a cup of coffee in the morning, despite their politics, but mostly Jake kept to himself. He turned on the big screen TV he'd splurged on last year, which made watching football games and golf amazing. There were worse ways you could spend the end of your days.

As Jake sat on the worn, brown corduroy sofa to eat his dinner—the same leftovers he shared with Milo—he turned off the TV. Sometimes the news depressed him. He grabbed a magazine from the stack on the coffee table instead. A story about the weak economy in upstate New York made him reflect back over his life.

"I need to stop doing that Milo. It's not good for me. After all, the past is the past, right? Can't do anything about it." Milo jumped up on the sofa so Jake could scratch behind his ears.

Jake had made a lot of mistakes, and he'd paid a high price for those mistakes. He had regrets.

Almost every day, Jake took Milo for a walk in Mission Bay Park, a short drive from his apartment, where they listened to the waves and watched the children play. They both needed the exercise. Afterwards, they would sit awhile to enjoy the sun and breeze and water. After having lived most of his life in the dreary Northeast, Jake never tired of the green grass and palm trees. People whizzed by on bicycles and rollerblades, getting a workout and enjoying the weather.

He loved to watch the kids play soccer and envied the dads who coached their children, something he'd never done with his own son and daughter. Usually, he and Milo went in the afternoon, after school. The cheerful voices and laughter filled the sunny park, making Jake smile.

One May afternoon, Jake and Milo sat on a bench in the park. Jake was reading an old Michael Connelly paperback. He liked that detective, Harry Bosch.

He felt her eyes boring into him before he saw her. The little girl ran over to him, interrupting his reading. "Hi. Can I pet your doggie?

"Sure," he said. "Milo likes kids. See his tail wagging? That means he's saying hello."

"His name is Milo?" she asked. "Like in the movie?"

Jake laughed. "What movie? I don't know if it's from a movie. I don't think I ever saw a movie with a dog named Milo. When I got him, he already had that name."

She looked about seven or eight. "Oh, so you weren't his first owner?" Skinny little thing with a bouncy blonde ponytail held in place by some kind of stretchy pink do-dad. She wore a pink hoodie, and black and pink striped leggings with purple sneakers, the kind with the rollers in the back.

"Right. He was a rescue."

"What does 'a rescue' mean?"

"It means the first people who had Milo weren't very nice to him. They hurt him, so the police took him away and brought him to a shelter."

"What's a shelter?" She had started to pet Milo, who sat on the ground, smiling with the attention. When Milo jumped up on the bench beside Jake, the girl sat down next to the dog.

"That's where they take dogs and cats nobody wants, or if they've been hurt." Why wasn't she in school? It was Wednesday morning. "They hope somebody will adopt them, give them a new home." He paused and looked at her. "You ask a lot of questions, you know that?"

"I know. That's what my mom says."

"So now it's my turn for a question. My name's Jake, what's your name?"

She put her face down on Milo's head to kiss him. "Zoe. I really like your dog, Jake. I wish my mom would let me have one, but she says no way."

"Zoe. That's a pretty name. I don't think I've ever known anyone called Zoe."

While they talked, Jake could hear a woman yelling into her cellphone. He glanced over to another bench. A hundred feet away, it faced the playground. The woman hopped up and started pacing around, her left arm waving in the air. She looked angry or upset.

As he watched her, Zoe said, "That's my mom."

He couldn't help but notice she paid no attention to Zoe at all.

Suddenly, she strode toward them, cellphone thrust into her pocket. When she got about thirty feet away, she yelled. "Zoe, you get back here right now! How many times have I told you never talk to strangers?"

"It's okay, Mom. This is Milo, Jake's doggie. He's really nice."

Did she mean me or Milo?

Jake stood up and extended his hand toward her. "Hi, I'm Jake O'Malley. You have a charming daughter."

But Zoe's mother ignored Jake's gesture. She grabbed Zoe by the arm, pulling her off the bench, and started dragging her back toward the playground. She twisted her arm—that had to hurt—and continued to reprimand Zoe for talking to strangers.

"Get into the car, Zoe, we're leaving."

Jake felt bad, because it looked like he'd gotten Zoe into trouble. He knew it wasn't his fault. After all, he hadn't approached Zoe. But still . . .

A week later, Jake and Milo drove to Mission Bay Park as usual in Jake's secondhand green Ford Escape. On this Friday morning, he hadn't brought his book. Instead, he brought a folding chair and a towel to dry Milo off if he wanted a swim. Lunch sat in a cooler in the trunk. He parked the car at the dog beach on Fiesta Island in Mission Bay, where Milo could run off leash. It was uncrowded on this weekday morning. Jake avoided the weekends when unruly dogs, who'd been cooped up inside all week, overran the place.

May gray had set in, so a chilly fog still covered the beach. That might be keeping some people away, which was fine with him. As soon as they got out of the car, Jake took off Milo's leash, and they started to walk on the calm side of Fiesta Island. No waves there.

After he scanned the beach, Jake breathed a sigh of relief. There weren't any of the big, bully dogs that often visited. They liked to descend in groups upon little dogs like Milo, owners oblivious, on their phones, not paying attention. Milo wasn't tiny, he weighed about twenty pounds, but his history of mistreatment had made him very timid. Jake hated it when those big, aggressive dogs came bounding over.

"Milo, wanna swim? It's nice and calm on this side. No big scary waves, like the other side." Milo wasn't crazy about swimming because, Jake supposed, he never had a chance to experience it until he was several years old.

Milo tentatively ventured into the water. Jake threw an old tennis ball out twenty feet. Milo dogpaddled out and carried it back in his mouth. After Milo swam and chased the tennis ball for a while they walked back to the car and drove over to the ocean side. Jake put Milo back on his leash. Then he found a good spot where Jake opened his chair and unfolded the towel so Milo could dry off.

"Look how foggy it is this morning," Jake told Milo. "Can't even see the rides at SeaWorld." Jake settled into his sand chair and dried off his buddy. "You know, Milo, I never get tired of this. Aren't we lucky we can do this any day we want to?" They watched the surf, smelled the tangy salt air, and listened to the waves pounding.

By eleven-thirty, the fog had burned off, and it had warmed up. Jake decided they'd drive over to the grassy area of the park facing the protected side of the bay. Jake had brought lunch for himself—a turkey and cheese sandwich, some chips, a chocolate chip cookie and an apple—and some treats for Milo. As soon as the dog saw Jake take the cooler out, he barked and jumped up and down with excitement.

Jake basked in the sun's warmth and ate his lunch. He fed Milo little pieces of turkey and cheese, his favorites, and tried to find a piece of cookie for him with no chocolate. Finally, Milo got his official dog treats. As Jake carried their garbage over to the trashcan, he looked up.

Zoe walked toward them. "Hi Jake. Can I pet Milo?"

Surprised that she'd remembered their names, Jake said, "Sure," pleased to see her. "If you think it's okay with your mom. She seemed kind of mad the last time you came over. I don't want you to get in trouble."

Today Zoe wore skinny blue jeans and a lavender sweater. "Oh, she's fine. Mom's in a better mood today."

Like the last time, her mom talked nonstop on her cellphone, sitting on top of a picnic table, her feet on the bench.

"So, how come you're not in school?" As usual, Jake wore what he regarded as his retirement "uniform:" sneakers, khaki cargo shorts, a tee shirt, and a hoodie.

"Well, I kinda am in school. Mom homeschools me, so this is how we take a break. Mom says I'm supposed to be getting some exercise. But there's no other kids to play with and usually Mom's on the phone. Right now, she's fighting with Dad."

Uh-oh. Jake had never liked the idea of homeschooling and was glad his ex-wife hadn't proposed it for their two children. "So why does your mom homeschool you Zoe?"

"She says there's too many Mexicans at school."

"Oh, I see." Why did she live in San Diego if she didn't like Latinos? "So, Zoe, since you go to school at home, do you have any friends?"

Zoe dropped her head and said very quietly, "Uh-uh."

"None?" Poor kid.

"Nope, not a single one."

"Well that's too bad. It sounds like you and me are in the same boat."

"What boat?" Zoe sat down next to Milo on the bench, with Jake on the other side. She'd been petting him nonstop. If Milo could have purred, he would have.

Jake chuckled. "In the same boat means we're in the same situation." He should have saved his cookie to share with Zoe.

"What do you mean?" Zoe asked.

Milo had moved and placed his two front paws in Jake's lap. Zoe got up from the bench and walked in front of the dog. She put her left elbow on his thigh and bent over to kiss Milo on the head.

"I don't have any friends either," Jake said.

"Well, maybe you and me can be friends, Jake."

"I think we would have to ask your mom about that. You know, I have a granddaughter your age, but I've never seen her."

"How come?"

"Because she lives far, far away." Not the real reason, of course. His daughter wanted nothing to do with him. Even though he knew he had a granddaughter who would be about seven or eight, he'd never seen her. One of Jake's biggest regrets.

"Hey, I know what," Zoe said.

"What?"

"Maybe you could be *my* grandpa."

"But don't you already have a grandpa?" She had no idea how much I would like that, Jake thought. What he wouldn't give for a relationship with a grandson or granddaughter.

Zoe frowned. "No, no grandpas at all."

"Zoe!"

Startled, they both looked up and saw Zoe's mother, sitting cross-legged on top of the picnic table, gesturing for Zoe to come over.

"Uh-oh, gotta go. Don't wanna make Mom mad."

"How 'bout if I go with you and see how your mom feels about us being friends?"

"Okay, Jake."

They got down from the bench and Jake grabbed Milo's leash. As they started walking toward Zoe's mom, Zoe grabbed Jake's hand.

Oh boy, that's not good. "Zoe, how would you like to take Milo's leash?"

She put her hand out for the leash. "Awesome! Can I?" She stood up straight and proud. As Milo pulled her forward, she looked back at Jake with a huge grin and walked toward her mom.

When they got to the picnic table, Zoe said, "Look, Mom, Jake is letting me hold Milo's leash. Milo is such a nice doggie. I really like him."

Zoe's mother scowled, and Jake reintroduced himself. "Hi. Jake O'Malley." What can I say that will reassure her and not annoy her? "So, I've enjoyed talking with Zoe. She's a great kid."

Finally, her mom said, "Hey. I'm Sasha. Nice to meet you."

Sasha had a hard look about her, too much black eye makeup, straw-colored hair with dark roots showing and pulled back in a messy ponytail. She wore skin-tight jeans and a blouse so low cut you could see almost down to her navel. Back in my day we'd call that cheap, or trashy, Jake thought.

After an awkward moment passed, Jake said, "I live pretty close, so Milo and I come here every day." He took the leash back from Zoe. "How about you?"

"Yeah, we're pretty close, too. Zoe, come on, we've got to get going."

"Bye, Jake. Can I give Milo a hug goodbye?" Zoe asked, her little ponytail bouncing around.

"Sure."

Sasha grabbed Zoe's arm. "Come on, Zoe, we need to get a move on."

Jake watched as they walked to their car, wondering what it was like for that sweet little girl at home. "Come on Milo. We should probably get a move on, too."

Over the next month, Jake and Milo saw Zoe in the park once or twice a week. Zoe came over and petted Milo, she and Jake chatted, and her mom called her back after a few minutes. Even so, Jake treasured those encounters. He tried to make small talk with Sasha to reassure her. It turned out they lived around the corner from each other in the same neighborhood.

Jake had an idea. Would Sasha agree to let Zoe take a walk with Milo and Jake at dinnertime? One afternoon in late May, he pitched the idea to Sasha as she and Zoe prepared to leave. He worried about proposing it in front of Zoe, in case Sasha said no, but he decided to go ahead and risk it.

"Since I live so close by you guys, how'd you feel about me coming over either before or after dinner with Milo and having Zoe take a walk with us around the neighborhood?"

"Yeah, Mom, please. Pleeease say yes. I reeeally wanna go."

"It would give you a little time to yourself or even to run an errand if you need to," Jake said.

Sasha hesitated, looking straight at Jake, who held her gaze. Finally, she said, "Okay, we could try that. When do you want to do it?"

"Tonight, Mom, tonight! Let's do it tonight," said Zoe.

Jake looked at Sasha. "We go pretty much every night, so it's up to you. Whatever works for you." Would she go for it?

"Okay, how about tomorrow night at six-thirty, right after dinner?"

As Zoe said thank you about a hundred times, Sasha gave Jake their address and said she'd see them tomorrow night.

So, Jake and Milo started going over to their apartment and having Zoe join them on walks at dinnertime, sometimes before, sometimes after. Jake didn't know what Sasha did while they walked—it was only about half an hour—but one night when they returned from their walk Sasha wasn't home, so they had to sit outside on the steps. Later, with some trepidation, Jake suggested Sasha might want to give a key to Zoe so she didn't have to rush to get home if she was running an errand, and Jake and Zoe could get inside. Sasha surprised him when she agreed after giving Zoe a lecture on what a big responsibility it was to have a key.

As the attachment between Jake and Zoe grew stronger, Jake began to think more about the family he left behind. His ex had divorced him many years earlier when his children were young because of his drinking. He couldn't blame her. He rarely saw the kids after the divorce, because his ex said if they tell me, even one time, that you've been drinking, you're done. By then they were old enough to know.

So, Jake didn't see them, preferring to drink on weekends instead. Eventually it caught up with him though, and the Postal Service sent him to rehab. By the time he got sober, the kids were teenagers involved in their own lives and no longer interested in seeing him, sober or not. He sent his child sup-port, and the kids turned out okay without him. He had to hand it to his ex, she did a good job.

He had no contact with his son Brian, now forty-five and married, working at a bank in London. His daughter Karen lived in Pittsburgh with her husband and daughter. His ex had let him know when his granddaughter was born, but when he tried to get in touch Karen made it clear she wanted nothing to do with him. He nursed a ton of regrets about all that. He should have kept up with those meetings that got him sober, which would have pushed him to make amends to his kids. Was it too late? Did he still have a chance? Every day he spent time with Zoe he thought about writing a letter to his kids, telling them how sorry he was that he'd messed up their lives. He still held out hope he might be able to piece things back together.

As summer approached, Jake wondered what would happen when school let out. What did homeschoolers do in the summer? Would they still come to the park?

Sasha and Zoe stopped going to Mission Bay Park. But by then, Jake had earned Sasha's trust, and she'd allow Zoe to go to the park during the day with him and Milo. The three of them would take walks, have picnics, and go swimming. Milo now loved playing in the water with Zoe. And Jake got a thrill out of watching the two of them splash around in the bay, barking and exclaiming with joy.

One summer day they played on the ocean side of the park. They watched the waves and listened to the noise over at SeaWorld, and Zoe said she's never been to SeaWorld. "Mom said it's too expensive."

Hmm, I haven't either, Jake thought. We're going to have to fix that. When he dropped Zoe off at home, he suggested to Sasha that the three of them have a little outing at SeaWorld. He made it clear it would be his treat. Sasha said she didn't want to go. Both Jake and Zoe's faces drooped when they heard that.

"But you two can go if you want to."

The next morning, bright and sunny, Jake picked up Zoe, who jumped around and chattered nonstop about their excursion. She looked so cute in her flowered dress and red sandals. Tickets cost seventy-five dollars each, as expensive as Sasha had said, and it would get more expensive when they got inside, and Jake learned how many things the admission price didn't include. No matter, it was worth the splurge. They were going to have a great time. They spent the day going from exhibit to exhibit and ride to ride. Jake found the quality of the animal exhibits disappointing. It seemed more like an amusement park than a marine park, but Zoe had the time of her life.

"What did you think of the killer whales?" Jake asked.

"Awesome! What was your favorite, Jake?"

"I loved riding on the Manta with you."

Jake took pictures of Zoe on his phone, but he had none of the two of them together. He finally asked a woman if she'd snap a photo of the two of them. They stood side by side, and when Jake put his arm around Zoe, she looked up at him with a huge grin.

After the woman took the picture, she looked at it to make sure it came out okay. "Great picture of you and your granddaughter."

Jake beamed.

For lunch, they ate hot dogs and fries. After that they saw the sea lions. Zoe loved how they barked so much. While they watched the silly antics of the penguins, Jake's favorite, he remembered a zoo outing when his children were young. His eyes glistened with tears.

They went on one last ride together, the Wild Artic. By then the lines for the rides had gotten too long and they decided to call it a day, both exhausted.

On the short ride home, Jake asked Zoe if she'd had a good time.

She smiled ear to ear. "Too bad Milo couldn't come. It was my most fun day ever."

Jake struggled to keep the tears at bay. Me too.

In September, homeschooling resumed for Zoe. Sometimes Sasha and Zoe met Milo and Jake at the park, and several times a week Jake, Milo, and Zoe took short walks together before or after dinner. Early one evening in October, Jake stopped by unannounced with a little gift for Zoe, a Monopoly game they could play together. He had contemplated asking Sasha if Zoe could come to his apartment occasionally for short visits, not an overnight or anything, maybe just a Saturday afternoon. She had allowed Jake to come to their apartment sometimes to read with Zoe or play games.

He walked up the stairs to their apartment and rang the bell. Milo jumped around with excitement, knowing he was going to see Zoe. No answer, so he knocked. "They must not be home," he said to Milo, sorry his dog would be disappointed.

As they started to walk away, Jake holding his surprise gift for Zoe, an older neighbor lady who had seen them there sometimes said, "They moved out two days ago."

What? Seeing the disappointment on his face, the lady asked, "Didn't they tell you?"

Jake hung his head, at a loss for words. How could this be? Could they really have moved without even saying goodbye? What could have happened?

They started back down the stairs, the neighbor lady saying something behind them Jake couldn't hear. He barely held back tears and struggled to make sense of what had happened. He remembered he had Sasha's cellphone number back in the apartment. He hurried Milo along, pulling him as they walk-ran the several blocks back home. When he called Sasha's number, it rang and rang before finally an announcement came on saying the number was no longer in service.

"You've got to be kidding!" he exclaimed to Milo, his fists clenched. "I can't believe this! How could they do this to us?"

He gave Milo a treat and together they plopped down on the sofa. Jake went round and round in his head, trying to figure out what could have prompted this unannounced move. How could Sasha do this to Zoe? Could she be so cold-hearted or self-centered that she couldn't see how much Jake meant to Zoe? Jake was her only friend, for heaven's sake.

He paced for the rest of the evening, unable to watch TV or read or do anything. He couldn't stop thinking about poor Zoe. Finally, at ten, he decided he might as well turn in. He got ready for bed, and Milo jumped up on the bed to comfort him, falling asleep curled up next to Jake. But sleep eluded him. He tossed and turned all night, trying to imagine what could have happened to Zoe.

The next morning, feeling like he'd been hit by a truck, he dragged himself out of bed and said to Milo, while feeding him his breakfast, "Enough is enough."

He sat down at his kitchen table with a yellow pad and started to write a letter to his daughter Karen. For weeks, thoughts had swirled around in his head. He knew he needed to do this, the amends long overdue. What could he say that might get her to reconsider allowing him back into her life?

Dear Karen,

I know it's been way too long, decades too long, but I felt like I had to try to make amends for what a terrible father I was to you and Brian. I was a drunk for most of your childhood. I made a lot of mistakes, and I have a ton of regrets. Your mother had every right to throw me out. I deserved it. My first mistake was choosing to drink instead of spending time with you and Brian right after the divorce. I was deep in my disease and acted like a complete jerk. By the time work made me get sober, you guys were teenagers and had lives of your own. You wanted nothing to do with me, and I understand that. So, I made another mistake. I gave up and left town and tried to forget what I was leaving behind. It was too painful. Although I sent checks, I made your mother be both mother and father. I think she did a good job. I know you've both made her proud.

When I was sixty, I retired and moved out to San Diego. I have made a quiet little life for myself here. I haven't had a drink in over twenty-five years. More than anything, I would like to see you, to meet my granddaughter, to try to make up for the past in some small way. Or at least talk to you about what happened and your feelings about it.

Karen, I'll understand if you're not interested, but I had to at least try.

Love, Dad

He included his address and phone number, said a little prayer, and put it into the mail. He had only one address for her. Hopefully if she had moved, his former employer would see fit to forward it.

Two weeks later Jake's cellphone rang. Every time the phone rang, which wasn't often, he hoped it would be Sasha and Zoe, telling him where they were, explaining what happened. He longed to hear Zoe's sweet voice.

"Hello, Dad. This is Karen. I got your letter. There's someone here who'd like to say hi."

Becoming Vice President

I still enjoyed the university's commencement ceremonies each May, even after all these years, annoyed at my cynical colleagues who had to be cajoled to attend. They claimed to hate the pomp and circumstance, but it could have been the wasted undergraduates concealing booze under their chintzy, rented regalia. I settled into my chair on the dais in my flowing black academic robes, the black velvet tam perched on my head, and listened to the university president's booming voice.

"Ladies and gentlemen, it gives me great pleasure to introduce our next vice president for academic affairs. Join me in congratulating Vice President Leslie Emerson."

Why had he chosen commencement to make the announcement? My promotion wasn't a surprise, but the occasion was.

The instant I heard the words "vice president," the long-forgotten memory of that nerve-wracking period of graduate school erupted into my mind.

Following the polite applause, President Nelson Harrington turned to face me. Grinning, he extended his arm in my direction. Crap. Did he expect me to address the crowd? Why hadn't he prepared me?

Panic rose in my chest. As I stood on shaky legs, my heart pounded. Sweat bloomed on my face and poured from my armpits. Is this what a heart attack felt like? Focus, Leslie, focus!

The first image to burst in my mind's eye was Peter's snowy white hair.

But the details of the affair bubbled to the surface like simmering caramel and began to ricochet across my mind. The next image to surface was his aging body, pale and lean from long-distance running, his only reprieve from constant work.

I rose and floated over to the podium, scrambling to make my rational brain work, to purge these images, to manufacture something—anything—to say, no matter how vacuous. I smiled and gazed over the beaming crowd, stalling for time, afraid I would pass out.

I sucked in some air. "Thank you, President Harrington. Graduates, this is your day, and I don't want to take up your time. I appreciate your vote of confidence and look forward to guiding the academic departments forward into the future."

More tepid applause.

I wobbled back to my seat, praying none of my distinguished colleagues—mostly men—would notice how roiled I was, how utterly disquieted.

The instant I sat down all I could think about was Peter back in graduate school. It would be hard to imagine a less likely sexual partner, if you could call him that, than that aging university vice president. What could I possibly have found attractive in him? Me, a lonely, poverty-stricken graduate student going through a painful divorce, struggling to complete my dissertation. Him, a distinguished sixty-seven-year-old administrator, not even terribly attractive. With the benefit of hindsight, I could see what a cliché it was. As in all May– December romances—ha! only Peter would call what we had a romance— it was the power I was attracted to, his privilege, hoping it might open doors for me. Why couldn't I see that at the time? Nausea settled in my gut.

When it began, I wasn't yet thirty. At the time, if you'd asked me, I probably wouldn't have described myself as pretty. Attractive, maybe. Slender and tan, with an earnest unlined face, full lips curled into a smile despite feeling stressed all the time about money and whether my professors would approve my dissertation. About whether I'd land an academic job after all the years of hard work.

And yet, I displayed my endless legs and braless breasts— it was the Sixties!—in short shorts and tank tops, clueless about their effect on a work-obsessed man in his sixties.

On the stage, Ph.D. graduates glided by one by one, sailing toward bright futures, smiling broadly as cameras flashed and family and friends applauded in the steamy auditorium. I barely heard a word though, my mind fogged, all of my mental energy obsessing about why I did it and what it said about me.

It was consensual, wasn't it? No one held a gun to my head. Or was I a victim?

I never expected the "relationship" to follow me across the country to my first academic job. Peter traveled constantly, finding excuses to fly to the city where I worked. He would beg me to meet him for sex in a seedy, no-star motel where he could be safely anonymous. We drank expensive vodka from a flask he always carried with him and had sex on germ-ridden, tattered bedspreads. Drunk was the only way I could fuck him. The smell of vodka still nauseated me.

After those encounters, three in all, I wondered if that's what it felt like to be a hooker, though not a single dollar had ever exchanged hands. If money was not the currency of this relationship, then what was? Peter got my youthful sexual body. But what was in it for me? What did I get in return? The satisfaction of a powerful man craving my body, finding me desirable, showering me with attention? Such a contrast from my soon-to-be ex-husband and the needy, immature graduate students who surrounded me. But were there other motives, too?

Eventually, I started to date another assistant professor and mustered the courage to tell Peter it was over. He became furious, unaccustomed to not getting his own way. At first, he told me I had no right. Later came wheedling, and eventually pleading. He said we could continue despite my having a new boyfriend. As if that were the issue.

Finally, he gave up. I breathed a sigh of relief when I heard he'd died several years ago, despite all that running. Now I was the only one with memories of that time.

As I marched down the steps and off the stage with the other faculty, the irony hit me.

Who was the vice president now?

Too Good to be True

Misty couldn't have imagined returning to the encampment voluntarily. The rag-tag bunch of teenagers had been living under that bridge abutment for months, sleeping bags, shopping carts, and empty water bottles littered everywhere. At first, the city let them be. Every so often, the cops arrived to roust them. The kids scattered, hooting and hollering, only to return later.

But when the street-toughened kids started hitting up tourists for cash and pilfering things from nearby stores to pawn or sell, people started calling the mayor. He told the police, "Get rid of them once and for all, any way you can, short of putting them in jail or beating them. I mean, they're kids—how hard can this be?"

Misty had been with them almost from the beginning, from the minute she'd escaped from the Russians last year. She'd found Ratso (who loved that character in the film classic *Midnight Cowboy*) and they'd become the de facto leaders, older than most of the others, a motley group of kids of every size and shade, some as young as thirteen. As bad as life was under the interstate, the lives they'd fled were unimaginably worse. At least here everybody shared, and no violence was allowed. Ratso made sure of that.

Then the police arrived in force. Those who couldn't run fast enough were scooped up by the cops and forced into white, windowless vans, brought to the station to see who had records and sent to programs for the homeless. Hours later they repeated the process until none were left.

"Thanks, officers," the social worker said. "You can just put her in that last interview room at the end of the hall." The cops had brought the girl to an agency charged with helping homeless teens, a longstanding problem in this California city.

"You got it, Amanda," Lincoln said. The young African-American cop frowned. "You're going to have your hands full with this one."

The two officers had brought in their young charge, each holding her under one armpit while she kicked and spit at them. She would have bitten them if her hands hadn't been cuffed.

"Says her name is Misty," said Hector, an older Latino cop who'd worked with juveniles for years. "No ID. No Social Security number. Gave her last name as Meadows. Misty Meadows." He chuckled. "Yeah, right, in her dreams. Seriously doubt she's ever laid eyes on a meadow."

The scruffy looking waif spewed epithets all the way down the hall to the interview room. "Let go of me, you bastards," she howled. "You fuckers are hurting me."

Lincoln sighed. "If you'd stop fighting like that, you wouldn't get hurt."

But Misty continued to struggle, periodically letting her legs go limp so she hung by her armpits from the officers' hands and had to be dragged.

Amanda pulled her light brown hair into a ponytail and returned to her office. Five minutes later the officers joined her. "Have a seat, guys," she said, pointing to two chairs across from her desk. "You locked the door down there, right?"

Lincoln nodded and tossed a set of keys on her desk.

"What else do we know about her? Like, how old is she?"

"Claims to be twenty-one," Hector said, his lined face skeptical. "But I'd say not a day over seventeen. No previous arrests, so we haven't been able to get much info on her. Maybe you'll have better luck."

Amanda shrugged. "I'll see what I can do. Sometimes they just won't talk."

"She's gonna be tough," Hector said. "Good luck."

Lincoln got up. "Let's get on the road, Hector. Still got another couple of kids from this bust to deal with."

Amanda grabbed some forms and walked down the hall to the interview room. She unlocked the door, looping the long cord with keys around her neck, and sat down at a small scarred, wooden table. "Hi, I'm Amanda. How's it going, Misty?"

The girl sat opposite her at the table in the small window-less room, refusing to look up as Amanda tried to engage her. "Where the hell am I?"

"You're at New Hope for Teens, a program for homeless youth," Amanda said. "We're going to try to get you some help, so you're off the street and safe. Let's start with your real name."

The girl studied her dirty fingernails. "Great." Sarcasm dripped from her voice. She fingered the fraying cuff of her dirty hoodie. "Misty Meadows."

Amanda considered her. Not quite emaciated. Long, choppy, dark hair. Skin-tight, flimsy jeans shot through with holes, the kind that came from years of wearing them day in and day out.

"Okay, let's go with that for now. So, Misty, how did you end up under the underpass with those other kids? That's gotta be a hard life.

"And by the way, everything you say will be confidential, unless you tell me you're going to hurt yourself or someone else."

Misty looked up, glaring into Amanda's brown eyes with her gray, wary ones. Her eyes darted around the room, settling on the table in front of her. She sighed. She'd heard all this before. Really didn't want to get into it. "Long story. You wouldn't be interested." Her voice had a melancholy, wistful quality.

"How do you know? I've got all day." Amanda moved her chair back and settled in. "By the way, are you hungry? Thirsty? When did you last eat?"

"Can't remember. Probably kill for a sandwich," Misty mumbled, motoring past her vow to keep her mouth shut. "And a Coke."

Truth was, she was starved and filthy and cold. Living under an overpass had gotten old. She missed Ratso though.

"We can do that." Amanda grabbed her phone from her jeans pocket and texted the request to her secretary. "It'll be a few minutes. While we wait, we can get to know one another."

"Oh goodie." She stared at the young social worker's freckled face, taken by the gold nose ring.

"So," Amanda said, "we were at the part where you were going to tell me how you ended up under the freeway."

Misty looked into Amanda's earnest eyes, sizing her up, trying to decide if anything could be gained by going into what had happened to her. What did these people want from her? She pulled her right foot onto the chair. "It beat working for those drug dealers."

Amanda squirmed. With furrowed brows she asked, "What drug dealers?"

"See, here's where the story starts to get long." Misty slid off her hoodie, revealing a skimpy black camisole, no bra. Virtually no breasts, her ribs like a washboard.

"Told you I have the rest of the day. And besides, we're still waiting for your food." Amanda stared at Misty's upper arm, where a tattoo instructed *"fuck me"* in cursive. "But before we continue, Misty, I'm curious about your tattoo." Her eyes bored into Misty's upper arm.

"Oh, this one?" Misty asked, looking down at her arm, slouching down in her chair, knee pointing toward the ceiling. Dirty feet clad in falling-apart sandals. "Yeah, when those Russians gave me this one, I started thinkin' maybe it was time to move on." She winced, remembering that day. The pain, the scuzzy tattoo parlor, the filthy scumbag who did it. Amazing it never got infected.

"So, you've got more?" Amanda asked softly.

"None as visible or interesting as this one." Misty fingered the tattoo, working out whether to get into it or not. Whether to trust this young Amanda. This social worker who claimed to want to help her. She'd met a few of these types in foster care. What could she get out of this?

Taking a deep breath, she continued, "None that say, 'rape me,'" like this one." Sometimes she got a kick out of shocking these people.

Amanda shifted her position. "What do you mean?"

"I keep telling you. It's a long story—"

"And I keep telling *you*, I'm all ears. Who are the Russians and why did they give you that tattoo?"

Misty considered how far back to go. The Russians or foster care? Or maybe what it was like living with her mom before that?

The food arrived, buying her time. Amanda handed the bag to Misty.

Misty opened it cautiously, sniffed. She grabbed the plastic-covered sandwich, unwrapped it, and peeled off the top piece of ciabatta bread. "How do you know I eat turkey? Or cheese? I could be vegan for all you know." She ripped open the small bag of potato chips, a few clattering across the table top.

"I should have asked you what you wanted. Sorry. You can take out the turkey if you don't eat meat."

Crunching chips Misty said, "Just messin' with ya. I eat, like, everything. It's not like the Russians gave us much choice. Ha, we were lucky to eat at all." She tore into the sandwich, mayo dripping down of the sides of her mouth.

"I want to hear more about the Russians and your tattoo."

"I prefer not to think about it as '*my*' but rather as '*their*' tattoo." She paused to take another mouthful, in no hurry to continue. Still unsure how much to say.

"Okay, fine, *their* tattoo." Amanda moved her chair in closer.

Misty popped the Coke open. It fizzed and foamed onto the table. She swallowed a big slug and belched. Was there any point in getting into this? Dragging out all this shit? She sighed again. "Okay, I'm gonna start when I was last living with my mother, which was when I was, uh, let's see, fifteen, I think. Before that it was foster care. Ancient history."

Amanda waited while Misty took another bite of sandwich.

"So, things got pretty bad with Mom. She, um, got laid off after she hurt herself at the factory where she worked. That job is why they let me go back after foster care. It's such a cliché now, but she, like, got prescribed those painkillers and got hooked. And just like everybody else, eventually heroin was, you know, way cheaper, so . . ."

After another gulp of Coke, Misty examined her sandwich, trying to decide whether to finish it or not. She was full, but she hated to leave part of a good sandwich. "Then she started staying out all night, probably hooking, so I was, uh, basically on my own. I was in another new school—my fifth or my sixth. Ninth grade, maybe? Anyhow, doing horrible as usual." She stopped to rewrap the sandwich remains in plastic. "Always hated school, but now I was, like, failing. They sent notices home to Mom, which I naturally signed for her. She didn't give a shit anyhow. Always told me I'd never amount to anything, and . . ." She stopped there and laughed bitterly. "Guess what? She was right!"

Amanda squirmed in her seat, playing with her ponytail. She nodded for Misty to continue.

"I started to, like, skip school and stuff, spending my time hanging out with friends, surfing the internet, all that shit. We used to go to this coffee shop with free Wi-Fi. It sucked, but you could play on your phone and drink as much coffee as you wanted for three bucks."

The only sound in the room was Misty munching on potato chips, washing them down with the last of her Coke.

"After a couple months, this nice-looking white guy with an accent starts coming over to our table to visit. He'd come, like, every day. My friend Taryn thought I was interested in him, even though he was old, like, probably his thirties or forties. So, she'd always leave. Said his name was Andrei. No last name.

"He was super nice in the beginning. Always, like, paying for my coffee, offering to buy me food. Telling me how pretty I was. Buying me, like, really nice clothes." She stopped, shaking her head, remembering how nice it was in the beginning, how her mother never asked her where she got the money for those expensive clothes.

Amanda listened, fingering the three stud earrings in her right ear.

Staring down at the table, Misty continued. "He gave me, like, a brand-new iPhone." She looked up to see if Amanda was listening. "That's how I got sucked in. And he told me there were lots more goodies where that came from, that I could make a lot of money. Was I interested? Of course, I was interested! Shit, I was only fifteen. How else was I gonna make money for an iPhone?" Her voice trailed off and she dropped her head. "Note to self: when it seems too good to be true, it always is. What an idiot I was."

"You weren't an idiot. You were young and naïve, being neglected by your only parent."

"Still, I should've known better. I should've known that my 'job'"—she made air quotes with her fingers—"with Andrei would not end well. When I was supposed to be in school, he had me sell drugs—heroin and meth—to people in little towns outside the city you could get to by bus. Piece of cake, right?"

She remembered those days, riding the bus, spending all day in these little shit towns, in these skuzzy neighborhoods he introduced her to, coming home each night with bundles of cash. "I'd come back with, like two grand. He'd let me keep, *maybe*, a measly two hundred bucks from it."

"Don't forget about the tattoo," Amanda reminded her.

"I'm getting to it. Keep your pants on." She shifted in her seat. "After a month or so, Andrei told me he had, like, a new place I could live, away from my mother, now that I had all this cash. Sounded great. Every teenage girl's dream, right?"

She stopped and tried to take a drink from her empty Coke can. "So, I got some stuff from my mother's and moved over to this place." She flung the can toward a metal waste-basket in the corner. It clanged off the side.

"How did that work out?" Amanda said, eyebrows raised.

"Ha! First of all, it was a dump. Plus, there were, like, all these other girls there—and a few boys—doing the same thing I was. Takin' the bus out to these different towns where we sold drugs. Every day. I didn't even get my own room!"

"What was it like living there?"

Misty paused to think. "Parts of it were fun, actually. Not the drug selling, but at night, like, with the other kids. Sometimes they'd let us go out together, clubbing—"

"But you guys weren't old enough to go to clubs, right? How'd you get in?"

"I'm pretty sure Andrei's friends ran these clubs. I mean, like, we had no trouble getting in. And they let us dance and drink and do whatever we wanted to. Nobody to complain. We partied all night and, you know, sold drugs during the day."

"How long did this go on?"

"A couple years? At first it wasn't too bad. Like, I knew I couldn't leave, they wouldn't just let me walk away from this. But I had a lot of money and we had fun at night. Then it changed." Shit, why did I even get into this? Misty thought.

"Changed how?"

Misty scratched at a gouge on the table. "I think it got taken over by some other Russians, 'cause all of a sudden Andrei disappeared. It was these other assholes. The mean guys." Misty stopped, thinking about the next part. What was the point?

Amanda asked, "Do you need to stop? Do you want to take a break? This is some pretty intense stuff."

Misty thought about it. "Maybe just a quick bathroom break."

When they returned, Amanda said, "So you were telling me about how things had changed after a while, when some new, mean guys took over."

Misty sat bent over the table, her head in her hands. It hurt so much to remember those fuckers.

"Misty you're doing great," Amanda said. "This is some really hard stuff."

Misty exhaled sharply. "Yeah, right." She gazed off at some invisible spot on the ceiling. "So, with Andrei, we had to, like, sell the same amount of drugs each day and bring the cash home. But with these new guys, at least once a week they, like, increased how much—"

"You had a quota to sell each day?"

"Yeah. In the beginning it wasn't too hard, but each time you reached your quota they raised it—"

"And what happened if you didn't sell enough?"

"At first, they just slapped you." Misty stopped, staring down at her lap, her hair a waterfall that covered her face, remembering when those beatings started. She looked up. "They realized if the kids looked all bruised up people would wonder. So, they graduated to punching in places you couldn't see—the lower back, the belly, the thighs." A shaky sigh escaped. "After that it got much worse . . ."

A single tear made its way down her right cheek. Maybe if she got this out she'd feel better?

Amanda grabbed a box of tissues from a cabinet, placed it in front of Misty. "Take your time. You're doing fine."

"After the beatings started, a couple kids tried to run. They always found 'em and brought 'em back." Misty grabbed a tissue, wiped her eyes, and blew her nose. "At first, they just beat the shit out of them, not caring that they were covered in purple bruises."

Amanda flinched.

"But they couldn't sell drugs again till the bruises healed. In the meantime, the kids still owed rent. And for food and stuff. If we didn't have the cash, we had two options.

"We could 'run a tab,' so to speak, against our future pay, whenever we started selling again, or we could agree to go to the, um, sex part of that club we went to."

Misty heard Amanda's intake of breath and looked up.

"Oh, Misty, I am so, so sorry."

Misty sighed. "Eventually, everyone, even the boys, whether they tried to run or not, had to agree to turn tricks. Which brings us to your original question, about their tattoo. If we couldn't make our quota, we got the tattoo, and had to go the club at night wearing just camies or a sexy bra and panties, allowing the 'guests'"—air quotes again—"to see the *fuck me* tattoos."

Misty batted away the tears now streaming down both cheeks and grabbed some tissues.

Amanda leaned across the table and placed her hand on Misty's arm. She glanced at her watch and said, softly, "Misty, we need to stop for today. But I'm so impressed with how courageous you are. I know you're not done with your story—I want to hear how you got out of there—but that's enough for today. The important thing is you're safe now. I've got some paperwork, then I'll drive you over to the house where you'll stay tonight."

Misty nodded.

"There are four other girls there. You'll have your own bedroom. The house is locked, twenty-four seven, with surveillance cameras. How does that sound?"

Misty shrugged. She wondered where Ratso was right now.

"I'll be back tomorrow after breakfast to figure out a plan for the future—"

"What future?"

Amanda drove Misty to the residence, a converted five-bedroom home. The staff let her choose some clothes. Misty took a long, hot shower, met the other girls, and sat down to a family-style dinner. Surreal how normal it seemed. She listened as the others talked about their days. Where they'd gone and what they'd done—school, some kind of construction training program, learning how to drive. Was that her future?

Misty didn't say much—she regretted how much she'd already said—and no one made her talk. She watched TV with the other girls after dinner until she couldn't keep her eyes open. That coveted room, all to herself? She dreaded going there, where she'd have to think about everything that had happened and what might happen next. But it felt good to wash her face and brush her teeth and get into a pair of pajamas and think about an actual bed, by herself. No beds under the interstate where everyone clustered together for warmth and safety. And the last place she slept with the Russians? A bare, urine- and blood-soaked mattress, with other girls, who held one another for comfort.

So why didn't she look forward to lying in that soft, clean bed, a whole room to herself? She tried to remember when she'd last slept alone. Must have been at her mother's apartment, a lifetime ago, on a pullout couch while Mom kept the bedroom for her "dates." It should have felt comforting, reassuring, safe. And yet as soon as she hit the sheets it felt as if she were free falling, no net to catch her. She couldn't breathe with that knot in her chest. Hostile thoughts invaded her brain, pinging like an arcade game. She couldn't decide what was worse, these marauders or the nightmares. As she lay on her back, arms folded behind her neck, struggling to keep the tears at bay, she heard a quiet knock on the door. Had anyone, ever, knocked on her door for permission to enter?

"Come in."

The house mother, Rhonda, poked her head in. "How're you doing, Misty? Settling in okay?"

Misty sat up and looked into her kind, brown face. "I guess."

"Let me know if you need anything."

"Thanks." Misty lay back down, exhaustion overtaking her, and fell asleep immediately.

The next morning, Amanda showed up at the house at nine-thirty. Using the fingerprints shared by law enforcement, she'd located Misty's foster care records and learned her real name: Britney Nowicki. Her last caseworker could find no information on her mother, which was moot anyhow, because Misty/Britney had just turned eighteen. She'd aged out of the foster care system. School dropout. Essentially kidnapped and enslaved by an Eastern European or Russian drug gang. Sexually assaulted. But technically an adult. Facing the world on her own.

They sat in the empty, light-filled living room, furnished like a house—rugs, upholstered furniture, lamps, tables. Amanda sipped a takeout coffee. "How are you this morning? Did you get settled in last night?"

"I did. Not a bad place." Misty slouched on the midnight blue sofa. "Where'd everyone go?"

"They're all out at programming of some kind. To be in New Hope, you need to be completing your education or enrolled in some kind of training program so you can get a job."

Misty chewed on her lower lip. Is that what she wanted for herself? She wished she could talk it over with Ratso.

"That's why I want to talk with you about your future. Or we could continue with your story, how you escaped from the Russians. Your choice."

Crappy choice. Both scared the shit out of her. In her head, she flipped a coin.

"Okay, let's talk about the Russians."

"So, how did you get out of there?"

Misty regretted her choice immediately. Could she trust this woman? Amanda had promised her confidentiality, right?

Amanda waited.

Heaving a sigh, head down, Misty started. "There was this one guy at the club, one of the fuck-me men, who liked me a lot." She looked up. "I was a lot prettier back then." She smiled, remembering her curvier self, with actual breasts and a soft smile. "He always asked for me. One night after I *serviced* him, I convinced him to take me to this place I used to go as a kid. It's up high, kind of on a cliff, and it looks down onto the city. At night, it's so beautiful. You can watch the lights of the city sparking below, like jewels . . ." Her voice dropped off as she remembered the multicolored, twinkling city lights.

"What happened?"

"He was already pretty drunk before we left the club." She remembered his erratic driving up the winding road. "I persuaded him to bring a bottle of Remy Martin. When we got to the spot, I was surprised there weren't any other cars. Usually it's packed, but it was cloudy that night." Her heartbeat quickened as she recalled what happened next. "So, I knew I had a chance to use my plan."

"What plan?"

Misty studied the texture of the red throw pillow she hugged. "I'd managed to sneak a steak knife into my purse, hoping it would come in handy one day. It was so cloudy he wanted to leave. But I convinced him to stay and listen to music and drink some cognac." She could still feel the cold, smooth surface of the knife blade.

"By then he was so drunk he was snoring. I stabbed him in the neck, over and over." She smiled, remembering how fucking good it felt. Disgusting pig never saw it coming. Blood everywhere. "He started screaming bloody murder, running around like a madman, and I jumped out of the car."

"What happened after that?" Amanda sat on the edge of her seat.

Misty raised her eyebrows with surprise at Amanda's interest. "I waited a while, hiding in the bushes." Would she ever get that picture out of her brain? Him staggering around like a bull after a bullfight, holding his neck, blood spurting out like a fountain, bellowing. The metallic smell of all that blood. "Eventually, between how drunk he was and all the blood he was losing, he collapsed. So, I tossed the knife off the cliff, got back into the car, and took off down the hill."

"Where did you go after that?"

"First of all, I was covered in blood. I had to ditch my clothes. And I had to get rid of the car. I remembered my mother's apartment, not even sure she'd still live in the same place. It'd been a couple years. But sure enough, she was still there. I got the key from where she hid it on the back patio and went inside. She wasn't home. I grabbed some clean clothes and threw the bloody stuff into the dumpster out back. And I just left the car there."

"Why?"

Finally, Misty looked up at Amanda. "I knew they'd be looking for it—either the cops or the Russians—and I was afraid they might know where my mom's apartment was, so I knew I couldn't stay there."

"Where'd you go?"

"Jefferson Park is about ten blocks away, so I walked there. Just found a bench and stayed till it got light." She paused, thinking about that night, sitting on that bench, unable to stop shaking. "I met Ratso a couple days later. He saw me hanging out there, figured out I had no place to go. He introduced me to the other kids."

There it was, the whole story, start to finish. So how come she didn't feel better?

Amanda couldn't get that girl out of her head. She'd worked with tons of runaways. How come this one had taken residence up there, nibbling at her sympathy? Misty was scrappy rather than pathetic, so that was one reason. A survivor. Brave. Tough, but also vulnerable. And now, having promised Misty confidentiality, Amanda had a dilemma. This girl had killed someone—a scumbag, to be sure—if in fact the story was true. Should she look into it? Report it? What would be gained by confirming Misty's story? But, more importantly, how could she help this girl?

Amanda returned the next morning to get Misty started on planning and paperwork. November rain *rat-tat-tatted* the windows outside, the sky a chilly charcoal gray. They talked about getting a Social Security number so she could work, signing up to get her GED, getting on Medicaid, working on getting her driver's license. They set up several appointments over the course of the next week.

"Sounds like I'm going to be busy," Misty said. She tried to imagine it, having a busy schedule. Was this how you got your life sorted out?

"You sure will be." Amanda handed her another form to sign. "Are you ready to talk about your future?"

"What does that mean, exactly?" Misty's future had rarely extended beyond the next day. With the Russians, all she thought of was getting out, and on the street, despite the freedom, she worried about the next meal.

"Well, what do you want to do with your life? What do you see yourself doing in five years, for example?"

Misty played with the zipper on her new blue hoodie. Five years? Way too long to imagine. "I'm gonna have to think about that." She couldn't make eye contact.

"Misty?"

She looked up to face the social worker.

"You need to do that quickly. In order to stay here you have to have a written plan that identifies your goals and a plan for achieving them. Use the rest of today to think it through, maybe talk to some of the women tonight when they come home. I'll be back tomorrow."

Goals? Nobody had ever asked her about her goals. On the street the only goals were finding food and a place to sleep, not getting hurt. If only she could talk to Ratso.

"Oh, I almost forgot. Here are the rules for New Hope. Make sure you read them, because breaking them could jeopardize your slot here." She handed Misty a two-page document. "See you at nine-thirty."

Misty returned to her bedroom, curled up, and read the rules. A shitload of things could get her kicked out—drinking or drugs, of course, but also leaving without permission, failing to sign out and say where you were going, not being back by curfew. Shit, her mother didn't even make her do that when she was fifteen. Almost sounded like jail.

But on the other hand, she liked her room and her own bed. Decent food. The other girls seemed nice. She *did* need to figure out what would happen next.

All day long she tried to think about her future. Getting a GED and a driver's license. What would a regular job be like, like in a store? It would be so great to have a paycheck, her own place, a car.

At dinner, the girls talked about their days. Working as apprentices at a construction site or child care center, attending community college.

"What's it like, learning construction?" Amanda asked Jolene.

"You know, it's pretty interesting. A lot of cute guys." She laughed.

"When will you be done?"

"I think I've got about another year."

Another year? Misty tried to imagine showing up at a construction site every day for more than a year. Or sitting in classes at community college. Never leaving New Hope without signing out. Following all the rules, day after day. Having no money except the small stipend they offered. On the street nobody told her what to do.

But she'd be safe! Nobody beating her up, forcing her to have sex. No stealing food or panhandling. No running from the police. A clean place to sleep every night.

She went to bed with all those bees buzzing around in her brain.

The next morning, Misty tried to eat breakfast with the other girls. She watched them leave for their activities. The closer it got to nine-thirty, the more restless she became. She still had no clue about her goals—did she even want goals? Her breathing speeded up.

After checking to make sure the staff person was busy in her office, she snuck into the kitchen and found a big, black garbage bag under the sink. Into it, she stuffed a loaf of bread and jar of peanut butter, some yogurts, the few articles of clothing they'd given her, and whatever personal toiletries she could scrounge from the bathroom.

She slipped out the front door and hightailed it down the street, hair blowing behind her, heart racing. Free! Grinning, she wondered how long it would take to find Ratso and the gang.

Dog Gone

"Oh my God, you are the cutest dog ever!" I rub Jezebel's tummy and smother her with kisses all over her little Cavalier King Charles spaniel body. She wags her tail like windshield washers, back and forth, and runs in circles.

I pour cream into my coffee as my husband Nash walks into the kitchen.

"Morning, Sydney. You spoil that dog shamelessly, you know that?" Mr. Tough Guy shakes his head but I catch him slipping her a piece of toast from his plate while he thinks I'm not looking. Now who's spoiling her?

"I was thinking of taking Jezzy on a hike, but it looks iffy. Didn't expect the showers last night." It rarely rains in May in Phoenix. Soft, gentle showers fell, what the Native Americans call a female rain. We desperately needed it. Probably wouldn't last for long. Since it was so cool, I wanted to take full advantage with a nice hike before the summer heat set in. Feeling optimistic, I'd donned a pair of hiking shorts, T-shirt, and hiking boots.

"Good, Jezzy could use a nice hike. It's supposed to stop soon, according to the weather app." He frowned. "Not going to the office today?"

Was he jealous? "Nope, taking a mental health day. I could use a nice long hike, too."

Nash looks skeptical. "Gonna be muggy though. Actually, looks like it's just drizzling now."

I take a quick look at the newspaper and make a smoothie. By the time I finish the front section and down the smoothie, the rain has stopped.

"Jezzy, wanna go on a hike?" Rhetorical question. She knows that word almost as well as "dinner."

The love of my life—and Nash's—starts barking like crazy and dancing in circles. God, she's so stinkin' cute!

"Okay, okay, keep your shirt on. I gotta get us water, and you need to get your collar on."

My phone rings. I look at the face. Shoot. Gotta take it. "Hi, Grandma. How are you?" She never calls me. Wonder what's up.

I listen and nod my head. She's not making a lot of sense though. "You know what, Grandma, I'm on my way out the door. Can I call you back later when I have time to talk? Okay, I'll call back this afternoon." Give me a chance to talk to Mom first and see what's going on.

"Okay, Jezzy. Let's get going." More frenzied barking as we head toward the garage.

There are tons of hiking places near where we live in North Phoenix. I debate the merits of several and decide on the Lost Dog Wash in Scottsdale. It's a little longer drive than some, but I haven't been there in a while. It doesn't get too busy and has jaw-dropping views. Give the weather a chance to clear so the trails won't be muddy.

Twenty-five minutes later we arrive at the trailhead. From the looks of the parking lot, the trail isn't crowded yet. The distinctive fragrance of the desert after the rain welcomes us as we exit the car. One of my favorite scents in the world. Can't describe in words what that smell is. Clean, for sure, but what else? Herbal, pungent?

We start up the rocky trail, and frantic Jezzy almost pulls me into a prickly cholla cactus. "Jezzy, knock it off! I know you're excited but stop pulling. You almost hurt me."

When the sun makes an appearance, the raindrops on the cactus spines sparkle like diamonds. Splendid day for a hike. And, so far, we're the only humans among the majestic saguaros and chollas. Frightened rabbits scurry away, their cottontails bobbing, while cactus wrens scold us for disturbing their solitude. The moisture has kept the dust down, so all we have to contend with is the rocky trail. Jezzy's nose twitches at eighty miles an hour, inhaling the delicious desert scents as she races back and forth between brittlebush and bursage. My theory is that the rains freshen up the zillion dog-pee smells on the shrubs, sending Jezzy into orbit. She wags her tail in circles and gives me her biggest dog smile.

We hike for almost two hours when my morning coffee and smoothie catch up with me. I consider peeing off the trail but reject that idea. First, hikers and mountain bikes now flood the trail. And second, not much cover, this being the Sonoran Desert. Not to mention the possibility of rattlesnakes and Gila monsters. The last thing I need is a snakebite on my butt. So, no, I'm not peeing off the side of the trail. I curse the absence of restrooms at this trailhead and envy guys who can just take a whiz wherever they like.

I quicken my pace so I'm almost running now, Jezzy panting to keep up with me. Once in the car, I remember a Starbucks ten minutes away. "Jezzy, we're gonna have to make a quick stop at Starbucks. I could really go for an iced mocha, anyway." She hops into the back seat and I give her more water. "You really enjoyed that, you little poochkins, didn't you? Lots of bunnies and ground squirrels and lizards to chase?" She rewards me with another huge smile.

I pull into the L-shaped strip mall and park in front of Starbucks, embedded among restaurants and little boutique-y shops and spas. Jezebel barks like a maniac as I step out of the car. Darn. It's against the law to leave a dog in a parked car in Arizona, so I'd better take her with me, even though I won't be gone long. But I realize another problem: She's not a service animal, so she can't come into Starbucks. I'll leave her outside with her leash secured on a chair and ask whoever's sitting there to keep an eye out. I'll only be a couple minutes.

But, unbelievably, there's nobody outside. I put the loop of her leash under the leg of a heavy metal chair. I run back to the car and get her plastic water bowl and pour in the remainder of her water in case she's still thirsty.

Inside, I'm surprised at how crowded it is at midday. I make a beeline for the restroom, inhaling the heady coffee aroma. By now I have to go so bad I can almost taste it, as my grandmother used to say. Damn, it's occupied! I dance from foot to foot for what seems like five minutes, my overfull bladder about to explode. I pray whoever's inside will hurry up. Two people queue up behind me. I want to check on Jezzy outside, but I can't risk losing my place in line. Finally, a woman dragging two whining kids exits the restroom, almost knocking me over.

I rush in and struggle to work the button on my shorts, almost peeing on the floor. "Darn these pants." I slap a paper cover on the toilet and plop down as the urine rushes out. Ahh, I sigh, relishing the relief.

I wash my hands and catch a quick glance at myself in the mirror. Ugh. My short brown hair is all plastered down under my white baseball cap. My skin glistens with sweat. Oh well, hopefully I won't run into anyone I know. Gotta get out of here and check on Jezzy.

I walk to the front of the shop and sneak a peek out the window at Jezzy. I don't want her to see me and start barking. Good, she's lying quietly under the chair. By the time I get in line there are several people in front of me.

The line takes forever. How badly do I want this mocha? The longer I wait, the more the coffee aroma makes me crave it. What are these people getting? One guy seems to be ordering coffees for his entire office. The woman from the restroom and the two kids are still arguing about what they want. Come on! I glance outside again to make sure Jezzy's okay. She's lying down, waiting for me, lapping water from her bowl. Such a good dog. I smile.

A few minutes later, the barista places my iced mocha on the counter. I grab the iconic green straw and walk outside, feeling guilty I have nothing for Jezebel.

But wait. Where is she? I look in every direction, but no dog. "Jezzy!" I yell. "Jezebel." The chairs outside are empty. I assume her leash must have come loose and call and call her. A panic rises in my chest, and my heart pounds. I search, I call over and over, but no Jezzy.

I scan the parking lot and start to freak out. I feel like I'm losing it, going crazy. Jezebel has no fear of cars, no sense to avoid them. Would a driver backing up notice her tiny body scurry by? Of course not. My mind refuses to think clearly.

Okay, Sydney, try to focus. Try to be calm. She's got to be here somewhere. Make a plan.

I rush back inside and say loudly, "People, I need your help. I tied my dog Jezzy to a chair outside—just for a minute." My whole body trembles. "She's small—about twenty pounds—and fluffy, brown and white. Has anyone seen her? Did anyone notice her run off?"

The murmuring stops. A couple people working at laptops look up. But no one says a word. My heart beats so fast I'm afraid it might burst through my chest.

My voice rises. "Please!" I beg. "Jezebel's never off leash and has no fear of cars."

Finally, a couple of people say they haven't seen her. Others shake their heads.

It finally hits me: Maybe someone stole her.

Darn it!

Back outside, I call her name again. I still can't believe she's actually gone. I make a quick loop around the shopping plaza, sticking my head into stores and businesses. I ask over and over if anyone has seen Jezebel. Nothing.

Crestfallen, I finally call Nash. I'd hoped I could avoid it because I'm afraid he's gonna rag on me. And he does.

"I can't believe you did that. Left her out there by herself while you—"

"Nash, I didn't have much choice! I had to use the restroom. I kept checking on her. Cut me some—"

"You should have just brought her inside. People do that—"

"She's not a service dog!"

"So what? Have you looked everywhere?"

My eyes fill with tears. "Of course, I have. I don't know what else to do. I glance around the parking lot, hoping to see Jezebel's adorable little face and wagging tail.

"Call the police," Nash orders.

As I Google the Scottsdale police phone number, I notice one of their squad cars drive in on the opposite side of the strip mall. The police car parks in front of AJ's Fine Foods at the other end of the parking lot.

I hot-foot it over there and when I arrive, I overhear two cops talking to an old guy.

"What does she look like?" asks the tall, handsome cop.

The poor guy looks even more frantic than I feel. Shaky, running his hands through his thin white, wild-looking hair, the poor guy's belly protrudes beneath his untucked shirt.

"Her name's Edith Newsome and she has dementia—"

"Okay," says the other cop, shorter and Latino. "We understand that. But what does she look like?"

"She's seventy-seven years old, and she has short gray hair. Not too tall. She has on a flowered dress, I think . . . and white sneakers." Agitated, his eyes dart all around.

On his thin, papery skin, blue veins show through on his pale lower legs and arms, and especially his hands, which are also covered in mean-looking purple bruises. He reminds me of my grandmother, the one I put off earlier. A shower of guilt washes over me.

"And when did you last see her?"

By now, a small crowd has gathered on the large patio area where people chat and eat lunch. Some people still sit at wrought iron tables, but others stand around the old man and the two cops.

"I saw her about fifteen minutes ago. I went inside to get her some iced tea. I thought she'd be okay for a few minutes." He's gotten more agitated. "She lives in the facility across the street." He points toward an assisted-living center. "I was just taking her out for a short visit."

As desperately as I want to talk to the cops about Jezzy, I feel for the old guy. Losing your dog is one thing, but your wife . . . No wonder he's so upset.

I stand on the periphery and watch the drama unfold. The two cops start to interview people sitting nearby, but nobody admits to seeing the old lady wander off. They seem to be getting nowhere. Why aren't they going store to store and asking inside? She can't have simply vanished.

The husband starts to wail and weep. The Latino cop tries to comfort him, but he keeps on.

I shift from foot to foot, checking the time on my phone, uncertain what to do. I'm eager for them to find Edith so they can turn their attention to helping me find Jezzy. Maybe I should put in a call to the police myself. I can't decide what to do, torn between wanting to help and wanting the cops to help me find Jezebel.

I have to do something, so I patrol the parking lot, looking for both the missing lady and Jezzy. The muscles in my neck and shoulders tense and cramp. The longer she's gone, the more likely she's been hit by a car. Or the people who took her will get away. I imagine a huge SUV flattening her. Fear parks itself in a toxic lump in my belly.

By that time, the AJ's crowd has dispersed, and the cops start going from business to business. I tag along and say to the tall one, "Can you guys keep an eye out for my dog at the same time. She disappeared from the front of the Starbucks over—"

The Latino cop whips around and scowls. "Miss, can't you see we've got our hands full with a missing *person*." He pulls out a card and hands it to me. "You're gonna have to call this number about your dog."

I stare at the card: animal control. Just then, out of the corner of my eye, on the opposite side of the parking lot, I spy a tiny old lady in a colorful dress. It appears she holds a dog on a leash. Wait, isn't that Jezebel?

I rush back to the old guy. I grab his arm, pull him up out of his seat, and drag him over to the two cops. "Is that her over there?" I point in the direction of the lady. "Your wife?"

He stops sniffling and squints in the direction I'm pointing. "Yes! That's Edith. She looks all right. Thank God. Oh, thank you, young lady." He wraps me in a bear hug while the cops watch.

All four of us take off toward her.

When we reach her Edith says, "Herbert, look who I've found. It's Finley. How come you haven't brought him to visit me?"

Herbert puts his arm around Edith. "No sweetheart. Don't you remember? Finley's been in heaven for a long time."

I call, "Jezzy." The dog strains at her leash to come to me, making little whimpering sounds. "Officers, this is my missing dog."

Edith holds on to Jezzy for dear life. She pulls the leash in tighter to her chest, and Jezzy barks. Edith pets her and tries to quiet her. "Shush, Finley. You be a good boy now."

"Edith, honey, this isn't our dog," Herbert says gently, putting his arm around her. "This dog belongs to this nice lady." He looks up at me. "I didn't catch your name."

"Sydney." What now?

The cops stand and observe the whole scene, looking back and forth between Edith, me, and Herbert.

Herbert tries to wrest Jezebel away from Edith. A small scuffle ensues.

Edith will not relent. "Leave him alone. He's my dog." She yanks the leash and pulls Jezebel behind her. "You're not taking him."

Again, Herbert attempts to pull Jezzy away. I'm afraid she's going to get hurt.

Edith starts to wail. Big, choking sobs. Herbert pulls out his handkerchief and hands it to her.

Oh, geez. Why don't the cops do something?

Just then, my grandmother's phone call from this morning pops into my head, giving me an idea. "Edith, how about this? How about if I get the phone number where you live and bring Jezzy by for visits. She won't mind if you call her Finley."

When she looks at me, Herbert manages to grab Jezzy's leash and hand it to me.

"That's so nice of you," he whispers. "But honestly, she won't even remember this after today."

"Maybe not, but I'm serious. I'd enjoy bringing Jezzy for visits, unless you think it would upset Edith, or she'd have a hard time letting Jezzy go."

Edith stops crying. The corners of her thin lips turn up into a smile. Her blue eyes crinkle at the corners, and her entire wrinkled face lights up.

My phone rings. "Hi, Nash . . . yep, I found her . . . uh-huh, she's fine. And guess what? She has a grandmother now."

Which reminds me, I still have to call my own grandma back.

Ambivalence

At 5:50 p.m. he sat in his car in the church parking lot and watched people stroll in one by one. All kinds of people. Mostly men, but women too. Some were well-dressed, probably coming from work, while others wore jeans or shorts. Most were older than he was, at least middle-aged, and nobody was in their twenties. Everyone looked so . . . normal.

Could the doctor be right? Was he really that bad? Had it actually come down to this? It seemed awfully extreme. But what about the diagnosis? He sat across from the doctor this morning listening as those two words dropped with a thud in front of him: liver disease. What? He was barely forty. He pulled the visor down and stared at himself in the mirror. He looked fine, brown hair in place. Well, his eyes were a tad bloodshot and his skin had an odd yellow tinge, but other than that . . .

This morning, the doctor insisted he needed immediate treatment. Probably detox but definitely rehab. He scoffed. Not going to happen. Thousands of dollars—who was going to pay for that? Certainly not insurance since he'd lost his job. Should have been more careful coming back from lunch after the bar.

He struggled to find the courage to walk inside, a headache pounding behind his eyes. He looked at his watch again. Six fifty-nine. Shit, Tim, just do it. Mobilize those legs. But his legs wouldn't move. Maybe if he walked in there instead of buying a bottle, Lisa would let him move back in, let him see the kids again. He could get out of that dumpy motel that was all he could afford since he got canned. Every time he thought of his kids his heart broke. Devon's words echoed in his head: "Why does Daddy keep falling down, Mom?"

He placed a trembling hand on the door handle and looked out the window, heart pounding. A guy hurried by, waved, and flashed Tim a friendly smile.

Seven-oh-three. They'd probably already started. Too late. Despite the devastating news, he'd almost made it through a whole day.

With shaking hands, he started the car, backed up and carefully pulled out of the church parking lot, ever vigilant for cops.

Her New Self

This time both kids showed up, as if they were staging a drug intervention. They sat in her living room on a Friday night, Adam and Rachel on the white linen sofa, facing her in the tapestry club chair. Like she was being interrogated.

"I didn't do it on purpose," Wendy said. "It was an accident." Was she whining?

Rachel stared at her tear-stained face and played with a strand of long, wavy auburn hair, a sure sign of her discomfort. "We *assumed* that, Mom." All snippy. "How exactly did it happen?"

Rachel was Wendy's oldest, almost thirty, an ambitious, still single, financial planner. She could tend toward high-and-mighty.

"The neighbor said you were even more upset than she was," said Adam. "Hysterical—"

"I'd hardly use the word *hysterical*. I was backing out of my garage on the way to get my hair done. I was kind of . . . preoccupied."

Adam leapt to his feet. "Preoccupied?"

He started pacing, always the dramatic child. In fact, he acted in community theater in his spare time, aspiring to write plays during his time off from being an estate attorney. Excellent interrogator.

Rachel interrupted her brother. "Adam, let her finish."

Now Wendy felt like she was on trial and started to weep all over again.

Rachel looked at her, eyebrows knitted. "Mom, try to get a grip and tell us what happened."

"I was backing out, and suddenly I felt this . . . this sensation . . . and I could tell I'd run over something." She held her head in her hands, staring at her lap. "I slammed on the brakes and jumped out of the car. My neighbor Jane was screaming and pointing under my car. Her little dog lay between the front and back wheels. All blood and white fur." Wendy started to sob and had trouble continuing. "It wasn't . . . moving. Oh my God, I killed the poor creature." She massaged her temples, paused, and took a deep breath. She looked up. "So, yeah, maybe I got a bit . . . hysterical. Jane adored that little thing. Walked it constantly."

"Why wasn't it on a lea—" Adam began.

Rachel interrupted, amber eyes flashing. "Adam, it doesn't matter."

Wendy had stopped crying. "I've apologized profusely and offered to pay her vet bills and buy her a new dog." Which she couldn't afford. It was some kind of expensive, froufrou breed. She wiped tears from her face and sniffled. "The truth is, I'm mortified. Beyond embarrassed. I should've been paying closer attention. I haven't been sleeping, and I'm always exhausted."

Rachel and Adam exchanged concerned looks.

"Mom," Rachel said, "we've had the sense for a long time that something's just not right with you."

Adam sat back down next to Rachel. "Especially the last couple of weeks. I hardly recognize you anymore."

So, they'd been talking about her.

"You used to be so active," Adam continued. "Going out with friends all the time, exercising, doing volunteer work. You had a full life. But lately . . ."

Rachel left and returned carrying a box of tissues she placed on the table next to Wendy.

"You haven't acted like yourself for a long time," Adam said, "and you really don't look good. Your face looks very . . . I don't know . . . puffy."

Rachel shot him a look and hissed, "That wasn't helpful, Adam."

Wendy didn't need to have her grown children tell her she looked like crap. Some days it was hard to look in the mirror at her lined face and dry, lifeless, dyed-brown hair. The sparkle had gone out of her hazel eyes.

"I'm convinced it's the medication, so I've been trying to get off it."

Adam gave Rachel a quizzical look. "What medication?"

"I started on an antidepressant when your father walked out on me—"

Adam shot up again, pacing. "That was almost five years ago, Mom."

"I'm fully aware of that, Adam." She stopped even trying to hold back her tears. "Do you want to hear about this, or would you rather keep berating me for something that was an accident?" She sat holding her head, crying softly again, and twisting a handful of tissues.

"No one's berating—"

Rachel shot him another one of her looks.

He sat back down, and his voice softened. "Sorry, Mom. I'm going to stop interrupting."

"After your dad left, I was a total mess. It felt like I was, I don't know . . . going under. I was also in full-blown menopause, which is enough to cause anyone to lose their mind. Sweating all the time. Couldn't sleep. Couldn't focus. My primary care doc prescribed Effexor, an antidepressant."

Adam grabbed his phone and started typing.

Wendy narrowed her eyes and frowned. Why couldn't Adam even *pretend* to listen? "I decided five years was long enough to be on that stuff. Didn't like how I was feeling—"

Rachel interrupted. "What do you mean?"

"Well, I've gained a lot of weight, for one thing." She looked over at Adam. "Obviously. And I have trouble sleeping. Sometimes when I get into bed, my heart races." She paused. "I always feel restless. And that damn sweating that started with menopause, it never stopped. I'm sick of it."

"So, what did you do?" Adam asked.

"Cut the dose in half, two weeks ago." She stopped and sucked in a big breath. Her voice dropped. "And now I'm completely freaking out. I can't sleep at all, so I'm pooped all the time. Sometimes when I stand up, I get dizzy—"

Adam stared at his phone. "Mom, listen to this. I Googled 'getting off Effexor,' and there's all kinds of posts from people complaining about how hard it is to get off that stuff. You need to go back to your doctor."

"I agree with Adam, Mom. Don't mess with this on your own."

"Okay, I will, but I need your support, not your judgment."

As they left the condo, Wendy heard Rachel say to Adam, "Man, I really need a run or yoga class after that."

Was she that bad?

Wendy sat across from her primary care physician, the genius who'd prescribed the Effexor. "I want to get off this shit completely. I'm miserable. I'm so distracted with racing thoughts it feels like I'm losing my mind. I killed my neighbor's dog, for God's sake."

That got Dr. Sanders' attention and he looked up from his computer.

"Get me off of this stuff, once and for all. I mean it." The examining room felt like it was closing in around her.

"Here's the thing, Wendy . . ." Dr. Sanders said.

"I don't care about 'the thing.' Get me off of it."

"Well, tapering off Effexor is not all that easy—"

"No shit. I know that. I've been trying on my own for a couple weeks." She couldn't stop tapping her foot. Up and down, up and down.

Dr. Sanders frowned. "Bad idea. How much are you taking?"

"I cut the dose in half."

"Oh boy, way too quick. How are you feeling now?"

Wendy summarized what'd she'd reported to Adam and Rachel, mentioned the neighbor's dog again. Then she teared up. "Sometimes it almost feels like I've got the flu. Plus, people at work tell me I seem spacey, that I have trouble concentrating." She got up and starting pacing.

Last week at her job as a school secretary, her boss and two co-workers sat her down in the break room when no teachers were around and read her the riot act.

"You're making a lot of mistakes," her boss Frank, the principal, observed. "You need to check your work more carefully."

Ellen, another secretary, said, "Wendy, you seem . . . tired or something. Are you sleeping?"

No, of course she wasn't sleeping, but she wasn't about to confess that.

"I gave you two things to do last week and I still haven't seen them," said Tara, the other secretary.

Crap. "Uh, maybe I misplaced them on my desk." How mortifying. Red splotches blossomed on her face.

"Okay, try to relax." The doctor's words brought her back to his office.

She shook away the embarrassing memory.

Dr. Sanders opened Wendy's chart on his laptop. "Let's see, how long have you been—"

"Five years."

"So, a long time. Hang on a sec. I need to check something." He studied the computer screen for a few minutes and turned to her. "You've got what's called 'antidepressant discontinuation syndrome.' Not that it's much comfort, but many people—not everybody—who try to get off an antidepressant experience it."

Who cared that lots of people went through this? She already knew that. "Are you telling me I'm stuck on these pills for the rest of my life?" She drummed her fingers on the chair arm.

"Not at all. But it's time for a psychiatry referral. Hang on." He typed on the laptop. "Okay, I found someone who specializes in antidepressant medications." He grabbed a referral pad, scratched out a few things, and handed it to Wendy. "Hopefully it won't take too long to get in to see him. Let me know what happens.

"Oh, and you should return to your prescribed dose."

That's it? A psychiatrist? Wendy shook her head. That's what he should have done in the first place, damn it. Why did this bozo prescribe it if he couldn't help people get off it?

The instant she reached her car, Wendy called the shrink's office. Despite pleading with the receptionist ("Is this an emergency?"

"No, I guess not."), the soonest she could get an appointment was three weeks. An eternity, given how miserable she felt.

She trudged home and called her best friend Grace, who'd listened to her complain for weeks. She wanted to find out how Grace's mom was faring after her recent move to an assisted-living facility.

"At least I know what it's called now. It's not my imagination," Wendy told Grace. "Antidepressant discontinuation syndrome. Fancy name for hell on Earth."

"When he first prescribed it, do you remember him warning you it would be difficult to get off of? Or was addictive?"

Wendy had put on her walking shoes while they talked and headed outside.

"I'm walking," she told Grace, who was probably wondering why she was breathing so hard. Wendy was trying to lose the weight she'd gained since menopause, the divorce, and starting with the drug. "Back to your question, no." She paused, huffing and puffing up a hill. "Hang on till I get to the top of this hill." She reached the top and bent over to catch her breath. She gazed out over the park, the trees finally leafing out, the grass a tender green. Spring lurked around the corner. Good thing. She didn't think she could stand another gray, cold day.

Wendy resumed. "I don't remember him warning me." Her head was such a mess back then. "And I don't think it's technically addictive, at least from what I've read on the internet. Not in the usual sense. But you do go through withdrawal."

"Isn't withdrawal what addicts go through when they stop?"

"I s'pose . . . I don't understand the difference." Wendy had entered the park, her favorite part of the walk. People whizzed by on bikes. Runners and dog walkers wove around the path as weak sun peeked through the gray clouds. A shirtless guy pedaled by on a bike, no hands, rushing the season.

"Remind me why you got on it in the first place," Grace said. "What's it called again?"

"Effexor. Evil shit. Brad the asshole had just left, and I'd completely fallen apart."

"Okay, I sort of remember now."

"The kids were worried about me. I was crying all the time, couldn't sleep. Absolutely on my last nerve."

"So, what's your plan?"

"Dr. Sanders said I need to resume my prescribed dose—"

"And are you going to?"

"I really hate to. The whole point was to get off this stuff. But—"

"Wendy, listen. You need to do what the doctor says. Hopefully, when you see the psychiatrist, he'll tell you how to do it right."

"I guess. I'm just so damn sick and tired of people telling me what to do and nothing working out right."

Wendy stopped. "How's your mom doing? Has she adjusted to that home?"

"She's okay, not great. Assisted living is a huge change, so it's been slow."

Wendy had lost both her parents early, so she hadn't had to deal with the painful aging process, seeing parents you loved slowly deteriorate. "Must be tough to watch. My heart goes out to you."

Wendy resumed taking the dose Dr. Sanders had prescribed. And within a week she felt a tiny bit better. But, damn it, she would get off this stuff if it killed her.

Wendy found Dr. Rockwell's office in a newish, two-tone, stucco building not far from downtown Wilmington, North Carolina. She took the empty elevator up to the second floor, praying the shrink could help her get her off this crap. Questions clattered around her brain. Would he be young or old? Warm and easy to relate to, or cool and distant? How long would she have to see him? What if she didn't like him, if he didn't understand?

She checked in with the receptionist and sat briefly in the small, serene waiting area—sage green walls, three beige upholstered chairs, a table with old *Southern Living* magazines. Not much time to agonize and fidget before the receptionist gave her a lengthy form to fill out. It demanded all sorts of personal information, pages and pages. She spent fifteen minutes completing it. How was she supposed to know whether any of her grandparents had mental health problems or heart disease? She drew a line through all the "no" boxes.

Finally, Dr. Rockwell came to the door and called her name. After a firm handshake, he showed her to her seat. Tall and nice looking, he had smooth skin, a patrician nose, and close-cropped salt-and-pepper hair. In his forties maybe. He sat in a chair next to the desk rather than behind it.

"What brings you in today?"

The voice inside her head screamed, if you'd read the form you'd know! She crossed and uncrossed her legs and couldn't stop her right foot from shaking. You're agitated, she told herself. Try to relax. She wondered what he thought, staring at this puffy-looking, mid-fifties woman with gray roots and a pinched face. Oh God, let's just get this over with.

"I'm trying to get off Effexor. My primary care physician was clueless about tapering, as he called it. I wish I'd never gotten on this shit."

"How long have you been taking it?"

It's on the damn form. She gave a tight-lipped smile. "Five years."

"Okay. Why did he prescribe it?"

He seemed very relaxed in a navy cashmere sweater and pressed khakis. His gray eyes were kind. Maybe he'd be okay. "I was in the middle of a nasty divorce and starting menopause. It wasn't going well. In some ways, it felt like I was physically ill. That's why I made the appointment. He suggested an antidepressant." She shuddered as she recalled those days of bewilderment and anger, furious with Brad but inexplicably longing for him at the same time. Hoping he'd reconsider.

"Do you know if he gave you a diagnosis of depression?"

Wendy shook her head.

He raised his eyebrows. "He didn't give you one or you don't know?"

"I don't remember him giving me one. Why's that important?"

"Effexor is a medication for people with serious depression and/or anxiety. It's intended to be taken for a time-limited period, not years and years." He paused. "Do you think it helped you with the symptoms you were presenting to"—he consulted the form—"Dr. Sanders?"

Of course, you moron, why would I have kept taking it? She inhaled a deep breath. Get a grip, she told herself. Stop being so angry. This isn't his fault. She struggled to keep the annoyance out of her voice.

"Yes. Within a couple months I was feeling much better. I stopped crying all the time and could sleep better. Wasn't a complete wreck anymore."

"Did Dr. Sanders ever suggest you consider counseling or a support group?"

That stopped Wendy in her tracks. He hadn't, but would she have taken the advice? "No, I don't remember him suggesting therapy."

Dr. Rockwell had this unnerving habit of peering, unblinking, directly into her eyes. Wendy fidgeted in her chair, wishing he would stop staring and move on to how she could get off the Effexor.

"The reason I'm asking is the symptoms—the emotions and behaviors—associated with grief and loss closely resemble those of depression."

"Like what?" she asked, more hostility in her voice than she intended.

"Well, you've mentioned crying and having trouble sleeping, being a complete wreck—"

Wendy started to tear up and said, "Getting divorced after twenty-five years was a nightmare. My husband was an absolute bastard." She jerked some tissues from the box on the table next to her and stabbed at her eyes.

"I don't doubt how difficult it was," Dr. Rockwell said, his gray eyes softening.

"Well, what are you suggesting?"

He uncrossed his legs and leaned forward in his chair. "That you might not have been *clinically* depressed or experiencing *clinical* anxiety of the type that warranted medication. That you might have benefited more from receiving supportive psychotherapy or being in a divorce support group. Most people get through divorces, even terrible ones, without medication that can be difficult to discontinue."

"Right. That's why I'm here," she said. "Why are antidepressants so fucking hard to get off of? I mean, virtually all the women I know are on one kind or another. Just about everyone."

"I'm aware of how widely they are prescribed, especially for women in your age group. Let me explain how they work." He steepled his long, narrow fingers. No wedding ring. "Most antidepressants boost a brain chemical called serotonin that's responsible for feelings of well-being and sleep. Your body gets used to having more serotonin in your brain—that's why you feel better. If you discontinue a medication like Effexor too quickly, your serotonin plummets and you feel like—"

"Shit. You got that right. I tried to get off it on my own by reducing my dose to half of what—"

"Way too fast."

She hung her head. "That's what Dr. Sanders said. Made me feel like absolute crap." She tapped her foot again. Let's get on with it. "What do I need to do?"

"I'll guide you through the tapering off process. But I need to warn you it will take longer than you think—"

"How long?"

"At least a year, maybe longer."

Wendy groaned.

"I know, it's frustrating." His voice was gentle. "And to make matters worse, you may still feel a little discomfort, even tapering slowly."

She heaved a big sigh and adjusted her position in her chair.

"Listen, I've gotten other people off Effexor, and I can help you, too. But you'll have to be patient and talk to me regularly about how it's going."

"Am I going to get depressed again? When I tried to get off the Effexor, I felt just like I did right after the divorce. The depression and anxiety came right back again."

"Hopefully that won't happen if we taper slowly. Meanwhile, I've got a homework assignment for you. I want you to do a little research."

Her eyes narrowed. "Homework? On what?"

"Google 'reactions to divorce.' I want you to learn about how people typically respond to divorce. Then I want you to think about how that compares with how you *personally* responded to your divorce."

She looked skeptical. "Okay."

"And we'll talk about that at your next session."

Worry furrowed her brow. "How often should we meet?" She worried about how much of this her insurance would cover.

"Let's start with once a month. We can adjust that depending on how you're doing and whether you think you need to come in more often. How does that sound?"

"Reasonable." Despite her initial reservations, Wendy found herself liking this guy. She didn't trust him yet, but maybe over time. He seemed sincere.

They wrapped up the session with instructions about how to start the tapering.

A week after her first appointment with Dr. Rockwell, Wendy's son Adam invited her to dinner and chose the restaurant, a fancy new French place. She arrived first and looked around. It was all plants and dark wood paneling. Tasteful jazz—Wynton Marsalis—played in the background. White tablecloths and flowers on each table. The aroma of garlic assailed her nostrils. The hostess seated her, and she opened the menu. The prices alarmed her. Adam had better be paying, because she couldn't afford this.

"Hi, Mom. Thanks for meeting me." She looked up. Adam stood there with a huge grin. He seemed about to burst. What was he so happy about? He leaned over and kissed her cheek.

"Hi, sweetheart."

Adam had started to lose his hair in his early twenties. By thirty he'd started to shave his head. He looked pretty handsome as he leaned down and kissed her on the cheek.

"How are you?" Adam asked. "Nice place, huh?"

"Are we celebrating something?"

He still wore a silly grin. "Not really. I don't need an excuse to treat my mom, do I?"

A waiter wearing a tux arrived and took their drink orders. Dry martini for Adam, Sauvignon Blanc for Wendy.

"How're things?" she asked. "How's work? How's Margaux? How're the house renovations coming along?"

"Whoa. Slow down, Mom. Work's good. Making progress on the renovations. Slow, dirty, and noisy. Driving Margaux crazy."

Margaux did IT work from home. Adam would not stop grinning.

Finally, Wendy asked, "What?"

"We're pregnant!"

"Oh, Adam, congratulations! I'm thrilled for you. So, we *are* celebrating." Curious they didn't tell her together.

"We are indeed."

The waiter returned with their drinks and they ordered, steak for Adam and halibut for Wendy. They chatted about the details of Margaux's pregnancy.

As they started in on Caesar salads, the conversation finally turned to Wendy.

"Did you ever go back to your doctor? I talked to Dad the other day, and he asked how you're doing."

She blanched. "Your father lost the right to know how I was doing five years ago when he dumped me."

"Geez, I can't believe you're still so angry after all this time."

She didn't respond, considering Adam's reaction. She *was* still furious, wasn't she?

The waiter delivered their dinners. Her first bite of halibut, finished in a lemony hollandaise-type sauce, was heavenly, the delicate flavor of the fish enhanced by the sauce. As it melted in her mouth, she thought about her feelings toward Brad, or as she still thought of him, "that asshole Brad."

Adam put down his fork and looked into her eyes. "So, what did your doctor say?"

"He referred me to a psychiatrist. I've seen him once. He's going to help me 'taper,'" she said, using air quotes.

"And?"

"Too soon to tell."

After dinner, as she walked to her car, Wendy thought, a grandchild on the way. What wonderful news.

She arrived at her second therapy session with notes from her research on the effects of divorce. She'd compiled quite a list.

Staring at the paper in her lap, the corners of Dr. Rockwell's lips turned up in a smile. "It looks like you completed your homework." Today he wore a white polo shirt and gray slacks. Why was she tracking what he wore?

"You actually call it homework?"

He nodded. "What have you learned about how divorce affects people?"

As she handed him the list her hands brushed his. She felt her cheeks redden and turned away abruptly. Did he notice?

He studied her list.

"Which of the things on this list did you experience while you were going through your own divorce?"

"I'd say most of what's on the list, except not a loss of identity or guilt. I was sad and angry and stressed out. When Brad first left, he didn't say right away if he would file for divorce or whether he might come back. It was a confusing time. My stress level was off the charts."

He nodded.

"I guess I felt . . . ashamed, maybe? Like a complete jerk. How could I not see how miserable he was? I guess we drifted apart. Apparently, I wasn't paying attention, preoccupied with my own life. Maybe guilt about that."

She paused, tapping her foot.

"Anything else?"

"When he finally said, once and for all, he wanted a divorce, I felt completely rejected. How do you not take that personally? I mean, I was furious, just enraged at him."

"Was he involved with anyone else?"

"Not that I know of. That should have made it easier, I guess. But I think it actually felt worse. That he was leaving me for . . . no one. That being alone was better than being with me." Her eyes glistened. She snatched some tissues.

"Divorce can be especially painful when you're the person being left."

He let her weep.

When she stopped, he asked, "And how about now? How many things from that list are you still experiencing?"

"Interesting question. I'm lonely. I still miss the companionship of marriage. And I guess I'm still kind of stressed. I got a crappy settlement, so I had to go back to work after Brad had encouraged me to quit. I worry about money." She stopped. "And as my son pointed out at dinner last week, I'm still angry."

"What are you angry about?"

Her eyes flashed. "Don't you think I should be angry?"

"You seem to be feeling defensive. Is there something I'm saying that's making you defensive?"

She demurred and took a big breath which she blew out slowly. "You're right. I do feel defensive. People close to me think I should be moving on, but I can't seem to do that. I'm not sure why. I suppose that's why I'm being defensive."

"Important insight. We'll come back to that. I realized when I went over my notes from our first session, I never asked you why you wanted to get off the Effexor, especially since you thought it was helping you."

"I've gained at least twenty pounds since I started it. Plus, even though it helped with the depression and anxiety right after the divorce, lately I don't feel much of anything at all. Except anger."

"Are you saying you feel kind of numb?"

"Kind of, I guess. Before the divorce I enjoyed life, but these last couple of years . . . Nothing makes me happy. Although it thrilled me to hear my son and his wife were pregnant. It felt good to be excited about something."

He sat silent. "That's kind of interesting, what you've said about why you wanted to get off the Effexor. Because some of these things you've mentioned, like weight gain and not being able to feel your emotions, are not usually reported as side effects of Effexor. And other things you mentioned, like sweating, could be caused by the Effexor, but something else might also explain them."

"Like what?"

"Menopause, maybe?"

She sat with that. Wasn't she done with menopause?

"A couple more things. First, we'll lower your dose again. And second, your homework."

Wendy laughed. "More homework?"

"I want you to think about how you would like to feel that's different from how you've been feeling."

The following week, Wendy's daughter popped in for a surprise visit.

"Let's take our wine and sit on the balcony." Although Wendy had hoped for a clear, starry night, an overcast April night sky greeted them. They put their feet up and chatted about this and that.

Finally, Rachel got down to the real reason for her visit. "How are things going with getting off the antidepressant and your visits with the psychiatrist? How many times have you gone now?"

How much of this did Wendy want to get into? She was close to her daughter, but Rachel was not the touchy-feeling type. "Twice. I didn't expect to like him, but I do. I think he's going to be able to help me. To feel better."

"Fantastic, Mom."

"Yeah, for the first time since your dad and I split, I'm kind of looking forward to the future."

Wendy got up and went inside to put on some music, Ottmar Liebert. She needed some of his mellow Santa Fe guitar—a touch of Spanish influence, a touch of new age—to get her into the right mood to talk to Rachel.

She returned and sat. "Guess what?"

Rachel rolled her eyes. "What Mom?"

"I've met a man I'm kind of attracted to. He lives here in these condos." She kept bumping into him, picking up their mail, or at the dumpster. He was nice looking, about sixty, gray hair and eyes, a tan face. Golfer maybe? "I think I might be interested in him."

"How well do you know him? Is he available?"

"No wedding ring, but who knows? That's not the point."

Another eyeroll. "What is the point?"

"Just that I'm attracted to him. For the first time since your dad left, I've actually given some thought to a new relationship."

May arrived, already warm with summer humidity on its way. Things had improved at work. She seemed to be better able to concentrate. No one complained about her focus or performance. She'd started to eat better and took walks almost every day. She'd dropped eight pounds, enough to feel lighter, more like her old self, despite having a ways to go. A woman who lived in her condo complex had invited her for coffee and she'd gone. She couldn't tell yet if they'd become friends, but it was a start.

When she saw Dr. Rockwell for the third time, she proudly reported all of it.

"The tapering schedule seems to be working okay?" he asked.

She nodded. "So far, so good."

"Great. How about your homework? Did you bring in something about how you'd rather be feeling than how you've been feeling?"

She handed him a piece of paper. On it she'd written she'd like to be in a romantic relationship, be less lonely, and have more close friends.

"Interesting. Other than the loneliness, what I see is a couple of changed life circumstances."

She blinked her eyes. "Maybe I misunderstood. I thought what you meant was how I wanted my life to be different."

"Last time, you talked about still being angry about the divorce and kind of numb, rarely excited about life. Are those feelings you'd like to change?"

"You're right. I would like to feel joy again. And the anger, the resentment, well . . . I guess I'm just resigned to it."

He leaned in. "You're not willing to work on letting go of your anger so you can move on?"

Wanting to avoid those piercing eyes, she looked at him, then glanced away.

"Because here's the thing. I'm going to be blunt here. If you're thinking about starting a new romantic relationship, I think your anger will seep into it and be a turnoff. It'll say you have unfinished business with your ex. I would hope by the time we finish this process and you're off the Effexor, you'll be able to focus on the future rather than the past, let go of your resentment, forgive yourself as well as your ex for—"

She leaned forward. "What do I need to forgive myself for?"

"It sounds like you're being defensive again—"

"Know what? You're right." She sat back in her chair.

"Last time you said you felt guilty you'd failed to notice your husband's unhappiness prior to the divorce. Is it possible you're actually angry at yourself? Maybe you need to forgive yourself for that."

He'd gotten close to the bone again. She chewed her unmanicured fingernails, unsure she wanted to go there. She crossed her arms over her chest, closing herself off.

"Wendy, to move beyond this divorce, you've got to do some difficult work. I think it would help to attend a divorce support group. In fact, that's your homework for next time."

She pushed back. "It's been five years. I don't see how sitting around with a bunch of pathetic, *dumped* old ladies like myself will help."

"You may be right. Most people there will be pretty unhappy. But they might not all be 'old ladies,' or 'pathetic.'"

"Maybe, but . . ."

"But what? What have you got to lose?"

"Oka-a-a-y."

"I hear resignation in your voice." He leaned forward and did that intent staring thing again. "Wendy, we're not in a battle here. I'm on your side. My goals are your goals. Getting you off the Effexor and helping you to find more a more satisfying life, to feel better about yourself, to be less lonely."

Her eyes moistened. "I know. I'm sorry to be so . . . so . . . obstinate? Sometimes, I can't seem to get out of my own way. That's what my friend Grace says anyhow." She crossed and uncrossed her legs. "All right. I'm going to open my mind"—she lifted and opened her arms expansively—"and find a support group."

"Excellent." He smiled. "Think of it as an experiment. Come back next month and tell me the results."

"Okay, an experiment. That works."

Just before she left, Dr. Rockwell again lowered the dose. "By the next time I see you you'll be at half."

The divorce support group met Tuesday nights at seven at a local community center. She drove to the first meeting, arriving at ten to seven. At 6:59, she wiped sweaty palms on her black capri pants, took a deep breath, and walked through a misty drizzle into the single-story, red-brick building. She found the room and stood outside, peering in through a tall, narrow window beside the door. Her stomach wouldn't settle down. About a dozen people of various ages sat around two rectangular tables pushed together. She walked in and took a seat. Several people smiled. The men sitting on either side of her nodded and said "hi." Another table with a coffeepot, white Styrofoam cups, and a plate of cookies sat against the wall.

She looked around the table. All but one woman was middle-aged or older. They looked like regular people, making her wonder what she expected. Most were dressed casually in shorts or pants, but a couple must have come from work, a man wearing a dress shirt and loosened tie and a woman in a white dress.

At seven o'clock, a thirty-ish woman said, "Okay, let's get started. Looks like we have a new member, so let's begin with introductions. I'm Brianna, the facilitator, a social worker from Family Services." Her long, straight-brown hair framed her plain, oval face. She smiled. "Let's go around the circle."

People introduced themselves. Brianna pointed to them one by one. How could someone Adam and Rachel's age possibly understand what it was like to be dumped after almost twenty-five years? This girl might not have even been born when Brad and I got married.

The man sitting to her right, wearing a turquoise polo shirt and navy shorts, introduced himself as Travis. Said he'd gotten divorced two years ago. He looked to be in his late fifties. Average looking, balding and with ruddy cheeks and a kind face. He wore a spicy cologne that made her smile. He smiled back.

No one offered anything more personal than how long they'd been divorced or how long they'd been coming. After Wendy introduced herself, the facilitator asked for topics for discussion. A woman named Julianna suggested "moving on."

"Good one," Brianna said. "Who wants to go first?"

For the next hour, people talked about how they were—and more often, were not—moving on. It surprised her how easily she could relate. The woman who'd suggested the topic, Julianna, could have been her alter ego.

"Being left for a younger woman just sucks. My kids keep bugging me about letting go of my anger toward their father and accepting reality. It's hard though. I'm whining, I know, but there's something about that anger I don't want to let go of."

Others murmured their understanding. Julianna's words could have tumbled out of Wendy's own mouth.

She waited to hear what Travis had to say and was disappointed when he passed.

Brianna turned to her. "Wendy, as our newest member, do you have anything you'd like to share?"

Taken aback, Wendy thought for a moment. She was tempted to demur when Dr. Rockwell's face popped into her mind. She took a deep breath. "It's been five years and I'm still feeling stuck. I want to move on. I'm lonely, but I'm having trouble letting go of my resentment toward my ex."

Lots of nods around the table. Brianna said, "Thanks, Wendy. That's all we have time for. Thanks for coming, everyone. See you all next week."

Wendy stood and grabbed her purse. A woman whose name she'd already forgotten approached. "Some of us go out for coffee afterwards. Would you like to join us?"

If Travis went, or Juliana, she would, too. She'd like to get to know them better. She hung around the periphery as people milled around and chatted, eavesdropping on their conversations.

She walked to the exit. Damn. Now it was pouring rain, and she'd forgotten her umbrella. From behind her she heard, "I've got room for two if you want me to walk you to your car."

She turned to see Travis, opening a huge green golf umbrella.

She smiled. "Oh thanks, that'd be great . . . Travis, right?"

"That's right. And you're Wendy." They hurried to her car, which she unlocked. Summoning up her courage she said, "Are you going for coffee?"

"Absolutely. You?"

"I'll see you there."

She ran in to the café through the downpour. She looked like a dishrag, her newly colored hair wet and frizzy. Soft jazz played in the background of the café, dark and cozy on this rainy night. Booths lined the walls, but the divorce group sat at a big round table in the center. Several people were already seated. Someone said, "Wendy, have a seat. Glad you came."

Despite having been introduced to these people in the group, it still felt like being at a cocktail party without the booze. But she spent an hour with them, chatting and laughing, getting to know them. By the end, she felt comfortable, eager to see them again, grateful they had welcomed her.

She attended the group the following week, and the week after that. And she continued to go out for coffee.

In early June, Grace invited her to lunch at The Mediterranean, their favorite café.

"Let's sit outside, even though it's muggy." Wendy said. "I love the striped umbrellas."

Once they had menus, Grace said, "You look great. Have you lost weight?" Grace was in great physical shape herself, a regular exerciser.

"Ten pounds."

"Fantastic. And your hair—"

Wendy smiled. "Got rid of the gray and added some highlights. Your gray hair looks so great on you, but mine just looked tired."

"Well, it looks great. How's it going with getting off the antidepressant?"

"Good. So far, I'm not feeling depressed or too stressed out, but I'm still at a quarter the dose."

"Still seeing the shrink?"

Wendy studied the menu. Should she have her usual Niçoise salad or try something new? "Yep, seen him three times. It's helping."

"I'm getting the Cobb salad again. Guess I'm in a rut. How's it helping?"

"He gave me a homework assignment—that's what he actually calls it—to attend a divorce support group."

Grace studied Wendy with her steel-blue eyes. "After all this time?"

Wendy closed her menu. "I know, right? But yes."

The waitress returned, delivered iced teas and bread, took their orders.

"I've gone four times."

"Wow. And?"

"It's helping." She gazed off at the overcast sky. "The kids and Dr. Rockwell made me realize . . . I've been carrying around this huge resentment against Brad—"

"I agree, for what it's worth."

"—that's just not doing me any good. The group's a good place to . . . they get it. How pissed off it makes me feel, being dumped after all that time." Not to mention how angry I am at myself for not realizing Brad's unhappiness. Dr. Rockwell was right. She took a tiny piece of bread and buttered it. "Plus, some of them go out for coffee afterwards and I've been going—"

Grace smiled at her. "I'm proud of you."

"Thanks. Proud of myself. I've made a couple friends, a woman named Julianna and a guy named Travis from the group, plus a woman who lives in my complex."

"And?"

Wendy couldn't believe how delicious the crunchy, seedy bread was after the weeks of dieting. "Well . . . you know, I've realized I'm not ready for another relationship yet. But I'm getting there. The fact I can even talk about another relationship . . ."

"Is good."

"And now I have someone other than you to do things with, to talk to. I don't feel quite as lonely. And I've started to let go of my anger and accept that this is my life right now. And it's not a terrible life. It's just a different life than the one I had before."

Driving to her monthly appointment with Dr. Rockwell, she noticed that fall was in full force. Resplendent foliage, with Norway maples decked out in vermilion dresses, other trees covered in pumpkin-colored and yellow leaves. And multicolored chrysanthemums everywhere, the essence of fall, her favorite season. How odd that she couldn't remember the past few autumns. She parked, got out of the car, and she paused to look up at the sky, a deep blue it never achieved during the humid summer. As much as she looked forward to the summer, she was always relieved to wave goodbye and welcome autumn back. She inhaled deeply. The air had a different quality, brimming with new clarity.

She sat in the waiting room, remembering how she'd dreaded these visits in the beginning, equating them with defeat or surrender. But this morning she eagerly anticipated her session.

Dr. Rockwell poked his head out the door. "Come on in, Wendy."

She looked up at him and smiled.

She settled into the soft chair and gazed around his office. It all looked the same and yet being there felt different.

"Good to see you, Wendy," he said. "How are things going?" Then he interrupted himself. "Wait. I have to say that, you know, your affect is different."

She gave him a quizzical look, eyebrows knitted together.

"Sorry." He chuckled. "'Affect' is shrink talk for your . . . emotional presentation, how you come across."

"Different how?"

"More settled, maybe. More at peace with yourself. Is that true?"

She contemplated his observation. Was she more at peace? "I think you may be right."

He consulted his notes and looked up. "You've been at a quarter the dose you came with. Still feeling okay?"

"As I was walking in here, for just a second, I thought I was almost happy."

A huge grin spread across his face. "Almost happy? You mean like your old self again?"

She sat with that. "I've been unhappy for so long I'm not sure I can remember what my old self felt like. So, maybe my new self."

Block Island

We'd flown into Boston and driven to Narragansett, Rhode Island, so Mom could see some of New England. Mom and Dad sat inside for the entire ferry ride from Point Judith and never stopped arguing the whole time. The day was so radiant I stood outside on the deck to feel the salt spray from the sparkling waves and listen to the seagulls squawk. Times like this made me hate being an only child. I was counting on this vacation away from their stressful jobs to bring Mom and Dad back together.

We could walk to the old inn from the ferry landing. We planned to rent bikes and go fishing and see Indian arrowheads at the Historical Society Museum, to spend a day at the beach. Mom's favorite thing was to dine *al fresco*, rarely an option in Minnesota. We'd eat fresh fish and clams. Maybe I'd get to try lobster.

By the time we checked in and unpacked, the sunny day transformed into a cloudy evening. We ate out on the hotel's deck overlooking the ocean, but the winds had kicked up, and we had to run back inside and get sweaters. The service was slow despite the dearth of diners. Where was everyone? Dad inhaled two manhattans before dinner, and they split a bottle of chardonnay. We overheard other diners talking about an incoming storm. A feeling of dread settled into my stomach.

"Stacy, why aren't you eating?" Dad said.

My long hair kept blowing into my face. I regretted not bringing a scrunchy. I tried to keep the conversation going so they wouldn't snipe at each other. When Dad started to slur his words, I knew a fight was inevitable. Mom didn't disappoint.

"James, couldn't you just once get through a vacation meal without getting shit-faced?"

Of course, if Dad hadn't been so drunk, he'd have seen how wasted Mom was, too.

We started back to our rooms. "I think I'll walk around, explore a bit, before turning in." I had my own adjoining room but couldn't bear to hear another fight. This one would be about coming on the trip so late in the season.

Mom nodded. Dad said, "Don't be too late."

I walked down to the dark deserted beach. Already, enormous waves battered the shore, and a gale wind blustered. Although the sand and spray stung my face and legs, I sat on the beach and listened to the surf roar. I let the waves' white foam tickle my toes and shivered.

Fifteen minutes later, I wandered back to the lobby to see what more I could find out about the storm. The desk clerk confirmed a hurricane was on the way. Landfall expected tomorrow. How had we not heard a weather report? Ah, that explained why Mom was able to get the last-minute hotel reservation.

The clerk reassured me the hotel was very safe—hurricane proof—but getting a spot on the ferry back to the mainland was unlikely, if the ferry was still running. It looked like we were stuck on this tiny island in the middle of the Atlantic.

I returned to the beach and had an overwhelming urge to walk straight out into the pounding surf, my slender, pale young body swallowed up and never seen again. If I had a sister, she could hold my hand and we would walk into the waves together.

How long would it take them to notice I was gone?

Not Everyone Can Be Saved

I

My phone chirped to alert me to Devon's incoming text.

Hi, Mom. R U okay? Just heard about Uncle Jed. How come U didn't tell me sooner?

Normally, back-to-back appointments during the day kept me from looking at texts. But a last-minute cancellation left me with an unexpected free hour.

I had no idea what my son was talking about. I hadn't heard anything *from* my brother or *about* my brother for at least two years. I started to text him back and thought, better to call. I had at least a half hour before my next appointment. But the call went right to voicemail. Darn! A feeling of dread settled over me.

I tried to get back to the messy will in front of me. By the time I read the same sentence for the third time, I quit. It always amazed me how many intimate things you learned about people's lives when you helped them write a will. More than once, I had thought how well my crazy family life had prepared me for this job.

Unfortunately, our family had sent Jed down a different path. The last time I'd seen him, he was living in a homeless shelter down in Long Beach. I barely recognized him. So thin, a skeleton really, sunken eyes flitting around, and twitchy. He must have been using meth. His once beautiful red hair hung in a long, matted, dirty mess. How long had it been? Three years? I had tried to talk him into getting into a drug treatment program—I even offered to pay for it.

"Thanks, Sis, but it would be a waste of your hard-earned money. Plus, my new girlfriend's staying with me here. She's not around at the moment or I'd introduce you."

Right, I thought, probably out scoring drugs. I asked if he was still on SSI—Supplemental Security Income—and he said he was. Drugs had so decimated my little brother the government considered him to be disabled. I left him with all the cash I had on me and drove back up to Santa Barbara.

I stared out the window at the view: peaceful, downtown Santa Barbara. White stucco buildings with terra cotta tile roofs, green lawns, Spanish-Colonial architecture. I could almost see the Santa Ynez Mountains in the distance. I worked in a small firm and although I wasn't a named partner, wealthy Santa Barbara was a handy place to be an estate attorney. I never would have imagined, growing up in my rough Long Beach neighborhood, that I'd have ended up as a lawyer, much less living in Santa Barbara. I made good money, owned a nice home within walking distance of the beach, and put my son through college. Couldn't ask a lot more out of life than that, especially with my roots.

My phone rang and I jumped. "Hi Devon. Tell me about Jed. What happened?"

"He died three weeks ago. How come you didn't you tell me?"

"Because I didn't know, that's why. How did you find out?" I was sitting in my office chair, shaking now. Devon told me he'd just found out Jed died in a hospital in Long Beach, or more likely on the way there in an ambulance, after overdosing on fentanyl. On one hand, I was shocked but, on the other, his death was not unexpected, given his history and lifestyle. The fentanyl surprised me only because opiates had never been his thing. He was all about stimulants. Stealing Mom's cigarettes in seventh grade turned into pot smoking by eighth, and by high school he'd graduated to crack. Later, it was meth. I didn't even want to think about what he did to get the money for drugs. The best-case scenario was probably petty theft, and the worst? Well, there were lots of worsts, like selling himself on the street. He was a nice-looking kid—freckles, blue eyes with enviously long pale lashes, full lips, a huge smile, wavy red hair, slight build—and I was sure plenty of men would have been happy to drop a hundred bucks for a half hour with Jed. I shuddered. Although I was sure he wasn't gay, I wouldn't be surprised to hear he'd died of AIDS.

"You won't believe this, Mom. I found out by accident on Facebook. Poking around on there today, I happened on a post by Gabriela saying she hoped her father had finally found some peace—"

"What? What do you mean?"

"I messaged her for details and that's what she told me. She found out from her mom."

Jed had fathered a child named Gabriela with a young Latina girlfriend early in his addiction, before he'd gone off the rails. They never married, but he still worked a little then and tried, in the beginning, to support his daughter and stay in touch. But he had no clue how to be a father. How could he? Our father was hardly a role model. In fact, it was a misuse of the term "father" to call either Jed or the man who impregnated my mother a father. I still refused to call him Dad.

I said goodbye to Devon and tried to pull myself together. I had three more appointments before the day was over, and I couldn't afford to fall apart. I could feel a migraine coming on. Yet all I could think about was big, cold glass of chardonnay. Weird, because I hadn't had a drink in twenty-five years. I drank a bit in my early twenties, but when I was pregnant with Devon, I stopped. Once he was born, I figured, why start drinking again? With my family history, I was like a ticking time bomb. So far, I was the only one who hadn't exploded.

II

At five-thirty, still fighting that headache, I finally left the office for the two-block walk through downtown to the parking garage. I passed a crowd of homeless people panhandling on the sidewalk. God, I hated homeless people. Why couldn't they get their shit together? But, at the same time I sympathized, thinking of Jed and his lifelong attempts to straighten out.

Without warning, insidiously, guilt overtook me like the Santa Barbara fog and settled into my bones. Should I have done more? Could I have done more?

I passed Santa Barbara Wine Therapy on State Street. Wine was exactly what I needed. Wine therapy. A tall frosty glass of chardonnay had my name on it. But I willed my Jimmy Choos to keep on walking. By the time I hit the parking garage, big fat tears started their journey down my cheeks. So consumed with choking sobs I could barely talk, I called my BFF Sara.

"Greer, what's the matter? I can hardly understand you. Are you okay?"

"Not really, no," I said, as I sat in my Lexus, in no shape to drive.

"See if you can calm down and tell me what happened." Sara worked part-time as a psychologist, accustomed to dealing with meltdowns. While she yelled at her two teenage kids to turn the TV down to give her some quiet, I took a couple of deep breaths and regained my composure enough to speak.

"Jed died. Three weeks ago."

"Wait, what? Your brother Jed, the homeless one? Three weeks ago?"

"My only brother. Yeah, the homeless one. I found out from Devon this afternoon." Although I rarely talked about my family history, Sara and I had been close since I had moved to Santa Barbara seven years ago. Given what she did for a living, over time, she had weaseled the whole sorry tale out of me.

"Greer, I can hear you're upset. Are you at work?"

"No. I'm sitting in my car in the parking garage." Sniffling, I searched in my bag for tissues.

"Right. I can be there in five minutes. Ten tops. Stay there and I'll come."

As I waited for Sara I stared at my bloodshot blue eyes in the rearview mirror, wiped the mascara streaming down my face, and smoothed over my messy blond hair. Five minutes later I watched Sara walk-run up to the garage where I waited out front. She looked like an old hippie—long curly brown hair, streaked with gray, a long flowy cotton dress covered in big, colorful flowers, taupe Birkenstock sandals. She threw her arms around me first thing and stared into my tear-stained face. We sat down on a nearby bench.

"Thanks for being such a good friend. I'm a friggin' mess. Finding out this way was like a sucker punch to the gut."

"When did you last see him or have any contact with him? I can't remember you saying anything about him in ages."

"I've been trying to remember that. It's always been tough to keep in touch because he had no phone or email or address. Probably three years ago. I made myself visit him at a homeless shelter in Long Beach. What a shit show." I dabbed my eyes as more tears flowed. "He seemed to toggle between the street—or maybe the beach—and the homeless shelter. When the street got to be too much, he'd drag himself inside. Our weather lets people stay outside forever if they want to."

"Was he clean?"

"I'm sure he wasn't. He looked like crap. Gaunt. That's probably the reason he'd never stay in the shelter for long—'cause they don't let you use. If you're high or have drugs on you, they throw you out and give your bed away to some other hapless soul who isn't drunk or on drugs."

"Did he ever try to get clean?"

"A bunch of times. As many times as he could get someone to pay for it. I footed the bill myself a couple of times. That last time I saw him I told him I'd pay again if he'd give it another try."

"But he said no?"

"Told me not to waste my money." I stifled a sob and blurted out, "Then why am I beating myself up, wracking my brain, trying to think of what I could have done so it wouldn't have ended this way?"

"Greer, you know that's ridiculous, right?"

"Why is it ridiculous?" How could she expect me to be rational?

"Do you want my professional opinion, or should I answer as a friend?"

Oh, God. What's the right answer to that one? I wasn't up for having to decide right now. "I don't care."

"Well, that was a trick question, 'cause the answer's the same, whether I respond as your best friend or a psychologist.

You did everything you could. More than most people would have done. My God, you virtually raised that kid!"

"I know I did, but apparently I didn't do a great job. If I had, he wouldn't have turned out so fucked up." I had a quick memory flash of getting Jed ready for bed when he was little while Mom worked the three-to-eleven shift at the hospital. Reading Maurice Sendak's *Where the Wild Things Are*, his favorite book. Sometimes three times before he'd drift off. Ruffling his beautiful hair, kissing him softly on the cheek. How could that sweet little boy have turned into such a miserable wreck?

Sara jerked me back to the present. "In reality, he never had a chance. *You* never had much of a chance. You're a freakin' miracle! You know that, right? You defied the odds. You buckled down and vowed you would get out of that morass intact, and you did. He didn't. Despite all you did, your dysfunctional mother and absentee father never gave that kid a chance at a normal life. Isn't your father the one who introduced him to drugs?"

"I don't know that for a fact, but it's pretty much what I've always assumed."

"Listen. Now it's the professional psychologist talking: Let go of that guilt. Nothing good will come of it."

"Okay. Thanks for listening. You're the best. I really need help figuring out how to get closure on this thing."

"That may happen. But some things in life we don't have the luxury of getting closure on, no matter what we do."

God, I hoped she wasn't right.

"Go home and take a walk on the beach. Or find a yoga class. Or meditate. Do something physical. Take care of yourself. I've got to run. Call me tomorrow, okay?"

"Good advice. I like the idea of a nice dinner and beach walk. I need to call Julian, too. I'll talk to you tomorrow." We hugged.

My futile commitment to save Jed was one of the unre-solvable issues that caused my marriage to disintegrate. But Julian was a good dad—a great dad, actually—and we got along well. Also a lawyer, he still lived in Scottsdale, and I needed to talk to him about this. Had Devon already told him?

III

Finally able to drive, I made the short trip home to my pale-blue, shingled Craftsman-style home on West Hayley Street. I threw my purse and briefcase on the credenza in the foyer and kicked off my shoes. I hated what heels did to your feet, but they looked so darn good. I sat down on the sofa to massage my aching toes and my cat, Jupiter, came running to greet me.

"Hi, Jupe. Yeah, I'll feed you in a minute." As I walked into the kitchen, he wound around my legs, threatening to trip me. "How was your day? Mine sucked. Thanks for asking."

It was already a quarter to seven. As much as I wanted to plop down on the sofa and veg, it would do me more good to take a walk. I went upstairs to change, thinking about what kind of portable snack would tide me over on my walk. I changed into leggings, sneakers, and a UC Berkeley sweatshirt. The shirt was a gift from Devon, now in grad school there to study journalism. I came downstairs and grabbed a protein bar from the kitchen cupboard, along with my phone and headset.

I left the house and turned east on Hayley, toward State Street, where I would hang a right toward the beach. I wanted to get there soon enough to walk on the beach for a while—maybe even sit and listen to the waves—before it got dark. Not a great place to be after dark. The evening was beautiful, still clear, but the fog would roll in any minute. I usually brought my phone on walks to listen to music and for safety. Tonight,

I wanted to see if I could reach Julian before it got too late. I knew he turned in early, because he got up at an ungodly hour, like everyone else in Phoenix in the blistering hot summer.

"Hey, Greer, how's it going?"

"Hi, Julian. Not great, to tell you the truth. Did Dev tell you about my brother dying?"

"He did! Boy, what a shock. When did you find out?"

"When Dev texted me this afternoon!" I walked straight into the ocean breeze. It had gotten chilly, despite being July. Good thing I had on a sweatshirt. I could already hear the Pacific. With the sound of the waves crashing and the tangy smell of the ocean, I relaxed.

"You're kidding! I thought he died a couple of weeks ago."

"Three to be exact. My family is so fucked up. Neither Gabriela nor her mother had the decency to call me and let me know. Nor did my Aunt Marilyn. After all I did for Jed. Gabriela, too." I started to cry, hard. And I neglected to bring any tissues. Shit.

"Greer, I'm so sorry. I can't imagine how hard this must be for you—"

"And yet I feel guilty! I know that's stupid—or at least Sara told as much—but that's how I feel."

"Well, I wouldn't say it was 'stupid,' but I would remind you I was there during those tough years. You did *a lot* for him, and for Gabriela—"

"I know, I know, and you thought it was too much. I don't want to rehash all those old issues, but I needed someone to tell me that . . . that . . . I don't know, that I did everything I could."

"You *did* do everything you could. *Of course,* you did! You did way more than any other reasonable person would—"

"But it wasn't enough." Finally at the beach, I took off my sneakers and carried them, walking through the sand toward the waves, listening to their roar. Occasionally, when I got too close to the waves, I felt the salt spray. Near the water's edge, I dodged jellyfish on the sand—beautiful, pink, speckled, stinging jellyfish, big as dinner plates, tentacles two feet long.

"Sometimes it isn't enough," Julian said. "Not everyone can be saved. Wants to be saved. I don't want to reopen those wounds either, but that's what I kept trying to tell you back then. That Jed, for reasons we couldn't understand, didn't want to be saved."

I loved how the sand felt on my bare feet. Still warm on top, but when I squiggled my toes down into the sand, it was damp and cool. Darkness settled around me and fog rolled in, so grabbed my shoes and turned around. "Julian, you were right. Jed didn't want to be saved, not then and not later. 'Cause I still kept trying periodically after the divorce—"

"Devon told me you did. You never gave up on him, but he gave up on himself. That's what I wish you could accept."

I sat down on a bench to put my sneakers back on. "I can't stop thinking about how much of a waste it was, his whole life. How much pain he caused to so many people. I'm glad my parents aren't alive to see this, even though I know they're the ones who produced this pathetic human being who wasn't equipped to deal with life."

"Listen, I'm glad you called, but I gotta go. Take care."

As I walked home, I realized tomorrow was Saturday. Yay! I needed some downtime, but I also knew I had some difficult phone calls to make. The prospect gave me an instant upset stomach.

IV

On Saturday I woke up to fog and gloom. Instantly, I started to obsess about these phone calls I had to make. I finished a bowl of yogurt and fruit and forced myself to follow Sara's suggestion and go to a yoga class, even though I wasn't in the mood. Maybe the yoga would distract me for an hour and be good for my head and my body. Help me to be as calm as possible before I picked up the phone.

When I got home, I made my first call, the most diffi-cult, to my Aunt Marilyn, my father's twin. I tried to think through what I was going to say. Marilyn's MO was to hijack a conversation and force it into whatever direction she wanted. You'd think my years as an attorney would have prepared me to counteract that, but work was work and family was family. I brewed another cup of coffee and sat down on my living room sofa. Taking a deep breath, I picked up the phone.

"Hi, Marilyn, it's Greer." Nice and neutral. "Happy Saturday morning."

"I know why you're calling."

Oh boy, here we go. Not, how are you? Or nice to hear from you.

"Why's that?" Trying to keep my voice even. Jupiter saun-tered over and jumped into my lap.

"You're calling about Jed."

"You're right." Breathe, Greer. Jupiter purred as I stroked him. "I was disappointed no one contacted me when it hap-pened. That I had to find out three weeks after he died, in a text from Devon, who found out about it on Facebook—"

"You sound angry—"

"Ya think? Wouldn't you be angry if no one told you about your own brother dying, and you had to find out through a Facebook post?"

"Calm down, Greer—"

"Don't tell me to calm down! Would it have killed you to pick up the phone and let me know when it happened?

I don't even know if he was cremated or if they had some kind of service or anything. How am I supposed to get any closure?"

"Well, to answer your question, we cremated him, and Gabriela asked if she could spread his ashes over the ocean—"

"Why couldn't you include me in that? After all I did for him over the years!"

Marilyn didn't respond.

"Huh? Why couldn't you let me know so I could have taken part in that?"

"I don't think the family—"

"The *family*? *I'm* his family? What do you mean, 'the family?'" Now, I was up and pacing, Jupiter long gone after hearing my raised voice.

"Well, I mean Gabriela, of course. And Estela." Gabriela's mother.

"Why should their preferences trump mine? I virtually raised that kid! Paid for rehab twice. The last time I saw him I offered to pay again. He said no. He wasn't interested in getting clean."

My father's family had been wealthy, but because my dad was as bad as Jed was, when my grandfather died, half of Dad's portion went into a trust Marilyn managed for Jed. That trust paid for a few rehabs, too. For years, I'd had power of attorney for Jed, but eventually Marilyn went to court and, with Jed's cooperation, wrested it away from me. When my father passed away, half of his part of the estate went to me, but Marilyn managed Jed's half.

"Greer, you seem to expect some kind of credit for raising Jed, as you put it, but as far as I'm concerned—"

"Don't you *dare* say, look how he turned out! How could he have turned out any different?" My simmering resentment was about to boil over. "After Travis was killed, Mom fell apart, and my father—your brother—was already long gone."

My father was a Vietnam vet. My mother met him while working as a nurse in the VA hospital in Long Beach. The war left him with an amputated leg and PTSD. He healed from the former but never the latter. He'd started using cheap heroin in Vietnam and picked it up again when he returned. They didn't know much in those days about treating PTSD. It devastated our finances. When Mom made him leave, I was eight and Jed was still a baby. Travis was born shortly thereafter, the product of an unexpected visit by my father, whose sexual advances my mother could never resist, no matter how strung out he was.

"Your dad did the best he could—"

"The best he could? What planet are you on? He was on full disability by then! Totally addicted! Using his disability checks to score drugs. He's probably the one who introduced Jed to drugs!" Neither my mother nor my aunt could look at my father with an ounce of objectivity. They both got hung up on the whole war hero image he liked to project. And Marilyn could never acknowledge the role of drugs in my father's premature death.

"Stop yelling. You don't know that. Your father would never use drugs with one of his children. He loved all three of you—"

"I don't doubt he loved us. But he never took one iota of responsibility for us, even before the divorce."

"Well, that might be your perspective, but I chose a different way to look at it."

Marilyn, the high and mighty, childless, living in Santa Monica off her inheritance. What was I thinking, calling her? "Marilyn, I need to go."

I hung up and paced, zooming back to those days after my father left. The only supervision my brothers got was from me, because mom worked full-time. But I had a life, too. School was super important. I figured out the only ticket out of the madness of our home life was success in school.

When Travis was six, he was hit by a car and killed. My father had already been gone for years, returning every so often to stir things up and seduce the boys into thinking they had an actual father. After Travis died, Mom went off the rails. She'd always been a daily drinker, but before the accident she'd kept it in check enough to work every day. After we lost Travis, she descended into hell, losing one job after another. If I hadn't taken over the finances, not a single bill would have been paid.

V

On Sunday, still reeling from yesterday's conversation with my aunt, I called Estela to see if I could clear the air. I knew it would be a tense call, so I walked toward the beach while I talked. I hadn't spoken to her in years, but amazingly, the cell-phone number I had still worked. She answered on the second ring. "Hi, Estela, this is Greer Larson. How are you?"

After a pause she said, "Not so good. Jed's death hit me hard." Strange, since she hadn't seen him in probably twenty years or more. He'd dropped out of her and Gabriela's life when Gabby was still a toddler. I remembered, because I started to send checks soon after he left. Even when I was in school and couldn't afford it.

"Actually, that's what I was calling about. I'm disappointed Devon and I found out from a Facebook post of Gabby's. After all I did for you guys, couldn't you at least have had the courtesy to let me know that he died?" I felt proud of myself for being assertive, working hard to not talk through clenched teeth. The silence lasted so long I thought the call had been dropped.

"Estela, are you still there?"

"Yeah. I'm trying to figure out what to say. You were never my favorite person, Greer. And you were never Gabriela's favorite person."

Shocked, I stopped walking and tried to keep my voice from shaking. "And why is that? I helped the two of you out for all those years."

"Yeah, you did. But when I needed you most, you weren't there."

I arrived at the deserted beach. "If you're referring to your request to take Gabby off your hands when she was a teenager, that's bullshit—"

"I couldn't handle her! I needed help!"

"How was that my problem? I had a son of my own and was a single parent, too. I worked sixty hours a week, struggling to hold it together! And yet I sent you checks every month you were more than happy to cash—"

"Of course, I did! What was I supposed to do? Jed never helped at all!"

"That's why I sent those checks, even though it wasn't my responsibility. I'm sorry if I expected—"

I was about to say "gratitude" when the line went dead.

That bitch hung up on me!

I stood and watched the waves, fists clenched, tears streaming down my cheeks. Why had I thought it was a good idea to call Estela? Now I felt even more upset. I had hoped for some kind of explanation, some reason they couldn't call me and include me in whatever they did to close the final chapter of Jed's pathetic life. But there was no closure here. I tried calling Sara, but it went straight to voicemail. In desperation, I called Devon. It seemed inappropriate, calling your twenty-five-year-old son when you were at your wit's end, but at this point I didn't care.

"Hi, Mom—"

Interrupting, I said, "Oh, Dev, I'm having such a tough time with this . . . I . . . I don't know what to say. I'm so sorry to bother you. I'm sure you must be busy with school—" I was sure he could hear me sniffling and sobbing.

"Mom, it's okay, it's fine. Has something else happened?"

"I made the mistake of calling Estela a few minutes ago . . . to find out why neither she nor Gabby called me about Jed. But all she did was tell me I wasn't their 'favorite person' because I refused to take responsibility for Gabby when she was out of control as a teenager—"

"Wait. What do you mean? What did Aunt Estela ask you to do?"

"Have Gabriela come live with us. You and me. Dad had already left, and you were about twelve or thirteen. I couldn't handle it. I was working long hours, trying to be a good mom to you. Hanging on by my fingernails."

"Well, that's ridiculous," Dev said, always the loyal son. "Expecting Gabby to come from California to Scottsdale and move in with us. Especially if she was too much of a handful for Aunt Estela—"

"And she never even said thank you for the checks I sent all those years!" I sat down on the sand. The waves rolled in. The gulls screeched in the background. But the salt air didn't calm me down.

"What checks?"

"I sent money every month, starting when Gabby was a little girl, because Uncle Jed never supported her."

"Wow, I never knew that. Mom, I'd have to say supporting her all those years was *way beyond* the call of duty. It absolutely was *not* your responsibility to make up for what Uncle Jed wasn't doing. You know that, ri—"

"That's exactly what I told her—and she hung up on me!" I started to cry all over again. Damn. I'd forgotten tissues again. "And I know this is stupid, but I feel guilty."

"Mom, I must say, that is stupid. But I get that you need to do something."

What a great son I'd raised. I wiped my nose and eyes on my sleeve—yuck. "Yeah, I do. What about if we went down to the homeless shelter and talked to some people there, tried to find his last girlfriend or something?"

"When?"

"How about next weekend you fly here from Berkeley on Friday night and we drive down to Long Beach on Saturday to visit the shelter? Say our goodbyes. Have our own little memorial service."

"Good idea."

VI

Devon and I got up on Saturday and drove the two-and-a-half hours to Long Beach. The shelter looked exactly as it did three years ago when I last visited Jed there: filthy, chaotic, smelling of urine and vomit, utterly depressing. We explained to the staff who we were and why we were there. But no one on duty claimed to have known Jed or anything about how he'd died. And they acted surly and uncooperative when we tried to find out anything about his so-called girlfriend. Maybe he'd spent no time there in his last year.

So, we left and drove instead over to Bluff Park where Jed had spent countless nights. We parked on the street and walked over the spongy, lush grass to the paved walk along the cliff, high above the beach.

"How did he get around?" Devon asked.

"He always had a rickety old bike I'm sure was stolen."

We walked along the cliff, enjoying the ocean breeze coming off the blue Pacific. I inhaled the scent of mint and lavender coming from a shrubby plant with purple blossoms I always called it catmint, although its official name is nepeta.

I climbed down forty-two steep stairs with Devon following and crossed the busy, paved bike and running paths to the wide, flat beach. We sat on the sand, gazed out at San Pedro Bay, I realized this might be Devon's first major loss experience.

Devon sat in the sand next to me. "I wish we had ashes to spread."

"Yeah, me, too." I settled my gaze on him, struck by how handsome and healthy he looked, with his auburn hair, wavy like Jed's but not as red, his clear blue eyes and tanned face, dressed in khakis and a crisp blue linen shirt. In contrast to my last memory of my emaciated brother in filthy, tattered rags.

"Mom, why are you staring at me? Are you okay?"

"Mm-hmm. Thinking how good you look today and how awful Jed looked when I last saw him a couple of years ago." Watching the waves, hearing them crash on the shore, over and over, felt healing.

"I hate to admit it," Devon said, "but I was taken aback at how bad the shelter was. Disgusting. I can see why Jed wasn't eager to spend any time there. It creeped me out."

"It *was* creepy. I'm sure those people who work there do the best they can with whatever meager resources they get. And they have to deal with those poor wretched souls, day in and day out. Crazy, drunk, high, violent . . ." I shuddered. "Let's say our goodbyes to Jed and get out of here."

We each said a few words and turned around to walk back to the car. As soon as I started the car Devon asked to go back to see the house Jed and I grew up in and my old neighborhood. I thought about it for a minute and said no.

"Come on, Mom. I want to see where you and Uncle Jed used to live."

"I don't think so, Dev." I kept my eyes on the road. "Not a good idea."

"Let's just drive by for a quick look. So I can see it."

"I said no!"

Devon was born in Scottsdale a few years after Julian and I finished law school at Arizona State. He'd never seen where I grew up. I understood his curiosity, but I couldn't go back there. Especially not today. Part of it was shame, but the bigger part was not wanting to go down that road again. Not having the stomach for revisiting the past. It was all I could do to handle the volcano that erupted when I heard Jed had OD'd.

"Geez. Sorry. You didn't have to take my head off." He slumped down and turned toward the window.

We drove in silence for fifteen or twenty minutes, the tension in the car thick as mud. Devon's body language told me he was upset, all curled in on himself, staring out the passenger door window. I owed him an apology, but I wasn't ready yet.

Finally, I said, "Dev, honey, please look at me. I'm sorry. I shouldn't have snapped at you like that. You didn't deserve that. It's just . . . this whole past week has really taken a huge toll on me—"

"I know it has, Mom—"

"Wait. Let me finish. I spent my childhood trying to take care of Jed and Travis. Doing the best I could because neither of my parents was up to the task . . . and even into adulthood. That's one of the reasons your dad and I ended up divorcing. He couldn't take it anymore." I kept my eyes on the road so I didn't have to look at Dev. "I don't fault him for that. I don't. The only reason I'm even telling you this is I feel like I owe you an explanation for not wanting to go back to that house."

"It's okay, Mom. Apology accepted. I get that, or at least I'm trying to. I knew your childhood must be pretty bad. After all, look at how Uncle Jed turned out. But you've never talked about it."

"You're right. I haven't. Only two people in the world know the whole story, and that's your dad and Sara. That's why I can't handle going back there today, especially not after the shelter. And especially after your Aunt Marilyn implied last Saturday that the reason Jed turned out to be a drug addict is because I didn't do a good enough job raising him."

"Wait. What?"

"Yep, that's right. She as much as told me I did a lousy job. She probably blames me for Travis dying, too."

"That's the second time you've mentioned Travis. Who is he?"

Shit. I forgot I'd never told Dev about Travis. "Travis was my youngest brother. He was hit by a car when he was six."

"Mom, are you kidding me? I never knew you had another brother!"

"That's because we never spoke of him again after he was killed. Grandma fell apart after that, and my father had already left. Nobody ever told Jed and me 'don't mention it,' but we knew. It devastated Jed. They were only a year and a half apart. Best friends." I was glad I was driving and had an excuse to keep my eyes on the road, afraid if I looked at Devon I'd start crying again.

I had his full attention now.

"Wow, your family was chock full of secrets, wasn't it?"

"Yeah, it was. There were only two things I wanted in life growing up. One was to do whatever was necessary to get out of that crazy household, and the second was to create a normal family for myself. And I almost succeeded."

"What do you mean 'almost succeeded'? You and Dad and I have a great family."

"I guess. Maybe. You turned out great, but I wish I could have kept us together."

"Mom, I have a great relationship with both you and Dad, and you guys get along really well."

"It thrills me to hear you say that, Dev." I was trying so hard not to cry.

After that, the car went quiet. I had given my son a lot to chew on, maybe more than I should have. But he was a mature twenty-five-year-old and a sensitive young man. As we approached Santa Barbara, I only half listened to Devon go on about one of his courses or a professor or an assignment he struggled with. I couldn't decide whether our trip to the shelter made me feel better or worse about Jed dying. I could hear Sara's words echoing through my brain: "Some things in life, no matter what we do, we're just not going to get closure on."

Looking for Solace Elsewhere

He laughed uproariously. "I thought that, too. I can't believe you were thinking the same thing."

Mark Webster was on his cellphone, talking to one of his colleagues—his *closest* colleague—Erin Rockwell. They had worked together for three years. Mark did the legal work for her agency, Berkshires Family Services in western Massachusetts, where Erin worked as a social worker.

He leaned back in his leather chair, legs sprawled out in front of him on the desktop. Jenna Webster migrated from the kitchen when she heard his laughter, standing just out of sight, peering surreptitiously through the French doors. He seemed so relaxed. She couldn't believe he was talking to that woman again. It had become every friggin' night. She wondered how often he saw her during the day, unable to remember him ever being this animated, even in law school. Mark was by nature an introvert. For the fifteen years they'd been together, she'd always had trouble getting him to talk, especially about his feelings.

He'd say things like, "What's the point in talking about it? It is what it is. Stop being so intrusive."

Maddening.

Tonight, Jenna watched him, striped tie loosened, blue linen shirt wrinkled after a long day, and remembered how attractive she once found him. The strong silent type, she'd told her sister. Since then, Mark's straight, salt-and-pepper hair had turned almost white, in contrast to his steel-blue eyes. He was so darn handsome. And still fit, breaking a sweat early every morning on the stationary bike.

Did he still find her attractive with fifteen pounds extra pounds and chestnut hair now streaked with gray? He used to love her freckles and upturned nose.

His voice lowered and she had a hard time hearing him. Should she move closer? She didn't want to get caught.

"I know. It made me angry, too," he said.

What were they talking about? And why did it have to be every night?

"No, I don't think it looks too casual. You look good in that—I think she'd love it."

What? Now he was complimenting her on her appearance?

She'd only met the woman once. Two years ago, she and Mark had invited Erin and her husband over on New Year's Eve. Erin was definitely attractive. Elfin, with short, spiky hair, bleached blonde at the tips, a competitive cyclist like Mark. She had an infectious smile and a spunky, bubbly personality, in sharp contrast to her sullen husband, Drake, who bristled with resentment about their recent move to Pittsfield for her job.

"How 'bout if we meet tomorrow for coffee or lunch? I know your schedule's tight." He laughed again. "I'm so glad you said that. I love the way you phrased it. We can work that through over lunch."

Was he actually grinning? Jenna couldn't remember when Mark looked so happy.

"Okay, Thursday. I'll let you know what I come up with. Call or text—better still email—if you have any more thoughts about it."

Lunch Thursday? Why? As he hung up, she hightailed it back to the kitchen, arguing with herself. One half of her said it was time to confront him about what was going on with Erin, right under her nose. How did he have time for all these calls and lunches with Erin when he rebuffed her attempts to get him to do stuff with her? Like last weekend when she'd asked about a movie and he claimed he had too much work.

But the other half, her better half, said she was being paranoid, that her imagination had spun out of control. The second half lost.

His footsteps creaked on the floorboards of their remodeled hundred-year-old farmhouse. Grabbing a sponge, she brushed crumbs from the granite counter into her palm. "Who was that?"

He didn't answer right away. "Erin." He picked up an orange from a fruit basket on the island and tossed it from hand to hand. "From work."

She aimlessly scrubbed the countertop, so she didn't have to look at him. "You seem to talk to her a lot—"

"Jenna, it's my job! We're working together on a complicated project. If I didn't know better, I'd think you were jealous."

Of course, she was jealous! He spent more time talking to that woman than he did with his own wife. She tried to keep her voice neutral. "And you need to talk to her every day, at home, after work? And have lunch with her?"

"You know as well as I do these projects take on a life of their own. They don't always end at five o'clock. Stop needling me." He turned and walked back toward his study, orange in hand, and closed the doors.

Needling him? So now she was a nag.

She kept her mouth shut after that. By the time Mark crawled into bed, she had already turned out the light on her side, unable to focus on her novel. It gnawed at her as she tossed and turned, weird dreams waking her. Was their marriage falling apart? He went along with her choice not to have children, but maybe he really did want kids. Their jobs took up so much time though. They didn't hike or ski anymore, like they used to. Shit, they barely ate dinner together. Instead of movies and plays, work and chores filled their weekends.

The first years of their marriage they talked at the end of the day and were never too tired to make love. Was that just a phase? Now, they rarely made love, going to bed at different times, both exhausted. Even on the weekends, he barely touched each her. How did other busy couples deal with this? They couldn't be the only overextended professional couple. And what about couples with children, like Maya and Adam? Their lives had to be even busier. So, it wasn't just being too busy. There must be something else going on.

She woke up exhausted. Mark had already left by the time she dragged herself out of bed. Despite trying to get it out of her head, worries of Mark's relationship with Erin intruded all day. She felt loopy.

Maybe she should try to find a private detective. Ha! Where would she find one out here in the boonies? And how would she pay for it without Mark finding out? Scratch that idea. Maybe she should see a counselor. All the therapists in this area knew one another though, so that was out, too. The last thing she needed was to run into a colleague or client in the waiting room. She had to talk to someone about this before it drove her berserk.

Maya had gone through this. Maybe she'd know what to do.

She'd met Maya at a previous job right out of law school at a firm both had come to hate. They bonded over their dislike of the work itself and the partners, old fuddy-duddies they loved to make fun of behind their backs.

First Maya, and later Jenna, had found jobs elsewhere, no mean feat in a small city in western Mass. Both loved the Berkshires, the fantastic hiking and cross-country skiing, gorgeous mountains covered with autumn foliage come October. Not to mention both of their spouses were committed to jobs they liked. So, relocating wasn't an option.

Over the past fifteen years, Jenna's relationship with Maya had gone through different phases. In the beginning, when both were single, it was drinks after work and hiking on the weekend, talking about anything and everything, especially their beaus. Later, when they both married, they sometimes included Adam and Mark for dinners out or dinner parties in each other's homes. That was the natural progression.

When Maya first talked about getting pregnant, Jenna raised questions about how Maya could manage work, her marriage, and a baby. How would there be any time left over for herself? Jenna certainly couldn't handle all that. From that point on, a frisson of tension ran through their relationship.

When Hailey was just thirteen months, Maya found out she was pregnant again—unplanned, which stunned Jenna. How could super-organized, competent Maya have allowed this to happen? Then Jenna asked the question that forever drove a wedge between the two women.

"Are you going to keep it?"

They still saw each other after that, rarely, but it was never the same.

Then Adam had had an affair a couple years ago, and everyone in the office found out about it. Maya would understand her dilemma, Jenna hoped. Humiliating, but they seemed to work it through, not wanting to disrupt their children's lives. Fine for Maya, but Jenna didn't see how she could gotten beyond something like that.

Big, fat snowflakes drifted to the ground. Piles of crusty gray snow dotted the parking lot, spring still months away. Despite the snowy day and icy streets, Jenna had persuaded Maya to meet at the Pittsfield Café. Inside, three men in watch caps and thick plaid shirts debated plumbing. Two young mothers carried hot chocolate to a table where bundled-up toddlers waited.

"I want marshmallows, Mommy."

"They don't have them here."

The kid started to whine.

Jenna already wished they'd met in Lenox instead, where they were less likely to bump into people they knew. But she knew Maya wouldn't want to drive that far in a snowstorm. Getting her to come out and meet for coffee on a busy Saturday, with Adam watching the kids, was a big deal. She must be desperate for adult company.

Jenna took a quick inventory of the café, relieved to see nobody she knew. Maya already sat at a table near the register with a coffee in front of her. Not ideal for a private conversation, but there were no other empty seats. Jenna walked to the counter, unwound her wooly red scarf, took off her puffy down jacket, and ordered. Her hand trembled as she picked up her cappuccino and plopped herself down across from Maya, facing the big picture window. The snow had already started to accumulate.

She looked over her left shoulder at the mothers and little ones and frowned. What were all these people doing here in the middle of a snowstorm? She'd hoped she and Maya would have the place to themselves.

The door blew open, a gust of swirling snow whooshing into the café. Two guys wearing brightly colored ski clothes marched in. As two other people left, the guys grabbed their seats. Jenna turned back to Maya and saw her eyeing the chocolate croissants in the display case. She'd put on weight since having the kids.

"Thanks for coming. How are Hailey and Ross?"

"They're okay, both recovering from colds, so everyone's cranky. They pick up everything in day care. I'm fried. It was nice to get away for a couple hours." She sighed. "Though now I'm gonna owe Adam big time."

"Sorry. Sounds tough." Poor Maya had dark circles under both eyes. Better her than me, Jenna thought.

"We've survived worse. What's up? I love the new haircut, by the way."

"Thanks. Mark's having an affair."

"Mark? No way."

"He's on the phone with this woman from work. Constantly—at home."

Maya blew her blonde bangs away from her eyes. "Yeah, but lots of people working together have long conversations about work." The coffee grinder roared. Maya's voice rose. "You know as well as I do our jobs have no boundaries."

Jenna raised a warning hand. "Shh. Keep your voice down."

"Stop being so paranoid," Maya said.

Was she being paranoid? "It's not just how *long* they talk. It's the *way* they talk, the tone of voice, laughing, being so . . . familiar with each other. You know Mark's an introvert. When they're talking, he becomes absolutely *animated*!"

"Sure, but they've been working on this project together for how long?"

"Two years." Jenna fussed with a hangnail.

"Right, so they know each other pretty well," Maya said, watching Jenna.

"Yeah, I know that. But when they talk it sounds so . . . *intimate*. It doesn't sound *normal* for a man and a woman who are just co-workers."

"It sounds like they've become good friends. Friends is a long way from an affair. Are you saying you don't think male and female coworkers can be friends? 'Cause you've had male friends at work."

Back at that first law firm, before they'd met their husbands, both Jenna and Maya had befriended a guy named Joel. They all worked long hours, and close friendships developed among young, single coworkers who spent so much time together. They often socialized after work, too—drinks on a Friday, a barbecue on the weekend, Tanglewood concerts.

"I've had male friends at work, you're right. But that was years ago, before I married. And we didn't have *intimate* relationships. We didn't talk on the phone at all hours, first thing in the morning and late at night."

Maya sipped her coffee. "How're you going to find out for sure?"

The tables were close together. Jenna glanced around. Customers came and went. People working on their laptops could be listening. She lowered her voice. "What do you think I should do?"

"Well, the direct approach would be to confront Mark."

"Obviously. But what if I'm wrong?"

"Jenna, listen to yourself! A minute ago, you were convinced he was having an affair. Now you're worried about being mistaken."

"I know that!" Jenna said, raising her voice. "And if I'm wrong, it's not gonna do much for trust in our relationship, is it?"

"Now you're the one who's talking loud. Calm down, okay? It's not going to help to get all upset." Maya unzipped her down vest. "So, this might be kind of radical, but what if you confronted the woman? Asked her straight out if she is having an affair with Mark?"

"Geez, I hadn't thought of that." Despite being a lawyer, assertiveness was not Jenna's strong suit. She could never have been a litigator, standing up in court and openly challenging people.

"Okay, let's say you're right," Maya said. "What then?"

Jenna wondered how long this conversation would last, fidgeting as she contemplated the thirty-minute drive home in the drifting snow. Squirming in her seat, over-caffeinated at this point, Jenna wrung her hands. "If he's having an affair with this woman, I don't know if I can forgive him."

"Yes, it's hard."

At the risk of offending Maya Jenna asked, "How did you manage that with Adam?"

Maya stared into her coffee. "A major low point in my life. At the time, I thought he was an absolute *bastard*. But you'd be amazed what you can forgive if you have to."

Jenna remembered back to that time, three years ago. She and Maya had drifted apart after her question about Maya's second pregnancy. Maya, in her embarrassment about Adam's affair, had withdrawn from everyone. Maya should have kicked his ass out the door, but she'd kept her mouth shut.

"But why would you say, 'have to?'" Jenna asked. "You make enough money. You could have left."

"Said by someone who obviously doesn't have children." Maya grabbed a tissue from her purse.

"I suppose that wasn't the right way to put it, 'have to.' Of course, I didn't *have to*. No one put a gun to my head. But aside from the kids, I was pushing thirty-five and not eager to be alone or start over again. We had issues in our marriage, things I played a part in, too."

Jenna watched Maya's expressionless face. Not a clue. "And?"

"So, we worked on things, and slowly it got better."

"Better enough to stay around."

"Exactly. Not perfect, but better. And certainly better for the kids." Maya unwound her wooly scarf. "Jenna, why're you avoiding my question?"

"What question? I'm gonna get another latte." Jenna got and stood in line.

"Better make that decaf," Maya said.

Jenna stopped in her tracks and walked back to the table. "What are you suggesting?"

"One, that you've had enough caffeine for the day. And, two, that you're avoiding my question about what you'll do if it's true Mark's having an affair."

"Okay, *Mom*, I'll order decaf and answer your question when I come back."

Jenna returned with her decaf latte, set it down, and sat. "I don't know. That's why I'm avoiding the question. Consider leaving Mark? I don't think I could ever trust him again. How did you and Adam resolve that?"

"He promised no more affairs. We went to counseling, and both committed ourselves to talking about stuff we were unhappy about rather than looking for solace elsewhere. As far as I know, he's been faithful to that."

Jenna blew on her latte. Maybe Erin wasn't the only problem in her marriage. Should she talk to Maya about the other stuff? Why was she so reluctant to go down that road? She totally got the whole don't-want-to-start-all-over-again business. She was pushing forty. She loved Mark and wanted it to be like it used to be. Who had the time or energy to look for a new relationship?

"What's this woman's name, Mark's colleague, at the counseling agency?" Maya asked.

"Erin Rockwell."

Maya burst out laughing, loud and boisterous. The skiing guys looked up from their conversation and glared at them. The barista behind the counter shook her head.

Jenna's face reddened. "What? Why are you laughing like that? Get a grip," she hissed. "You're making a spectacle of yourself! People are staring at us."

Maya held up her hands in a stop gesture. "Sorry." She continue to laugh softly, head down.

"I really do *not* appreciate you laughing at me. I'm a total wreck over this! My marriage is at stake here." Maya had been through this. How could she find it funny?

"I get it. But here's the thing. Erin Rockwell's the counselor Adam and I saw." She finished the last of her coffee. "And guess what?"

Jenna was so not up for guessing games.

"She's gay—" Maya said, hand over her mouth, suppressing a laugh.

What was she talking about? "No, she's not," Jenna insisted. "She's married. She and her husband came to our house once—"

"Maybe, but not anymore. They divorced over a year ago when Erin finally realized she was a lesbian. She's madly in love with a woman she met awhile back. They're a couple. There's no way Mark's having an affair with her."

Jenna's cheeks flamed. Could this be true? Her lower lip trembled. A fragment of that eavesdropped conversation from Mark's phone conversation popped into her head. The bit about her outfit looking good. Hadn't he had said something like, "I think she'd love it?" Could the "she" be Erin's girlfriend?

Never in a million years would she have imagined this. Could Maya be right? Thank God, she hadn't confronted Mark or Erin. How humiliating that would have been.

"Why don't you look relieved?" Maya asked.

Staring at Maya's smile, Jenna shook her head. "Dammit!" She grabbed her latte and purse and raced for the door. She couldn't get out of there fast enough.

As she strode out into the snowstorm, she could faintly hear Maya laughing.

Now she was stuck dealing with everything else that was wrong with her marriage.

Good Intentions

She'd followed the unfolding story of the Rohingya with the obsessive fascination of someone passing a multi-car wreck on the freeway, slowing down so as not to miss a single detail of the tragedy. She moved back and forth from the newspaper to the internet. Throughout the fall of 2016 and into 2017, she couldn't stop herself. It felt like watching a huge building full of people catch on fire and burn to the ground with no fire-fighters anywhere in sight. Would no one intercede?

She mentioned the genocide to friends and colleagues, but no one knew anything about it. Eventually she found a Facebook page called Rohingya Women Network and decided she must take action, to help in some way.

That's how Keira Meadows found herself in London on a long layover en route to Bangladesh. With time to kill, she called her best friend back home.

After exchanging pleasantries about the flight, Naomi wasted no time in getting right to the point. "I hope you know what you're doing, Keira."

Naomi said taking a leave from Keira's job as a psychologist at a Minneapolis college health service to volunteer at a refugee camp was a terrible idea. Dangerous, but also futile. It was not Keira's responsibility to resolve this problem on the other side of the world. "It's not too late to change your mind, you know."

But it was. Keira had committed herself. Heathrow's international terminal bustled around her, constant announcements in multiple languages blaring overhead. Men from Saudi Arabia in robes and women in colorful saris and black burkas, eyes peering out, dragged their carry-ons through the packed waiting area.

It was the middle of the night on the East Coast. Who ese could she call? She knew could count on her dad, a Unitarian minister, for support.

A groggy voice answered.

"Hi Dad, it's Keira. I'm at Heathrow—"

"Is everything okay?"

"Sure, it is, Dad."

But instead of providing validation, someone else who cared about her questioned her decision to volunteer at the Kulupalong Refugee Camp in Bangladesh, just over the border from Myanmar.

"I know you want to help, sweetheart, but are you sure this is the right thing to do?"

Didn't they understand she was an adult, a professional woman, with a set of skills she could use to help these needy people on the other side of the world?

When she finally boarded the plane in London on her way to Dhaka, Bangladesh, she couldn't get comfortable, now second guessing her decision to go, on the verge of tears.

You made the right decision, she reassured herself. You need to do something important to help. And you could get the time off. Looking for a distraction, she pulled out the *Psychological First Aid Training Manual* the aid agency had sent to her, even though it was likely to be a review of everything she already knew, probably duplicating her clinical training and experience.

And mostly it did, except for the troubling parts, like the need to respect the local culture. What did she know about Muslim women, or Rohingya culture, except that women and children were often viewed as possessions, lacking human rights?

And wasn't she already aware of the need to be mindful of her own prejudices, so as not to let her biases affect her work?

Finally, the interminably long flight ended. She assumed someone from the aid program would meet her at the Dhaka airport to escort her to the refugee camp. Instead, she saw a small, dark-skinned man at the luggage carousel with a card bearing her name. In broken English, he announced she needed to board a bus for what would be a fourteen-hour trip to Kulupalong. Exiting the airport for the bus terminal into the moist heat felt like walking into a wall. Still stiff from the plane ride, her limbs fought to walk through air that felt like warm Jell-O. She struggled to suck in enough of the hot, moist air to breathe.

She boarded the rickety bus and thrust her suitcase into the overhead rack. She squeezed into a seat next to the window, crawling over a woman already seated with her two young children on her lap. Glancing around, she saw not a single Caucasian. The overcrowded bus wasn't air conditioned, but only she seemed to notice how stifling it was.

Finally, they wheezed out of the bus station. Her stomach rumbled. She hadn't thought to buy food, nor to exchange currency. She wondered about the length of the trip and how many stops there would be. Would her American credit card be accepted to buy food? Despite the humidity, her throat was parched. She needed water. Did anyone else speak English?

The long, hot, bumpy ride allowed plenty of time to worry. As the brown and barren countryside passed by, her heart raced. Maybe Naomi and her father were right. As sweat soaked her exhausted body, questions flooded her mind. When she tried deep breathing to calm her agitation, the sulfurous smell of her neighbor's body odor filled her nose. Babies cried.

Passengers got off and on at small towns and villages. No place looked promising for water or food or U.S. credit cards, so she tried to sleep, jouncing around, stomach growling. Eventually, in a cloud of dust, they rumbled into Cox's Bazar, a coastal city near the refugee camp, considered a tourist spot with great beaches. Not the least interested in beaches, she hoped someone there would speak English so she could figure out how to get to Kulupalong.

Keira located a driver who spoke enough English to get her to a currency exchange kiosk and a store where she bought water and packaged snacks. He made the short drive to the camp.

As she left the car, a heavy rain poured down, making the heat even more oppressive. Puddles and cocoa-colored mud covered the ground not occupied by makeshift dwellings that stretched as far as the eye could see. As soon as the car sped away, she realized she still hadn't solved the problem of finding her destination, the Women & Children Aid Program.

Keira scanned the horizon as rain soaked her hair, clothes, and suitcase. The Kulupalong Refugee Camp sprawled for acres in every direction, boggling her mind. Tent-like shanties sat shoulder to shoulder, constructed from bamboo poles and white and blue plastic tarpaulins. The camp teemed with thousands of people, scurrying in every direction. The stench made her cover her nose. Most of the residents seemed to be women and children.

How would she find her aid program? Despair started to set in until she noticed a mobile health van a short distance away. She made her way towards it, dragging her suitcase, trying in vain to avoid the pools of muddy brown water, her feet getting heavier as thick, sticky mud clung to her shoes. A queue of about thirty people waited in line.

She elbowed her way to the front. "Hi, I just arrived from the States. I'm looking for the Women & Children Aid Program. Does anyone here know where they're located?"

"Welcome!" a guy boomed. "Let me see if I can free up somebody to take you over," he said in a British accent. "As you may've noticed, they're no roads yet, so I can't give you directions."

He disappeared inside the van. A few minutes later a small, dark woman in a red headscarf emerged and introduced herself as Laila in accented English. "I'll take you to the program," she said.

For the first time, it struck Keira she wouldn't be able to communicate directly with the people she'd be helping.

The rain stopped as they wove single-file around puddles and a maze of dwellings filled with women and children. Finally, Laila pointed to a large, beige canvas tent with a sign announcing, Women & Children Aid Program. She thanked Laila, marveling at how she knew her way around.

"I'm Keira Meadows. Just arrived from the States," she announced to the first person she saw inside the tent.

"Really? I wasn't even expecting you." Lanky, pale, and quintessentially British looking, with almost-white eyelashes, a woman stuck out her right hand. Keira shook it. "Jocelyn Smith," the woman said. "Another pair of hands. Fantastic!"

Jocelyn looked as exhausted as Keira felt.

"Okay, let me introduce you to our small staff, although most are out helping residents," Jocelyn said. "How much do you know about the situation here?

"By the way, have a seat," she said, pointing to a wooden bench. "You must be exhausted from your trip. And here's a towel to dry off. You're soaked."

"I have a good idea about the past few months," Keira said, drying off as best she could. "The Myanmar soldiers burning the Rohingya villages and slaughtering so many of the people. I've been following the news and doing research on the Internet—"

"So, you're up to speed. What's your professional background?"

"I'm a psychologist—"

"Brilliant. Mostly what we do is triage and provide psychological first aid—"

"Yes, I read the manual on the plane." Keira struggled to take in everything she saw outside through the rolled-up tent flaps, a kaleidoscope of color. Women with bright-colored headscarves walked in all directions, trailed by small children in ragged clothes, speaking an unfamiliar language.

"So, you know we're essentially putting Band-Aids on gaping wounds." Jocelyn stopped and shook her head. "You kind of get used to it, but most of these women have been raped—gang raped—and have witnessed family members—parents, husbands, children—being *butchered* by Myanmar's security forces."

Keira winced at the word "butchered."

"We hear the same stories over and over." Jocelyn sighed.

Keira didn't know what to say. "What's it like for a Muslim woman who's been raped and whose husband has been killed?"

"Devastating. No good options. At least they're safe here and can get food and medical care. I have no idea what they'll do when they leave here. How they'll support themselves. Even their families often view them as damaged goods, though everyone knows those fucking soldiers beat the crap out of them . . ." Her voice trailed off again as she fought to regain her composure.

Sensing Jocelyn's discomfort, Keira wondered if she would ever get used to it. "Okay, so how does it work? What should I do?"

"Righto. Sometimes we have people come here looking for help. We ask what they need and try to point them in the right direction. The recent arrivals, for example, they might have a fresh injury from the sexual assault, so we refer them to a mobile health van. Oh, and they don't speak English, so you have to have somebody local with you who's bilingual—often a man, unfortunately—to translate. Sometimes it's hard to round up one of these translators. They're super busy."

A large blond man burst into the tent, tan, strikingly handsome. "So, mate, what's happening?" Noticing Keira, he said, in a strong Australian accent, "G'day. Trevor here. Who're you?" He thrust out his meaty right hand.

Blushing, Keira introduced herself and shook Trevor's hand, cringing from his almost crushing grip.

"Got something Keira can help you with?" Jocelyn asked.

"I do, indeed. Got a teenage girl, fourteen maybe, who just arrived by herself. Kind of a mess. Won't talk to a man. Soon as I locate a female translator, let's go find her and see what we can learn." He turned on his heel and left the tent.

"Are you a psychologist?" Keira asked Jocelyn.

"Social worker."

"What're the most common trauma symptoms you're seeing?"

"Pretty much what you'd expect." Jocelyn sighed deeply. "Lots of nightmares, crying, can't eat. Even people who weren't directly victimized witnessed loved ones being killed or hurt. Pretty much everyone's in terrible shape." She shook her head.

"And are most people willing to talk about what happened?"

"A few—enough to keep us busy. But a lot of them, they're too scared."

A frisson of fear ran through Keira. "Scared of what?"

"Retribution from the Myanmar soldiers. Or, if they have a husband, they don't want him to know they were raped. Or unmarried girls, if someone raped them, afraid they're not going to find a husband."

Keira blew out a stream of air. "Whew."

"Yeah, they're things about Rohingya culture that can be . . . uh, challenging from a Western perspective."

Keira recalled the manual, the parts about culture and prejudice. Was it prejudice to disapprove of having to keep your rape a secret from your own husband? Or to judge a young man who wouldn't marry a girl because she had been raped? Suddenly overcome with exhaustion, she wondered where she'd be sleeping.

Trevor marched back into the tent with a young, dark-skinned woman in a yellow print headscarf. "Keira, this is Mumtaz. Ladies, let's see if we can track down that recent arrival."

As they left the tent, Keira asked Trevor, "Are you a psychologist or social worker?"

"Nah. Paramedic. Lots of experience working with people in crisis. This is my third refugee gig. Most recently Syria and before that Sudan. Wouldn't have thought it possible, but this place is actually worse."

As they picked their way around shanties and mud, Keira asked, "How so?"

"The sheer scope of it—half a million people pouring in over a few months' period, largest refugee camp in the world—and how traumatized the people are." His voice turned bitter. "And that Myanmar is trying to totally *eliminate* the Rohingya minority, but Bangladesh doesn't want 'em either." He shook his head in disgust.

After a short walk, they reached an area on a steep dirt hillside. Shanties as far as the eye could see. How could Trevor remember his way around this seething mass of humanity? He said to Mumtaz, "She was around here. Can you ask those people if a young girl recently arrived here by herself and where she is?"

Mumtaz talked to several women dressed in ragged, dirty clothing. Four half naked, skinny brown toddlers, eyes wide with fear, hid behind the women's, multicolored skirts.

Mumtaz pointed a short distance away. "They think she's inside the tent over there."

"Okay, let's see," Trevor said.

They headed over, and Trevor greeted the group in the tent in the local language. I need to learn some of the local language, too, Keira thought. Mumtaz talked to them, and they pointed to a young girl sitting on the ground in the corner, weeping.

"Let's see if she wants to talk," Trevor said. "What she needs."

The three of them walked over and joined her on the ground. Mumtaz spoke to her briefly.

"She says she'll talk," Mumtaz said. "What do you want me to ask?"

Trevor looked at Keira. "Do you want to take the lead, mate?"

Taken aback, unsure she was ready or whether she'd ever be ready, Keira hesitated a moment then nodded uncertainly.

Should she start with whether the girl came alone or whether she needed medical attention?

She turned to Mumtaz. "Ask her if she has any injuries, if she needs medical attention."

Mumtaz and the girl conversed, and Mumtaz said to Trevor and Keira, "She says she is bleeding down there," pointing to the area between her legs.

Keira grimaced. "Okay, tell her we can take her to the mobile health unit and ask if she has anyone else who can go with her."

After talking to the girl again, Mumtaz said to Keira, "She says she came by herself, that she doesn't know anyone. She's in a lot of pain and has trouble walking."

"Tell her we're sorry she's in so much pain and alone, that we'll help her over to the health van," Keira said. "Ask if it would be okay if you and I put our arms under her armpits and helped her walk." She was acutely aware of Trevor watching the interaction.

Mumtaz conferred. "She said that would be okay."

So, with Trevor trailing behind, Mumtaz and Keira helped her walk.

Keira looked back at Trevor. "Should I try to get her to talk about what happened to her?"

"Have at it."

Looking into the girl's tear-reddened eyes she said, "My name is Keira. What is your name?"

Mumtaz translated. "Her name is Yasmine."

"Yasmine, what a pretty name," Keira said. "Yasmine, do you want to talk about what happened to you?"

Again, Mumtaz translated, and they spoke for a few minutes. Mumtaz turned to Keira. "She walked several days from Rakhine without food or water. After soldiers burned down her village she had to hide in the mountains. Before that she watched soldiers slaughter her husband and two children, including her month-old baby."

Keira tried not to react, but her stomach lurched. She had read this kind of thing but hearing it from this young girl caused a visceral reaction. How could someone this young already have two children? She barely looked thirteen.

Mumtaz continued. "The soldiers took turns raping her. She says she wishes they had killed her. She does not know how she will live after losing her family."

"Tell her how sorry we are." Keira readjusted her arm supporting Yasmine and wondered, what next? "Ask her about her parents."

Yasmine and Mumtaz conversed again. "She said her mother was already dead and the soldiers also killed her father."

"Jesus," Keira whispered. It came out without her even realizing it.

"Careful," Trevor said.

When they arrived at the mobile health unit, Trevor explained to the health professionals, two men and two women, what they needed. Suddenly, Yasmine started to struggle, protesting, and pulling away. Mumtaz held on and spoke to her.

"What's wrong?" Keira asked.

"She is afraid the men will touch her, which Rohingya culture doesn't allow," Mumtaz said. "I reassured her only women will treat her, that there is a curtain for privacy."

Finally, Yasmine agreed to receive treatment. Mumtaz would stay with her and bring her back to the Women & Children tent afterwards.

Walking back to the tent, Trevor asked Keira, "So, what do you think so far?"

She hesitated. Thoughts ricocheted around her brain as she tried to process what she had already experienced. "I have so many questions. I'm not sure where to start." They walked a few paces. "Like, how is it a girl so young could already be married and have two children? She's just a child!"

"You're right, but the Rohingya practice child marriage, arranged marriage, where young teenage girls are typically married to an older man. And they want to have as many children as possible, especially because of the ethnic cleansing, but also based on the belief that a married woman—a mother—is safe from other men—"

"Yeah, and we saw how well *that* worked," Keira said bitterly. Suddenly exhaustion settled over her, like thick smoke. "Where will I be staying?"

"Every other week half the staff stay in the tent, on cots in the back. Primitive quarters. The next week you get to stay at a hotel outside the camp in Cox's Bazar. Not fancy, but a real bed, a bathroom instead of a stinkin' latrine with barely any privacy, and clean running water."

"I could sleep standing up at this point."

Trevor took her to the tent. Approaching nine o'clock, darkness had fallen. Jocelyn gave her something spicy to eat over rice and showed her to her cot. As she fell asleep, still fully clothed, she overheard Jocelyn ask Trevor how she did.

"Good," he said. "Real good. I think she's gonna be okay."

Two months passed, each day much like the previous. Keira worked with Trevor and Jocelyn. To some extent, she did seem to get used to it. She helped women and listened to their stories, assisted by various translators. After a while, a disturbing sameness to the stories emerged, each one a version of the first one she'd heard from Yasmine. So many rapes. So many family members slaughtered. So many nightmares. So many young widows with little kids. She helped the mothers find food for their children, many of them severely malnourished, skinny, sick with chronic diarrhea and distended brown bellies, eyes bulging from skulls with skin stretched tight.

New aid organizations arrived almost daily, but so did more families, thousands of families. So many refugees poured in that the camp soon overflowed, and people began to set up camp outside the official perimeters.

Before long, Keira had learned her way around the camp, even absent any roads. One day as she walked with a translator, Mohammed, to meet a young mother, she could hear and see a commotion nearby. A crowd had gathered around a man and woman who shouted at each other. Keira and Mohammed stood at the edge of the crowd and watched a shirtless man, his brown chest slick with sweat, clad in a dirty sarong and sandals. He yelled at a cowering woman, whose hands protected her head. She wore a blue headscarf, yellow blouse, and long, wrinkled patterned skirt over muddy bare feet. As the man slapped her, over and over, she cringed and wailed. Keira flinched at the sound of each *thwap* against her bare skin. The crowd murmured around them.

Keira's heart raced. "What's happening, Mohammed? Should we try to do something?"

"Oh no, ma'am," he said. "He is her husband. Another man told him he saw the wife being raped by the soldiers in their village, before they arrived. His wife had not told him. Now he is so angry his wife has been . . ." Mohammed stopped.

Keira finished it for him, spitting out the word, "defiled." Now she was damaged goods in their eyes. Wasn't it bad enough someone raped the poor woman—probably gang raped—maybe while her children watched? Now she had to contend with her husband punishing her for it, as if it were her fault, as if she could have prevented it?

Then a teenage boy joined the man in hitting the woman, the sounds of his slaps ringing in Keira's ears, while the woman keened and moaned, blood dripping from her nose.

"Who is the boy?"

"He is her son."

Keira's face contorted in pain. She wiped away tears.

Seeing her tears, Mohammed said, "At least they are not stoning her to death."

Hardly consolation. Suddenly Keira couldn't stand it. Not for another minute. The stench of the camp, the smell of fetid latrines and human sweat insinuating itself into her nostrils. The crush of people, fighting one another for food, for water, for medical care. The lack of privacy. The heat, the unbearable humidity, always wearing damp clothing, always feeling dirty. She couldn't bear any of it, not for a second more. It was too hard. The Rohingya culture, what Burma had done to these wretched people, the Bangladeshis who wanted to send them back.

And yet, what could she do? She felt powerless. "Mohammed, I have to go back to the tent."

"Ma'am?"

"I need to go back."

Keira burst back into the tent. Jocelyn sat at the table, doing paperwork. "I can't do it anymore. I know I have two months left on my volunteer commitment, but I don't think I can do it. I can't bear it another minute."

"Wait, wait. Slow down. Sit. What happened?" Jocelyn's brow furrowed.

Keira sat hunched over on the bench and told her about the incident she'd just witnessed—the crowd, the son and husband beating the woman for getting raped. And she started to cry, big heaving sobs, dribbles of mucous pouring from her nose.

Jocelyn came over and put her arm around her, saying nothing. Eventually she said, "This work is so difficult, so . . . taxing. Is there anything that would make you consider staying?"

Keira shook her head. "I need to feel like I'm making a difference. That someone's life is actually better for me being here."

"But you *are* making a difference! You're great at this work. I've heard you. I've seen you. And not only with the women, with the children too. Their lives *are* better because of you."

"I thought I knew what I was doing coming here, that my work with sexual assault victims at the college prepared me for—"

"Nothing prepares you for this."

"It's so ironic. Yesterday I had this great idea. To recruit some Rohingya women, the ones who've been here a while and are doing okay, and train them to deliver psychological first aid, like we do. And if it worked, we wouldn't need translators, 'cause they'd already know the language and the culture."

She looked up from her lap and stared into Jocelyn's pale blue eyes. "Here's my dirty little secret. I *despise* this misogynist culture that hates women. That thinks girls and women are just to be *fucked*, to pop out another kid each year, to haul your water and cook your food." She stopped to rest. Venting rage took so much out of a person.

Jocelyn didn't say a word, just gazed at Keira's tear-stained face and let her spew her venom.

Keira stood up and started pacing, her voice raised. "Prejudiced? You bet, and I don't even care! I don't even *want* to change."

"Keira, please," Jocelyn begged. "Don't decide when you're so emotional. At least sleep on it. And I love your idea to train the Rohingya women to deliver the psychological first aid. I think it would work. Let's do it."

Keira nodded and walked back to her cot, but she'd made up her mind: she had to get out.

Later, she heard Trevor come in. He was talking to Jocelyn, but she couldn't make out what they were saying.

He walked over to her cot. "Hey, mate. Heard you had a bad day."

She'd grown to love his Australian accent.

"Joce tells me you're thinking about leaving. Don't do that, love. We need you."

Shit. He was going to talk her into staying.

Keira packed her luggage while he continued.

"She told me about your idea, about training the Rohingya woman to do what we do. Brilliant. Just what we need. I'm all in."

"It's too late. I'm *spoiled*. I've grown to dislike some things about this culture to the point where I can't be *effective* anymore—"

"Keira, we've all felt that way at times. It can be so hard to take. But you *are* effective, I've seen you. You did great work with Yasmine. She's much better than when she first arrived. Come here, you need a hug."

She made a face but stood up, and Trevor encircled her with those huge, muscular Australian arms. She started to cry again, wetting his already damp white T-shirt.

"Go ahead, love, cry it out. Sometimes that really helps. But don't go home mad."

If only she could save just one person . . .

In the end, Jocelyn and Trevor talked Keira into staying. They worked together to develop a little program to recruit Rohingya women, to train them to deliver psychological first aid to new, traumatized refugees who arrived daily. The challenge pushed Keira to her limits. These women were illiterate, uneducated, and it all had to be done through translators. But after they finally trained a group of ten, Keira and Jocelyn could not stop grinning as they watched the women practice on one another. Warmth radiated through Keira's body as she witnessed the women's transformation from victims to empowered human beings, using their own experiences and new skills to help other refugees. Quivering with excitement, she couldn't wait to set them loose on their first group of new arrivals.

But she couldn't persuade Yasmine to join the group. She had kept in touch with her, ultimately finding a group of older women who had taken her under their wing. Yasmine was doing better than when she arrived—not crying constantly, eating—but still showed signs of deep depression, withdrawal, and nightmares. Keira worried about suicide.

Without consulting Jocelyn or Trevor, neither of whom was American, she concocted a plan to get Yasmine to the United States as an unaccompanied minor. After some research online she learned the United States was taking refugees from Myanmar, although the application process was long and arduous. She contacted her father and convinced him to have his church sponsor her in Vermont, working on a plan during the weeks she spent at the hotel in Cox's Bazar, where the internet was iffy, but the international phone service worked. She contacted the American embassy in Dhaka, Bangladesh, and they referred her to the American embassy in Rangoon, Myanmar.

For some reason, they rarely answered their phone. Once she got through, she had trouble finding the right person and had to leave a message.

Time was running out. She had hoped to have arrangements in place before she approached Yasmine, not wanting to make a promise she couldn't keep. But, with just a week left at Kulupalong, she couldn't put off the conversation.

She found Mumtaz and they tracked her down. When Yasmine saw them coming, she started talking right away to Mumtaz, who translated.

"She says she hasn't changed her mind about learning the psychological first aid."

"Tell her that's not why I'm here."

"Why *are* you here?" Mumtaz asked.

"Because I want to make arrangements for her to come to the U.S. as an unaccompanied minor. Can you explain that to her?"

Mumtaz frowned and looked puzzled.

"Do you understand?" Keira asked.

Mumtaz nodded and started talking to Yasmine. After some back and forth, Mumtaz said to Keira, "She doesn't want to go."

"What do you mean?"

"She says no. She's not interested."

"Please ask her why not. She'll be able to go to school there, to get help, to have a better life."

Shaking her head skeptically, Mumtaz again spoke to Yasmine at some length. Yasmine got very animated, waving her arms for emphasis, shaking her head no.

"What did she say?" Keira reached out to take her arm, but Yasmine yanked it away.

"She says she does not know anything about your country, she does not speak your language. She is too old to go to school."

"But she's *not* too old," Keira insisted. "And she *can* learn English. Tell her."

"Ma'am, she has made up her mind. Please don't pressure her. Be respectful of her choice."

Hearing those words was a slap in the face. How could Yasmine not want the better life the United States would offer her?

Mumtaz said a few more words to Yasmine, who walked away.

Baffled, Keira mumbled thanks to Mumtaz and walked back to the tent, thinking of other ways to approach Yasmine to convince her to come to America. As Jocelyn and Trevor were talking, Keira interrupted with, "You won't believe what happened!"

She told them about her plan and Yasmine's refusal.

Trevor looked at Jocelyn, then at Keira. "I'm not all that surprised, mate."

"What? How could she not jump at the chance to get out of this . . . this . . ."

"We think it's pretty bad here—horrible even—and it's certainly worse than her village," Jocelyn said. "But it's familiar, it's her culture, it's all she—"

"But her culture is so awful to women! I mean, what are her chances here, really?"

"Probably not good by your standards," Trevor said, "but it's what she knows. She's just lost her whole family . . ." His words trailed off.

"Wouldn't her prospects be better—"

"Not in her mind," Jocelyn said. "Her whole life's been turned upside down."

Keira's shoulders slumped and she let out a sigh. Her body felt heavy with disappointment. She couldn't even rescue this one person.

As if reading her mind, Trevor said, "Yasmine doesn't need to be saved. She needs to heal a bit more and find a new path forward. And she will. I know you don't feel like you've helped her, but you have. Just like you've helped those women we recruited to do psychological first aid. They're survivors. You're just going to have to be satisfied with that, love."

Just then, they noticed Yasmine standing in the doorway to their tent. Her head bowed, she walked over to Keira. Looking up with a tentative smile on her face, Yasmine wrapped her arms around Keira, soft as butterfly wings. Gazing at her face she whispered, in English, "Thank you for trying to help me."

Keira's mouth dropped open. A huge smile brightened her whole face.

Trevor grinned. "What did I tell you?

To Be Forgiven

She dreaded having to make the amends, but it ate away at her.

"It's time," her sponsor said. "Put on your big-girl pants. You'll feel better when it's done."

In previous attempts at sobriety, Laurel had never gotten to AA's steps eight and nine: Make a list of people you've harmed and make amends to them all. "All" was unimaginable, but Mom? Just start there, Laurel, she thought. How badly could it go? Her mom had Parkinson's, but Laurel was up to the challenge. After all, she was coming up on two years and spent almost every weekend helping at her mom's place.

So, Laurel drove north from Scottsdale to upscale Carefree where her mother, Joanne, lived. On the way, she rehearsed what she planned to say. Not just an apology, but how she'd changed.

She arrived and her mother let her in. Laurel's voice caught in her throat when she took in her mother's appearance. Face all pasty and gaunt, hair askew. In just two weeks the Parkinson's had taken its toll.

"You should have just let yourself in," Joanne said, still in her pajamas at noon.

"Why'd you make me get up?" Her voice sounded soft and raspy.

Oh boy, here we go, Laurel thought. Rail thin, Joanne hobbled into the kitchen, her posture stooped.

"What do you need me to do today?" Laurel asked.

Her mom picked up a list from the counter. Laurel spent several hours making her way through Joanne's list. She dusted and vacuumed, did two loads of laundry, emptied the dishwasher. She drove to Safeway and CVS, buying groceries and refilling prescriptions.

At four, housework and errands finally completed, she heaved a big sigh. It was showtime, time to sit down and get it over with. But dammit, where was Mom?

She found her in the bedroom, napping. Shit, now what?

Laurel gently nudged her awake.

"Damn you, Laurel," Joanne said. "I just fell asleep. And you know how much friggin' trouble I have sleeping."

"Sorry. How about some tea, Mom? There's something I want to talk to you about."

Joanne dragged herself out of bed, gray hair matted and tangled as a bird's nest. "By the way, a young man called here looking for you the other day."

Laurel eyes narrowed. Young man? "What did he want? Did he leave his name?"

"Just said he wanted to get a hold of you. I wrote his name down somewhere." She rummaged through a basket of junk on the counter. "Okay, here it is. Ryan Murphy." She handed the scrap of paper to Laurel.

But Laurel didn't need to look at it. Oh, dear God. Her legs felt wobbly.

"Who is this guy? I gave him your number, and when I asked him how he knew you he said something about being your son."

How had he found her? What could he want after all this time?

216

"Did he reach you?"

Laurel shook her head, thoughts racing.

"Who is he?"

Laurel slumped onto a chair. "Nineteen years ago, that bastard who abused me, Rick Murphy, got me pregnant." She paused, her breath ragged. "And forced me to have the baby."

"Wait, you had a kid? You never told me that."

"I was drinking, deep in my disease. Rick threw me out, kept the baby. Wouldn't let me see Ryan even after I stopped drinking. I finally gave up—"

"You mean you abandoned him? I can't believe you walked out on a poor defenseless baby."

Laurel fought to keep her mouth shut against the thick, red rage that bubbled up in her. "Shut up, Mom. You have no idea what you're talking about—"

Joanne egged her on. "I raised four kids—"

"And look how they all turned out! A drug addict, an alcoholic, a prostitute, and one in prison. Great job, Mom!"

"Maybe I wasn't the best mom, but I never abandoned you kids."

Laurel pounded her fist on the table. "What are you talking about? You absolutely did! That night you went to the bar and left eleven- and twelve-year-old boys—practically delinquents already—in charge? The fire? Child Protective coming? How about sending us to Aunt Alice's house the next day without even telling her we were coming? Have you conveniently forgotten how we ended up in three different foster homes, while you carried on with your latest lowlife jerk? How is that *not* abandonment?"

Joanne's nostrils flared. "That wasn't my fault! I told the boys not to cook." She stood, walked to the counter and stared out the window. "Stupid neighbors had no business sticking their noses in where they didn't belong—"

"Mom, the fire department saved us from the apartment burning down! That's how Child Protective got there, not because of neighbors being nosy."

"Well, if my sister had just agreed to look after you kids for a few weeks, it would have all blown over. She owed me that."

"Sending four kids across the country to a relative's house on a Greyhound—by themselves!—without even having the courtesy to let your sister know we were coming?" Laurel leapt up and paced. "That's fucked up, really fucked up! I was gone for almost two years!"

Joanne turned to face Laurel. She opened her mouth to speak.

"Shut up. I'm not done. And then, if that wasn't bad enough, you refused to believe I got sexually abused by one of the older boys in the foster family—"

"I *still* don't believe it! You made it up to try to make me feel guilty. You always were a liar. If that happened, why didn't you say so right away?"

"Because I was scared! Because I didn't think anyone would believe me! Because I thought I'd get in trouble!" She was shrieking now, frothing against this pathetic, sick old woman. "Because I was just a kid whose mother didn't care enough about her to not leave her home with two irresponsible brothers. A mother who couldn't get her shit together to be a half-decent parent. Who cared more about partying than taking care of her kids. And, *you* have the nerve to criticize *me* for abandoning Ryan?"

Joanne sat down and thrust out her chin. "You have no clue how hard it was to raise four kids by myself!"

"Who asked you to have four kids? You weren't equipped to take care of even one!"

At that, Joanne stood up and charged toward her.

Afraid her mother might hit her, Laurel dodged out of the way.

"Get out of my house!" Joanne yelled. "Now. Before I call the police."

Laurel grabbed her purse and marched out to her car. She sat in the car and trembled, her hands too shaky to even start the car. Hot tears of rage sprang from her eyes. She knocked her head on the steering wheel over and over. Why did she think making amends would work? What an idiot she was for even trying, for thinking her mother might forgive her. That they could ever come to a place of peace.

Her mother was the one who should be begging for forgiveness! Here she was, sacrificing her precious weekend time to help this wretched woman, and all she asked for in return was forgiveness. Understanding. Acceptance that she'd done the best she could with what she'd been given. Laurel had had no idea how to care for that innocent little baby. How could she with a mother like that?

So much for amends.

Every inch of her body felt bruised and every pore screamed, "I need a drink!"

Children, Untethered

Weighted down with my heavy photography equipment and overnight bag, I rush out of the airport and nearly bump into my partner Marisol, a reporter from the same newspaper. "So, this is Arizona. The heat is . . . it's like walking into a furnace." I wipe sweat from my brow. "But I'm surprised by how humid it feels."

Marisol looks up at the pale blue August sky. On the chunky side, Marisol, with her brown skin and shiny black hair pulled back in a ponytail, hails from the Southwest. That's about all I know about her, since this is our first assignment together. I usually work with a different reporter, but they've paired me with her because she's from the area. Hopefully that'll be helpful. Time will tell.

"Yeah. Welcome to the desert during the summer monsoon. Are you ready for this?"

Did she mean the weather or the assignment? I'm not sure I'm ready for either. I'm not exactly dreading the assignment, but . . . "As ready as I'll ever be, I guess," I reply. Did she say monsoon? Is she kidding, or do they really call it that? "I wish I knew more Spanish."

As we head for the rental car, Marisol yanks her Rollaboard up over a curb. "Don't worry. I'm bilingual. You won't need to know Spanish. Just focus on getting some great photos."

"But I want to be able to understand what these kids are saying to one another."

We're about the same age, Marisol and I—mid-thirties—but I'm a tall, red-haired, freckled, white guy with a rusty beard from the Northeast. We couldn't look more different. We rent a compact car and set off toward a small city bordering Mexico. The children's shelter is a two-hour drive. I offer to drive, wondering whether she'll think that's sexist, but she readily agrees. As we drive through the desert, a steady river of eighteen-wheelers rolls toward us, the unrelenting sun glinting off their shiny windshields. Bright yellow, diamond-shaped signs warn of blowing dust.

The desert surprises me, although I can't put my finger on what I expected. It's so extreme, so austere. And dry, of course, but unbelievably so. The sere grasses and shrubs blend into the buff-colored dirt. Or is it sand? Dark, craggy mountains loom in the distance. My town in New Hampshire has mountains nearby, too. But it's so lush and green there by comparison, with so many huge old trees. In this harsh landscape, only an occasional tree survives. How the hell does anything grow here? It takes two hands on the steering wheel to keep the car on the road in the wind that blusters across the highway.

"Do you know the names of the plants out here?" I ask Marisol. Not that there are many.

"Of course. I grew up around here. Like what?"

"What are those wispy, rust-colored bushes?"

Marisol reaches into the back seat to grab something out of her bag. "Usually they're greener, but they're stressed by the drought. Creosote bush."

I laugh. "Why are they called that?"

"'Cause that's what creosote is made from, silly."

I chuckle again. "Really?"

She takes a sip of water and nods. "Yep, their roots and leaves smell like creosote. You know, like railroad ties."

"Everything here looks sharp and prickly."

"Best to assume everything you meet in the desert is out to kill you."

Whoa. "What was it like, growing up near the Mexican border?" Having spent my childhood in tight-laced New England, I imagine it would be like another country to grow up in this alien landscape.

"Probably not all that different from anywhere else."

Yeah, right. Okay, so she's all closed up inside. I'd read Latinos play it pretty close to the vest when it comes to outsiders. Which makes me all the more curious. Although I have all sorts of questions about what it would be like living this close to Mexico, I'm afraid of offending her and don't want our relationship to get off on the wrong foot. So, I bite my tongue and hope she'll open up as the day unfolds.

We drive another half hour and cross something labeled "Coyote Wash."

"What exactly is a wash?" I ask.

"A mostly dry stream bed that can become a raging river after a big rain."

Huh. Every so often, little whirlwinds of dirt swirl up into the air. "Look at those." I point.

"Dust devils," Marisol says.

I marvel such a thing really exists. The desert holds all sorts of surprises.

An hour into the flat, boring drive, the vast, cloud-filled sky morphs from blue to dark gray as towering thunderheads overtake it. "Have you been watching the sky?" Hard not to notice.

"We're driving straight into the monsoon," Marisol explains.

"What exactly are monsoons?" I ask, apprehension creeping in.

"They're these intense summer rainstorms—thunderstorms—that are typically accompanied by extreme winds and torrential rain in a short period of time."

Soon, enormous drops pelt the windshield. An astonishing bolt of lightning lights up the sky, followed immediately by a sonic boom. We both jump. That was close!

Twenty minutes later, I find myself gripping the steering wheel so tightly my knuckles turn white and my hands ache. The windshield wipers clack furiously. I've never experienced rain like this. When hail starts hammering the car roof, I yell to Marisol, "Have you ever seen a storm like this?"

She shouts back. "Pretty common here during the monsoon."

After that, conversation becomes impossible. It's all I can do to control the car. Several times I almost end up on the shoulder and have to yank the steering wheel to the left to get us back on the road.

Finally, Marisol bellows, "Chase, how can you see?" She sounds mad—or is it scared?—and motions for me to pull off to the side.

I'm more than happy to oblige, relieved to stop driving in those conditions, and pull off the road. My hands need a break.

"Make sure your brake lights are off," Marisol warns.

While we sit by the side of the road, I contemplate what awaits us at the children's detention center. I wonder if I'll grasp enough about what it's really like there for the kids. I'm looking forward to some powerful, heart-wrenching photos that will make my editor glad he sent us all this way.

I peer out the side window. Nothing is in focus, and white covers the ground. Holy shit. The car's temperature gauge shows the temperature has dropped thirty degrees. When the battering gets even louder—how the hell big are these hailstones?— I wonder whether the newspaper will be responsible for damage to the roof of the car.

Thank God it's too loud to talk, because the silence would be awkward otherwise. Marisol yells at the top of her voice. What I think I hear is, "I hope we're not going to be late" and later, "These storms don't usually last too long." I worry about being late too, about missing the opportunity after traveling all this way.

Finally, it lets up and we drive the rest of the way, me speeding to get there on time. We arrive to see a chain-link fence topped with razor wire surrounding the immense, pale gray, one-story facility. We stop at a booth in the middle of the road at a gated security checkpoint. When I roll the window down, the smell of ozone fills my nostrils. Marisol leans over my lap and flashes her press pass at the guy in the booth.

A stern-faced Latino wearing a dark green uniform says, "Hand it over, please."

While he studies it, Marisol says, "They're expecting us."

Finally, the guard waves us through, and the gate creaks open. We drive through a huge, half-filled parking lot toward the buff-colored building, directed by someone waving a flag. He points to where we should park. I can still make out the yellow wheel-spokes logo of the former big-box store.

"They must've spent a fortune on renovations," Marisol says, shaking her head in disgust.

As soon as we get inside, we pass through metal detectors. Security people warn us no cameras or cellphones are allowed. We hand over our cellphones. Seething, I turn in a heavy nylon bag containing three cameras. When a guard tells Marisol she has to relinquish her purse, she frowns and shakes her head but says nothing. They assure us all our possessions will be secured and returned to us when we leave.

I am shocked and pissed. Why did I drag all my damned photography equipment along if I can't use it? What's a photo-journalist even doing on this trip? I'm half inclined to call my editor and find out if he'd had any inkling this was going to be an issue. But there's no way he'd send me all this way if he didn't think I'd come back with some kick-ass photos.

What these officials don't know is that I carry two cell-phones, a work phone and a personal iPhone. I hand over the former and hang on to the latter, making sure it's on silent. Even Marisol has no idea I carry the second phone. If I get in trouble, so be it.

Once we're inside, the officials guide us, along with the other invited journalists, to a windowless conference room lit too brightly by fluorescent lights. That's when I notice how hot it is—no A/C. I wipe my already sweaty brow, turn to Marisol, and mouth, "Are they kidding?" I can already feel sweat stains the size of watermelons under my armpits. And the smell. Not a bad smell, an antiseptic, institutional smell. Like bleach, or a hospital.

We sit around a rectangular conference table in uncom-fortable molded plastic chairs. The officials provide us with no refreshments, not even water. Tells you what they think about journalists. Despite the humidity, I'm thirsty, and I curse my-self for not bringing water along. Although they might have confiscated that along with all the other stuff we weren't al-lowed to bring in.

I count twelve other reporters or photographers. The briefing starts with more ground rules, delivered by a govern-ment employee in a tight charcoal suit. In this heat. He's tall, with black, greasy, slicked-back hair, and a bulbous nose on his ruddy face. I almost feel sorry for him.

"No questions while the tour is taking place. And absolutely"—he pauses, looking around at the group to make sure no one misses this point—"no conversations with the children. Any rule that is broken," Charcoal Suit warns, his gut sticking out, "will lead to immediate expulsion."

Boy, these guys must have a lot to hide. We're getting a taste of what it must be like to be a kid in here. A small taste.

Another official enters the room, a middle-aged bald guy wearing a short-sleeved polyester dress shirt and bolo tie, and the real propaganda begins. With a fake smile on his face he drones on and on, delivering an obviously canned lecture, about why the United States needs such facilities, about how humanely the children are being treated. How there are toys and recreation and healthy meals. In fact, these children are being treated so well, he argues, they're actually better off here than they were in their home countries.

Right. I pray no one can see the outline of my phone in pants pocket. The heat makes me zone out as the official continues. Sometimes, I tune in to buzzwords and phrases we'd all heard before. Zero tolerance, illegal entry, criminal offense, deterrence, unaccompanied minors.

I turn to look at Marisol. This guy's dissing her heritage. She's taking notes, looking up periodically, frowning and shaking her head. This must be killing her.

How can the people who live here stand this heat?

"We probably feed these illegal aliens better than what they get in their home countries," Bolo Tie says, a shit-eating grin now plastered on his face. "And each child has their own bed. They're not all piled in together, like they probably are at home." I'm dying to smack that stupid grin off his face.

Each time I hear the word "alien," I blanch. These are children, for God's sake, asylum seekers, without their parents, not creatures from another planet!

Charcoal Suit announces, "Ladies and gentlemen, we will have ten minutes for questions before we start the tour."

Marisol wastes no time. "How many migrant children are in the custody of Health and Human Services?"

Charcoal Suit claims he doesn't know.

She persists. "I've heard it's over eleven thousand. Does that sound right?"

"I have no idea," he says, not even trying to keep the annoyance out of his voice.

Another reporter asks how many are housed in this facility.

"About three hundred," the official says.

Marisol consults her notes. "If this facility fills, where will you house new children?"

"Above my pay grade," he says.

She turns to me and whispers, "Jesus, this guy's an asshole. Can't he do better than this?"

Other reporters ask questions, but the officials offer similarly vacuous responses. Finally, Charcoal Suit announces it's time for the tour.

We see rows of bunk beds in large dormitory-like rooms and then we see classrooms. Outside, we watch boys play soccer and chase each other around in the heat. They're probably used to it, given their home countries. I'm desperate to shoot some stills, but the officials had warned us no photographs without permission.

I approach Bolo Tie. "Can I have my equipment back just to take a few photos of the boys playing?" I assume it'll be futile. They don't want any of this recorded, but I have to at least try, conscious of the iPhone in my pocket.

The official shakes his head.

It seems so innocuous though, kids playing soccer. If not this, then what?

A few of the reporters are taking notes. Others whisper amongst themselves. I overhear one guy say how much he wishes he could talk to the kids. We troop back inside, just as two armed Border Patrol agents in green uniforms are dragging a gangly, young brown-skinned boy into the room. He looks about seven or eight, my son's age.

Marisol leans over and whispers, "I'm sure they didn't intend for us to see this."

"Absolutely not."

The kid fights like a wild animal caught in a trap, arms and legs flailing. The guards can barely hold on to the wily little guy as he writhes and pulls to get away.

Reluctant to miss a moment of the disturbance, I mouth, "Holy shit," with a quick glance at Marisol. Her almost-black eyes look worried. She's scribbling on her pad.

Without looking at me she whispers, "Fuck. That kid's gonna get hurt. I sure wish you could film this."

I look over at the grim expression covering her face, her full lips pursed in a straight line. I shake my head and lament not being able to capture the disturbing image.

Suddenly, it gets more interesting. The two officials leading the tour yell to the Border Control agents in Spanish. The agents look over toward us, momentarily relaxing their grip on the small boy. He takes full advantage, kicking their legs. He sinks his teeth into the arm of one guard, who lets go and yelps with pain. Another reporter winces as he watches. This kid knows how to fight!

More yelling back and forth between the officials and the Border Control agents. The kid's screaming, too. I silently curse again how little Spanish I know. I lean down to Marisol and ask, "What are they saying?" and the two officials rush over to the fracas.

She translates. "The guy in the short sleeves keeps ordering the guards to get the kid out of here. The guy in the suit is warning them not to hurt the kid."

"What about the kid?"

"I'm having trouble understanding him. It sounds like, 'Let me go, you're hurting me.'"

With our babysitters gone, I consider whether I can whip out my phone and grab a couple of pictures. Nah, better not risk having it confiscated.

The entire group of journalists waits, transfixed by the scene. A few talk quietly amongst themselves.

After a couple of minutes, the kid gives up, probably exhausted—who knows when he last ate or slept?—and the agents manage to drag him out of the room. The officials return to our group. Charcoal Suit gives us a big, fake grin. "Sorry 'bout that. Some of these kids can be difficult. But those Border Guards are trained to handle troublemakers."

What a slimy bastard. Two reporters try repeatedly to ask questions about the incident, but Charcoal Suit says, "No comment."

On our way out, we observe another young boy, maybe six or seven, sitting alone on the green linoleum floor in a corner of the cafeteria, sobbing. A mop of curly black hair falls over his face. He uses his ragged red T-shirt to wipe his nose. His wails give me goosebumps. Where the hell is the staff?

As the rest of the group continues on, Marisol and I hang back to watch. An older boy, maybe sixteen, enters the otherwise empty cafeteria. He's nicely dressed in navy shorts and a white T-shirt. He looks up when he notices the crying child, glances around, and after some hesitation scurries over to the little guy. He squats down in front of him.

"Look at that," Marisol says.

The younger boy, dressed in tattered brown pants, continues to cry with his head down as the older one puts his arm around him.

I decide to sneak a photo of the poignant moment. As I start to pull out my phone I look up and see Charcoal Suit walking toward us. Shit, missed it.

"Let's go, people," the official says. "The tour is over."

Dammit! After we get outside, I ask Marisol, "How is this not a concentration camp?"

Sadness fills Marisol's eyes. I wonder whether she's about to cry. Her shoulders droop and she covers her face with her hands. She walks slowly behind me as we trudge back toward the car.

I managed to keep it together until the teenage boy went over to comfort the sobbing little kid. The little guy looks so much like my son, Tyler. Skinny, with the same curly dark hair, the same summer-browned skin. My eyes fill, and my voice catches in my throat. I want to punch the guy in the suit who ordered us to move along. How can the people running this place be so heartless?

The teenage boy was walking through the cafeteria when he heard the crying. The sounds came from a little kid in the corner, a skinny kid, dressed in filthy pants and worn sneakers. He lifted up his ratty red T-shirt to wipe his tears, revealing his bony ribs.

What should he do? The boys' cries made his skin prickle. The little kid was Carlos' age—Carlos, his little brother, who he'd left in El Salvador. Rogelio bit his lip. The grownups had told them this morning about how they needed to behave when the newspaper people came through.

"You need to smile," the guard said. "And not talk to anyone, even if they talk to you," they told the children in Spanish, to make sure they understood. "Anyone who breaks these rules will be punished."

That word scared him. That's what the gangs threatened back in El Salvador. Punishment. That's what happened to his father. Punishment meant death, so he fretted for the little boy. Would they beat him? Or worse?

His heart told him to walk over to the kid and see what was wrong, but his head was scared he'd get into trouble. He'd worked so hard to get this far. The newspaper people were still in the room, and the big boss men were with them. He fingered his soft white T-shirt and caressed his new navy-blue shorts, the nicest he'd ever owned. The kid's crying was making him *loco*. He had to make him stop.

Rogelio took off across the room toward him. He squatted down and faced the boy. "What is your name?" he asked in Spanish

Silence.

"What happened? Why are you crying?"

Nothing.

He sat down in front of the boy, cross-legged, glancing around the room again. "Where are you from?"

Nothing.

"If you don't stop crying, you're going to get in trouble. Stop and tell me what's the matter."

The crying stopped, but the boy still didn't answer, just wiped his tears and dripping snot on his arm.

Rogelio moved closer, sitting beside him, and put his arm around the young boy's bony back. He gave a furtive glance around the room for staff. No sitting on the floor, and children were not allowed to touch one another. He didn't want trouble, but he had to do this, to comfort this little kid. "I am Rogelio. What is your name?"

The boy looked up and said, "Yulio Ortiz. I came from Honduras. They took away Mami. And my baby sister and brother."

"How long have you been here?"

"I barely just got here. First, we were in a place they called the ice box. Freezing cold. That's where they took *mi madre* away. Mami has watched over me my whole life. Now she is gone," he wailed, and started to sob all over again.

"Yulio, you have stop crying. It won't help, and you're gonna get in trouble. Tell me about your family, little brother."

The boys sat on the floor, side by side, their legs out straight, and Yulio began the story of his journey. He and his Mami and sister and brother left their home in Honduras many months ago. The gangs had killed his Papi because he wouldn't let them use his taxi to deliver drugs.

"For a while, Mami worked to get enough money to pay our rent and buy food. But after *mi abuela* died, there was no one to take care of baby Liliana. So Mami couldn't work anymore. The bad men knew she was having trouble, so they grabbed me from school and tried to get me to work for them. I was so scared."

Rogelio's brow furrowed. He knew Yulio's story because it had happened many times in El Salvador. Three of his friends had lost their fathers to gangs or drug dealers. The gangs were everywhere. "What happened then?"

"Mami said we had to escape to the United States, but we had almost no money. We found some other friends at church who were running, too, and we started our journey. Sometimes we took the bus, but mostly we walked and slept on the ground. One time we climbed on top of a train, but they threw us off. Many days we walked through *el desierto* until we arrived at the border. I thought when we got here everything would be all right. I am so tired from walking . . ."

Rogelio waited for Yulio to finish his story. "*Hermanito*, that sounds very hard, but someplace, you still have family. Me, there is no one left in my family except my little brother. I came home one day, and *mi madre* was gone, disappeared. I searched and searched but couldn't find her. Losing your mother hurts so much, I know. I came here with some other boys from El Salvador who had lost their families, too. Mami once told me we have some relatives in this country."

"How is this place?" Yulio asked, looking around the room, his eyes still red from crying.

"Not too bad. The food is good, but not like at home. We have a clean bed to sleep in. We can play outside, and there are some games and stuff." He pointed to his chest. "They give you new clothes. Sometimes, they teach us English. If we behave, we can play video games or watch movies. I try to make friends, but the other boys, they come and go. I miss my friends back home."

Yulio nodded. "I can't wait to see Mami again and to go back to school. Mami told me when we live here, I can have ice cream every day. That I can join a soccer club and see movies. Where do you go next?"

Rogelio shrugged. "Before *mi madre* disappeared, she told me about some *familia* we have in a place called Nevada. Asylum, she said to ask for. I didn't know that word. Nevada is many miles away, to the north. But still hot, *el desierto*, Mami said. If I can't find them, I don't know what I will do."

"Will you go back to El Salvador?"

"Oh no, I cannot. MS-13 will surely kill me. At least here I am safe. God willing, it will work out. I will just have to go back to school or find a job somehow, find someplace to live. Being on a soccer team sounds fun. The people here are good, they will help."

Marisol and I trudge to the car in silence. Her head is down. When I ask if she wants to stop for food, she doesn't make eye contact and just shakes her head. Is it the heat or what we just witnessed?

The trip back to Phoenix is interminable and exhausting. Another thunderstorm disturbs our late afternoon drive back to the airport. Thunder rumbles, and cracks of lightening split the sky again. No hail this time but pounding, deafening rain that keeps us from talking. It's just as well. I'm too churned up inside to talk. In the car, Marisol looks all turned in on herself, curled up against the door and pretending to sleep.

So, we drive in silence.

On the plane, we don't have seats together. I try in vain to work on my laptop and read a novel I brought with me, but I can't focus. The harder I try not to think about that place, the more I obsess about it. I can't purge the image of those two boys together. Or the phony smiles on the faces of those government bureaucrats, so smug as they talked about how the children were better off in that prison they euphemistically call a shelter than they were back home.

Were they better off there? Maybe in some ways. Safer. Clothed and fed, with comfortable beds. But did that make up for being alone, not having your family, having no idea what would happen to you?

After barely speaking for two hours, we leave the airport in our separate cars. I put some loud Bruce Springsteen on the radio, anything to distract me, as I make the long drive through the night to my suburban home. Usually, even when I arrive this late, my wife Kelsey waits up. Not tonight. It's after one. With barely the energy to drag my bag upstairs, I find Kelsey in our bed, cuddled up with our youngest, three-year-old Peyton.

I stand at the door and watch them sleep, listening to the rhythm of their breaths, and can't decide whether to be relieved or disappointed Kelsey is asleep. Relieved, I guess. I need to talk, but I'm not sure I can. Instead, I stagger down the hall to Tyler's bedroom. As I debate whether to kiss him and risk waking him up, I study his room. Colorful soccer posters adorn the blue-painted walls, and toys lay scattered on the floor.

I need to kiss this kid, no matter what. I bend down and place a gentle kiss on Tyler's cheek. I can't resist ruffling his curly, sweaty hair. He murmurs something and rolls over, never waking, safe in his bed.

"I love you so much it hurts," I whisper, choking up.

As exhausted as I am, I'm too restless to sleep. I shuffle back downstairs and grab a beer from the fridge. Sitting at the kitchen table, I twist open the amber bottle, drain half the beer in a single gulp, and study the label on the Molson bottle. What a waste, this day. I never got to shoot a single photo. Marisol will write the story, but the world won't see what we saw today, those two boys, that place. I'm eager to read her piece, but I also wish I could talk with her. I decide to call her tomorrow, even though I'm guessing she won't want to talk about what we saw. A shiver of fear shoots through me as I realize this is the country Tyler and Peyton will grow up in.

Finally, the sobs come, and I don't even try to stop them.

No Choice

By the time you limp into the dusty, overcrowded refugee camp, barefoot and starving after days of walking, blood no longer runs down your thighs. Relief settles over your ravaged body like an embroidered silken shawl. You have survived, but still there is pain down there. Maybe there will be others like you, young girls whose virginity and families were destroyed.

So many people massed together. As you meet each woman you say, "I need help."

They point you to a network of muddy, winding paths that lead to a big, green canvas tent with a large red cross on it. When you appear at the tent opening a woman says, "Welcome. Come in. What do you need?"

"I have nothing," you say. "I have been walking so many days."

The worker looks into your empty eyes. "Are you alone?"

You adjust your headscarf and nod. "I am Arafa. My family . . ."

"Please come, sit down," the worker says. "Do you want to talk?"

You sit in silence.

"How old are you, Arafa?" asks the woman, her eyes full of concern.

You hang your head. Only your parents know the answer, your age the least of your problems.

You yearn to speak about the unspeakable, but the words catch in your throat like a dried-up piece of bread. What good would come of that? Shame is a filthy rag that blankets your body. Will talking find you a husband?

As you sit, the memories monsoon your mind. Everyone knows what happened to you. It happened to so many for so long, of course they know. Many watched it happen, first in your village and later in the forest as you tried to escape. As if escaping from that horror were possible. Whole families destroyed. Whole villages burned to the ground.

They watched you sob and scream and beg for mercy as your virginal body was desecrated by government soldiers. You had already seen other girls fight back. After the soldiers smashed their heads with rifles, still those poor girls were debased. So, you don't resist.

And you witnessed others die, again and again. Babies tossed against trees, fathers shot or burned, mothers violated, like you. When, finally, you get away, you can barely walk, your pain almost unbearable. You hide in caves and behind trees and bushes, terror your constant companion. Will there be more soldiers? You hope the worst is over, but what if . . . ?

How does Allah allow this to happen?

You try to remember what safety feels like. To be home, with your father and mother and the little ones. Maybe death is better than this.

"Let me help you find food and clean clothes and a place to stay," the health lady says.

And you nod.

The health workers find you a new family. You share their crowded tarp-and-bamboo shelter. Samira and her husband let you watch their three young children, who remind you of your own lost brothers and sisters, while they look for work.

You don't notice you no longer bleed every month. Not right away.

Months pass. When the rainy season begins, your belly starts to swell.

When Samira notices, she hisses at you, her black eyes flashing. "You must leave. You will bring shame on my family." She spits on ground. "You have betrayed us."

You become confused, desperate. You are frightened to visit the medical tent again—men work there—but what choice do you have?

You force yourself to follow the well-trodden paths, teeming with other displaced and desperate people. Rain still falls, the sky dark with clouds. You take the longer route, to avoid the stinking communal latrines, covered with buzzing flies. You jump to avoid puddles, but the hem of your blue skirt hangs sodden and muddy.

At the tent, a woman welcomes you and smiles. "I am a nurse. How can I help you?"

You look down your skirt, barely hiding your swollen belly. Her eyes follow yours. When she puts her arm around your shoulder you flinch. "I'm so sorry," she says. "It looks like you're six or seven months along. Are you alone?"

You nod, unable to meet her eyes. Has she noticed the dark circles pooling beneath your eyes?

"Have you had any medical care yet?"

You shake your head. Not in your whole life. You cannot hold back your pain any longer. Tears moisten your cheeks. Sorrow spills from your cracked lips. You tell her what happened in your village and the forest and being humiliated by Samira's family, your voice as coarse as sandpaper.

The nurse listens with soft, kind eyes and nods with understanding. "Many girls have had this happen. We have a place you can stay until your baby is born."

A place where you can hide your shame, she means. Now that no man will want you.

You disappear into that dark, damp place with other girls, your secret hidden away from society's judgment. Girls like you, who found out too late about their unwanted babies. Abandoned by your own people, a culture that abhors rape victims, despite knowing it is not their fault, that they had no choice.

You learn when your baby is born that there are men who will take it away, who will pay a small sum of money. Who knows what will happen to the baby after that?

Your eyes now shine with hope. Now, maybe a man will want to marry you.

Solo

Matthew Spence strolled into the Bar Association committee meeting exuding confidence.

I turned to Emily, my BFF who worked at his firm, and whispered, "How well do you know him?"

Matthew and I had crossed paths at the courthouse but had never worked together. I was still in my first year of practice, whereas he'd been at it for years.

Emily whispered back, "Not well at all. You interested?"

"Maybe. Love the salt-and-pepper hair. Looks like he works out, too."

She frowned and whispered, "But you're already dating Logan."

Matthew sat down across from me and got started. "Thanks for coming everyone. Appreciate you taking time out from your busy days to volunteer for this project. As you know, it involves sentencing reform—"

My opening. I jumped in with a question. "Hi, Matthew, Sarah Davidson. What exactly is the sentencing issue we're going to address?"

"Good question, Sarah. We're going to look into what is likely to be a disparity in sentencing between whites and

African Americans. It's going to be pretty intensive work involving a fair amount of travel to New York."

I'm not sure I heard much after that. When the meeting ended Emily asked, "Are you in? I'd like to do it, but I know the firm won't let me be away from the office for all that time."

"I've already checked with my boss. He thinks it would be good for our firm to have me involved. So, yeah, I'm going to do it."

The committee's next meeting required an early morning, three-hour train ride to New York. Despite my efforts to arrive early at the train station, venti coffee and briefcase in hand, I barely made it.

As I scanned the crowded train I heard, "Sarah?"

I turned toward the male voice and saw Matthew Spence, motioning for me to approach.

"Hi." He patted the seat next to him. "We've got a long ride ahead of us, but I'm sure we both brought work. Promise not to bother you."

"What luck. I was so late I was afraid I'd have to stand the whole way." I sat down, put my coffee in the holder and opened my briefcase. But, distracted by the spicy scent of his aftershave, I was having trouble concentrating. After a half hour, I asked some questions about the project. He answered but seemed more invested in the work he'd brought.

But the ride home from New York was different. We caught the 3:30 train back.

"I'm going to get a glass of wine," I said. "Interested?"

"Sure. Red, please." He took his wallet out and handed me a twenty. "This is for them both."

I considered offering to pay for my own and decided against it. "Thanks. Be right back."

When I returned, I asked, "How do you think the day went? Was it what you expected?"

He took a sip of wine and looked pensive. "Better than I expected, I guess. I thought we might encounter some resistance from the court staff, but everybody seemed co-operative. It's almost as if they already know about the sentencing disparities. Maybe this'll go more smoothly than I'd anticipated."

We continued to talk about the project, and I shifted into asking more personal questions—how long he'd worked for his firm, where he worked before that, where he lived. Using my most lawyerly interrogation skills, I managed to learn a lot. Reticent at first, after that glass of wine, Matthew opened up.

"Have you got kids?" I couldn't believe my chutzpa. The wine had loosened my tongue as well.

"Two, boy and girl. Ethan finished Cornell last year and Marissa is at UConn."

So, he must be at least in his fifties. "Is your wife a lawyer, too?" Totally pushing my luck, but he didn't seem offended.

"No, she works in the corporate world. As the years have passed, we've discovered we . . . have very different values and have drifted apart."

What exactly did that mean? I looked at him and waited.

"She's grown much more conservative and is all about making money, so we've separated . . ."

That sounded promising. As much as I wanted to know more, I forced myself to shut up after that. Didn't want to be too intrusive. If he wanted to say more, he would. Couldn't wait to talk to Emily later.

After I drove home from the train station, I changed and headed to the gym. I wasn't really in the mood, but Emily and I had a workout date. Plus, I wanted to talk to her about Matthew.

We found adjoining elliptical trainers and got our cardio workouts underway.

Emily asked, "How was the trip to New York?"

"Very interesting," I said, as mysteriously as I could.

"Come on, girl, dish." She laughed.

"Okay. The work part went well. Matthew thought it went even better than he'd hoped. Over wine on the ride back, I found out more about him."

"Like what?"

"Like his dream job would be to write fiction—"

"You're kidding. I never would've imagined."

"And he's separated from his wife."

Emily stared straight at me and asked, "And given you're already dating a married man, why would that matter, Sarah?"

Her frosty tone annoyed me. "I don't know. It probably doesn't." I was breathing hard now, trying to do a high-intensity interval, despite talking to Emily. I'd already burned two hundred calories.

"How are things going with Logan? You haven't mentioned him lately."

That's because I knew how much Emily disapproved of my seeing Logan. So, I avoided talking about him and tried to dodge the question.

But Emily came right back at me. "So, Logan?"

"Okay, I guess." Huffing and puffing, working on another interval.

"What does that mean?"

She wasn't letting me off the hook, was she? "The answer to the question you asked before, why does it matter that Matthew's separated? It matters because I need to believe there are more available men out there, in case things with Logan don't work out."

"Does that mean Logan hasn't made any progress on divorcing his wife?"

"Correct." And with that, I hopped off the elliptical and headed over to the free weights.

When I glanced at my phone after the gym, a text from Logan said he'd meet me at my house. I knew he'd expect dinner—that was our pattern—but I just wasn't up for it.

I called him. "You can stop by, but I picked up a salad on the way home from the gym. I'm too tired to cook."

"Really? All right."

I could hear the disappointment in his voice. Too bad. "I'll see you whenever you get there." We needed to talk about Maine.

He got there at seven-thirty, walking in without ringing the bell or knocking. "Hi," he said, kissing me. "How was your trip to New York?"

"Good. It's going to be an interesting project."

What was it about this guy that kept hooking me? His sexy, dark, Mediterranean looks for sure. He was bright and articulate, as invested in his job as a college professor as I was in my career. And he could be fun, but also moody. We'd fallen into a pattern after a year where we hardly ever went out. We stayed home and watched TV and had sex. That was it.

"Shall we go upstairs?" he asked.

"I haven't showered since the gym. I need to clean up." I wasn't sure I wanted to make love, but I wanted a shower, for sure.

"How about if I join you?"

"Fine."

He climbed into the shower behind me, and we made love. I went from not really being in the mood to being totally into it. Because that's the thing about Logan. He was a great lover, knew how to please me sexually. He'd bothered to figure out what turned me on. It mattered to him that I have orgasms, just like he did. Emily would have said, so what?

We dried off. I slathered myself with lavender-scented lotion and put on my bathrobe. "We need to talk about the summer. I want to plan a vacation."

"Sure. Where do you want to go?" He got dressed. I refused to let him keep a robe or other clothes at my house.

"The beach somewhere. I'm thinking Maine. Someplace less crowded than the Cape or the Jersey shore."

Let's go," he said. Back downstairs, he grabbed the remote and sank down on the sofa. I put my feet in his lap.

"Maine would be fine. Never been there, but I'm game. When?" He rubbed my sore feet.

"Probably after this project is over. Like, August, before your semester starts. Would that work?" I'd be desperate for a vacation by then. Logan got his summers off, but with this project, I'd be working overtime.

"Okay, just fill me in on the details."

"Fine." I yawned. "Listen, I'm going to turn in. I'm exhausted. I'll talk to you tomorrow." That meant I wasn't inviting him to stay the night. He'd have to go back to his apartment.

I appreciated that he didn't argue, although he moped his way over to the door. "Sleep well, and I'll see you tomorrow."

"Love you."

"Me too." And I closed the front door.

The sentencing project had begun in late May, and about halfway through the summer, and despite everything I told myself about how crazy it was, I found myself falling in love with Matthew. I used all my lawyerly arguments to try to convince myself how ridiculous it was for a forty-five-year-old woman involved with one man—a man who, though separated from his wife, would probably never get divorced—to fall in love with different man, also still married, albeit separated. It felt crazy. I couldn't sleep. Distracted at work. Eating Oreos nonstop.

One day in July, after the gym, Emily suggested getting a glass of wine.

"Sure, what's up?" We met at our favorite downtown bar, McSorley's, all dark wood and plants, and grabbed a table in the corner. While soft jazz played, we each ordered a chardonnay.

Before our drinks even arrived, Emily said, "Sarah, you know you're my best friend, right?"

I nodded.

"And I love you."

Uh-oh. "Yeah, of course," I said. "I love you, too."

"And best friends tell each other when they're doing something really stupid or self-destructive, right?"

Shit. I nodded, dreading what came next. The waiter delivered our wine. "Could we have some pretzels or some kind of munchies?" I asked. I needed something in my empty stomach, already churning in anticipation of what Emily was going to say.

She just blurted it out. "You need to dump Logan! Now, and once and for all. To save yourself. You're falling apart."

And I thought I'd been hiding it so well. She waited for me to respond. The waiter delivered our pretzels. I grabbed a couple, stalling for time. "I've been thinking about it, Em, I really have. He's obviously not gonna get divorced. I've been trying to work up the courage to do it."

"I don't get why that requires courage."

Easy for her to say, happily married for ten years. "I guess I don't want to be alone."

"What is it about being alone that scares you?"

"It's not that it *scares* me so much as . . ."

The waiter started to approach and Emily waved him away, waiting for me to continue.

"I guess it pisses me off. I mean, I don't need a guy to take care of me. I earn a good salary, own my house . . ."

"Yeah, and . . ."

"That's less attractive to guys than you might think! Most men in our age range assume women need men to take care of them. That's not what I'm looking for."

"What are you looking for? And why are you so convinced you won't find it?"

"Companionship. Someone who can make my life better. Intimacy. Physical, but also emotional. Logan, for all his faults . . . well, we have a great physical relationship."

"But that's not a good enough reason to put up with—"

"I know, I know. You're right. I've had all these arguments with myself already."

"So?"

I drained the last of my wine. "Okay, Em, I'm going to make a promise—and I want you to hold me to it—that I will break things off with Logan before the summer's over. There's just one complication."

Emily rolled her eyes.

Logan and I planned—and paid for—that Maine vacation together in August. I desperately needed it. After working my tail off all summer, I needed a break.

Depression consumed Logan more than usual all summer. His depression sapped my energy. I gave so much, but I got so little back. He was sucking the life right out of me.

I planned to break it off when we returned from Maine, without thinking it through. A few days before we were scheduled to leave, we had an argument.

"You don't really seem to be looking forward to this week in Maine," I said. "Do you still want to go?"

Long silence. Fuck, he was going to cancel.

Finally, "Not really. I'm feeling really crummy."

What else was new? The vein in my neck pulsed. This was a no-win situation. I could make a big issue out of it, insisting he go, but he'd probably sulk and act like a victim. Or I could say we didn't have to go, lose a bundle of money on the seaside cottage, and miss out on the ocean and lobsters. Or option number three. I took a few deep breaths to calm myself.

"I've had no time off this summer, unlike you, and I deserve this vacation." My jaw tensed. "You can stay home if you want, but I'm going regardless."

"I'm concerned about being away from Jessica for that long," he said.

A week? Jessica, his spoiled fourteen-year-old only child, managed to manipulate both of her parents into getting whatever she wanted, including a horse. She talked back, misbehaved, and generally acted like a little princess. Which was what I secretly called her behind Logan's back: The Little Princess. Every prospective stepmother's nightmare.

My heart beat faster, as sweat poured into my armpits. I'd never taken a vacation alone. What would it be like, a week in Maine, by myself? But I felt really stubborn. Wait, wasn't there someone from work who said she'd be in Maine during the same week? Maybe I could get together her with a couple times. Maybe she'd take pity on me because Logan had cancelled out on me at the last minute.

Logan sat there, a big, pathetic lump, saying nothing.

This was the last straw. Snap. Besides, I had already promised Emily to end the relationship, and now this.

Screw it.

I could hear Emily's voice in my head from that day at McSorley's, urging me on. I inhaled a deep breath. "Logan, I've had it. I'm not getting enough from this relationship to make it worth what I'm investing. It's time for me to move on—"

"Wait, Sarah—"

"I'm not done. You've promised you'd divorce Susan. You moved out a while ago, but it's obvious you're never going to leave her emotionally. This is over. This whole vacation fiasco is a good time to do it."

He sat silent for a long time and finally started to weep. Ugh, I hated it when men cried. I squirmed, while he got up and paced. I grabbed a taupe pillow off the couch and hugged it, resisting the urge to comfort him.

"Please, Sarah, don't do this to me," he begged. "You know I love you." He sat all curled in on himself on the sofa. "We talk all the time, I'm here almost every night. We have great sex. What am I going to do without you?"

I wondered that, too, but I didn't care anymore. I let him cry for a minute. "I'm sorry, but you've had lots of chances and time to get yourself together and decide what you want to do. I'm tired of being strung along. Every deadline you set for leaving comes and goes, and you're still married. Enough is enough! The reality is, I'm just not in love you with anymore. My emotions have shut down on me. I'm tired of waiting and feeling disappointed."

He walked into the bathroom, returning with some tissues. "I know I've had a lot of trouble ending things with Susan, but it's mostly because of Jessica. I'm just afraid of what this is going to do to her."

Not my problem.

"Sarah, please reconsider. I know you're disappointed about my not coming to Maine, and I'm fine with your going alone."

As if he had a say in that.

"We're good together. I just need a little more time. I *will* leave Susan. Please give me another chance."

By that time, the tears had turned to sobbing for both of us. How had things deteriorated to this point? Too upset to argue, I told him I would think about it and asked him to leave.

That night, while I packed, he called me three times, reiterating his intention to divorce Susan and begging me to reconsider. All I'd say was I'd think about it. But, in reality, all I could think about was extricating myself from this morass. And Matthew. I thought about Matthew, although I had no idea whether he was any more available than Logan.

I drove to Maine by myself early the next day, found the cottage, and got in touch with my friend. She'd already been there a few days, surprised to hear I'd come by myself. I battled traffic to join her and her husband at the beach and at dinner a couple of times. But they were staying two towns away, so I spent most of my time alone. Solitude turned out to be more interesting than I expected. It gave me time to think about my relationship with Logan. I couldn't get excited about continuing to see him, but at the same time I dreaded his reaction if I told him the truth and could feel my resolve to end things weakening. I hated feeling indecisive.

But never mind, I was on vacation. During the day, I walked on the beach, took a chilly swim, or hiked. I found a couple of yoga classes and ended up tan and fit. For dinner, I bought fresh seafood and cooked it for myself, reading a good book while devouring clams and fish. At night, I read some more or watched something on Netflix. I wandered through booths at an outdoor art show and bought an oil painting. At a hip local independent bookstore, I found a beautiful journal for myself. I'd always intended to start journaling, so this solo vacation presented the perfect opportunity. And writing in the journal gave me a new perspective.

I decided I'd see Logan under three conditions. First, I wanted to date other men, on the off-chance Matthew was available, although I knew it would drive Logan crazy. Second, he had to return my house key, if only because of the symbolic value associated with it. Finally, I wasn't willing to see him every day and cook him dinner at night. If he wanted to see me, he'd have to make formal dates. No more taking me for granted and treating me as a pseudo-wife.

The day I worked this out, after I got back to the cottage, a gorgeous bouquet of flowers awaited me on my doorstep. The card read, "I miss you and love you. Can't wait to see you when you get back. Logan." I leaned over to smell the roses. Then I carried the whole bunch out to the Dumpster.

The remainder of the vacation passed quickly once I resolved what I'd tell Logan when I got back. I dreaded the moment when he realized I wouldn't change my mind and I really wanted out. Unless he met my conditions, our days as a couple were numbered.

When I pulled into my driveway, Logan sat on my front porch. Crap.

He helped me unload my luggage. "I'm so happy you're home. Can we talk?"

I heard his voice crack.

"Can I please just relax for a minute? The traffic was brutal." I didn't even try to keep the annoyance out of my voice. I'd forgotten how needy he could be.

In the kitchen I said, "I'm going to have a glass of wine, do you want one?"

"Sure. While you were gone, did you think about our relationship?"

Not, "Did you have a good time?"

"I did."

"And are we good?"

What planet was he on? We were so far from good . . . I walked into the living room with him following like a sad puppy.

I took a deep breath and exhaled. "Logan, I'm only willing to continue seeing you under three conditions. First, you need to return my key. Second, I'm done with cooking for you every night. Sometimes is fine but—"

The look on his face was priceless. His mouth dropped open and he gasped. "Sarah, wait—"

"I'm not done. Please don't interrupt. Third, I want to date other people."

He leapt up from the couch. Pacing the living room, he yelled. "Are you crazy? I've been faithful to you. I've been so good to you." He paused. "What's his name?" And finally, pathetically, "Sarah, I love you so much I just can't share you with anyone." His eyes welled up.

Shit, was he going to cry again?

"So, don't even think about dating other people."

Sarcasm dripped from my voice. "You don't *own* me," I hissed. "What right do you have to tell me who I can spend my time with, you who are still married to another woman you speak to several times a day? Faithful, my ass!"

"I'll tell you any goddam thing I want, Sarah."

For a moment, I thought he might be softening and about to apologize for his aggressive stance and tone. I relaxed a little. Big mistake.

"I'm so glad we never had *babies* together, Sarah. It's lucky you turned out to be *frigid*."

He knew I hated that word, especially as it applied to women like me who are unable to bear children. The problem with Logan was that you could never really let your guard down around him. He always zapped you when you least expected it. What had I ever seen in this guy?

"I've changed my mind. I want out," I said. "Immediately. No room for negotiation. Give me my key. This. Relationship. Is. Over!"

He pouted, holding back tears, but handed over my key. Face beet red, fists clenched, he stomped out to his car, pulling out of the driveway and down the street on shrieking tires. I let out a huge breath.

I couldn't wait to call Emily. She was going to be so proud of me.

My first week back to work I had a meeting of the Bar Association committee on sentencing. I looked forward to seeing Matthew.

In the bathroom, getting ready, I coached myself in the mirror. "Sarah, see if you can get up the nerve up to ask him out."

But my alter ego asked, "Should I try to find out if he's available first, or just ask and risk embarrassing myself?"

Putting on mascara, I answered, "What the hell? What's the worst that could happen?"

My alter ego answered, "He says he's in a relationship or has reconciled with his wife, and I'm a little embarrassed. I can handle that."

Labor Day weekend fast approached, including an outdoor jazz concert I'd enjoyed in the past. I'd decided to invite him.

Thursday morning, I took special care getting dressed and applying my makeup. Matthew chaired the committee, and I hung around until people drifted away. He asked how my vacation in Maine had been. I hadn't even remembered mentioning that to him. I took it as a good sign.

Should I be honest? Nah. "It was great to get away. The weather was good, and I love the ocean. Got to do some hiking, read a few books. Thanks for asking. How've you been?"

"Good. Busy. Looking forward to a long holiday weekend. Have you got plans?"

Putting on my biggest smile I said, "Been thinking about going to that outdoor jazz concert on Sunday. Any interest in joining me?"

"Jazz? Yeah, I love jazz. It's on Sunday, you said?"

We walked out to the parking lot. "Yep, Sunday afternoon. Weather's supposed to be great. What do you think?" I tried to act relaxed, despite my beating heart.

"Sure. Sounds like fun."

Getting my nerve up again, I said, "How about a picnic? Should we do that?"

I watched him considering.

"That'd be fine, what can I bring?"

We were at his Acura, so he stopped. I thought for a minute and said, "How about if I bring a main dish and some kind of dessert and you bring a salad?"

"That works. I think I know where you live, and my house is on the way to the concert. Why don't you come to my house, and I'll drive us from there? One o'clock?"

He knew where I lived? "Great!" I was so damned proud of myself.

The day of the concert brought abundant sunshine, not too hot or humid. I drove to Matthew's house in the suburb next to mine, we packed up his salad in my cooler and hopped into his car. We drove from his house to the concert location, just beyond the state line in Massachusetts, over country roads. Typical New England—trees and streams and a profusion of late summer wildflowers.

Although we enjoyed the concert—how could we not on such a splendid day?—we were both a little disappointed with the music. No one act lasted very long—three songs at best—perhaps because of the need to fit so many performers into one afternoon. Sitting outdoors on the lawn, people felt free to talk throughout the various performances, so annoying and rude.

We ate our picnic during the intermission. I'd brought a cold Indonesian noodle and chicken salad with peanut sauce and a fruit salad for dessert, along with chocolate chip pecan cookies I'd baked that morning. To drink, I'd brought a nice chardonnay and lemon-flavored sparkling water. Matthew's salad looked delicious, with arugula, radicchio and Bibb lettuce, strawberries and gorgonzola. When he realized he'd forgotten the raspberry walnut salad dressing he'd made, his cheeks turned red. I found it kind of endearing. No matter, we ate his salad anyhow, *sans* dressing, along with my noodle salad, and had a lovely meal. Over our picnic, we chatted about the music and got to know each other better.

"So, you're not actually divorced from Melissa right now?" I asked, fighting to control my inner dialogue about going out with another man who was still married, despite being separated.

"I moved out months ago, but she won't give me a divorce, even though she's the one who wanted the relationship to end. I can't figure her out."

"Sounds like you're kind of stuck." I realized after I said it that it was probably the last thing he wanted to hear.

"You're right, I guess. At least we didn't have children together."

"I thought you had two?"

"Actually, I do, from marriage number one. They're launched. Out of college and on their own."

Not knowing what to say at this point, I decided to keep my mouth shut. The conversation skirted sensitive territory for me, and I preferred to avoid it altogether.

The remainder of the evening passed unremarkably, and we rode home in silence, having spent the last seven hours together. In his driveway, Matthew hurried over to open my door. Next thing I knew, he pulled me toward him and kissed me hard. Not a peck on the cheek, a long, slow, romantic kiss.

Two days later I called him to let him know CNN was going to interview someone we had worked with on the sentencing project, so he might want to watch it. He said his TV was on the fritz, so I invited him over to watch it at my house.

He arrived at nine-thirty, a half hour before the program. Although I wasn't sure this was a date, I'd put on makeup and fixed my hair, spritzing myself with perfume. I pulled on black leggings and a long, sheer, silk shirt. When I inspected myself in the hall mirror on the way to the front door, I liked what I saw: a lanky woman with wavy red hair and bangs, freckles, still tan from the beach.

When Matthew arrived, he grazed my cheek with a quick kiss, which set my heart off. I disappeared into the kitchen to pour us some iced tea, and we chatted as we waited for the program to begin. Finally, it came on and we watched intently for an hour. The interview with the man we knew lasted a total of one minute, and he said nothing relevant to our project. What a waste of time. Oh well, at least I got to see Matthew again. I kept waiting for him to leave, but he sat nestled into the sofa. I got up and put some Miles Davis on the stereo.

When my cellphone rang, I kicked myself for not turning it off. After it rang a second time I got up and silenced it.

"Do you need to answer it?" Matthew asked.

I didn't feel like being interrupted at the moment. Besides, it was after ten o'clock.

"Nah, it can go voicemail."

Then ten minutes later I heard it buzz again from across the room. It must be Logan. No way I'd talk to him. Plus, if it was him, it must be driving him crazy not to be able to reach me. Maybe I was being kind of passive-aggressive about the whole thing. Too bad.

"Boy, you get a lot of late-night phone calls."

"Sure seems that way, doesn't it?" Miles' soft horn moaned in the background.

Midnight had come and gone. When I looked over, Matthew's eyes were closed, so I closed mine, too. Still, the kiss surprised me, soft and tentative. As I responded, he began to kiss me more deeply, although not quite passionately. That would come later, I hoped. Then, much to my delight, Matthew put his hand under my shirt. He'd seemed so shy I didn't really expect he'd be so "forward" this soon.

But the more I enjoyed it, the more thoughts of Logan intruded. Suddenly, the doorbell rang, startling both of us. I decided to ignore it. But it rang again and again. It could only be one person. I was mortified. What was Matthew thinking?

By that time, I was all disheveled. My bra hung unhooked, my shirt partially unbuttoned, hair a mess, face flushed. Afraid Logan would just barge right in—the unlocked screen door was all that stood between me and an undoubtedly enraged Logan—I rushed to the front door.

He started in immediately. "Where've you been? How come you haven't been answering your phone if you're home? Whose car is that in the driveway? It's that guy you've been working with, that other lawyer, isn't it? I knew you were seeing someone else!"

As he started to talk, I stepped outside and pulled the wooden door shut, hoping to spare Matthew some of this unpleasantness. But with all my windows open, he'd still be able to hear. Logan was shouting at the top of his lungs.

My heart felt like it could burst right through my chest wall. I tried to breathe and calm myself, hoping not to provoke Logan to become any more upset.

"First, it's none of your business who is in my house with me," I said. "I told you more than a week ago this relationship was over. And let's not forget who's married here and who isn't. And as for not answering your calls—"

"You're really a whore."

I smelled alcohol on his breath.

He yelled so loud I realized that not only could Matthew hear it, but so could my neighbors, not the kind of folks who'd relish being awakened on a weeknight after midnight by that kind of language. My whole body tensed up.

"Look, you're out of control, and you need to leave right now." My heart raced. "I'll discuss this with you tomorrow when you've had a chance to calm down." I felt like I was going to puke.

He paced around my front yard, agitated. "*I'll* decide when I'm ready to leave," he said, his face contorted.

I backed up the steps on my small front porch. "I'm calling the police. I'm not kidding. Get off my property. Now."

He paced for a few seconds longer, glaring at me, finally heading toward his car. When I finally let myself breathe, I realized I'd been holding my breath. He sped off, screeching tires and all, and I walked back into the house, shaking all over. Oh God, now I had to deal with Matthew.

I walked into the den. For a few moments neither of us said anything. I sat down next to him. "I'm so sorry."

"All you okay?" Matthew asked. "You're shaking all over."

"I guess so. That was awful, and scary. I intended to tell you about my ex sooner, but it didn't seem relevant until a couple of days ago." I couldn't seem to stop blabbering. "You'll probably never want to see me again after this. I'm sure you're wondering what you could be getting yourself into. I feel so humiliated."

Matthew said nothing. Please say something, anything, I implored.

Finally, he asked, "So, what's the story? Who is this guy?"

"I've been in the process of ending the relationship. It had nothing to do with you. I knew he'd be upset, but I never anticipated something this bad. I guess I should have, 'cause he's got a temper. I'll completely understand if you never want to see me again."

"I wasn't thinking along those lines," Matthew said wryly.

For some reason, that struck me as funny, and I started laughing hysterically.

"Actually, I figured something was going on from various things you've said. Like going on vacation by yourself a few weeks ago. But don't feel you owe me an explanation."

"Well, I kinda feel like I do." So, I explained as well as I could what I thought Matthew needed to know about my ill-fated relationship with Logan. He didn't say much, which was typical, as I would soon learn. I felt all jittery. What did he think about all this? He listened attentively and didn't seem to be scared off by what had just happened, much to my relief and amazement. At about one-thirty he left, saying he'd call soon.

And so, we became involved. Logan eventually calmed down and stopped chasing me around in his car, threatening to sue me, and doing other nutty things. Matthew and I went on dates, made love, and spent the night together once every week or ten days, always at my house. Most other days we spoke on the phone, at least for a few minutes, and sometimes at length.

I grew to appreciate his sharp mind and subtle wit. His divorce became final, although he never talked about it. I never did learn much about his grown-up kids. We even took a couple of vacations together. Each time, I thought when we returned our relationship would move into a new level of intimacy. But it didn't and we both maintained our separate lives.

A year passed, but our relationship didn't seem to be going anywhere. Eventually I confronted him—gently—and asked what was going on.

"What do you mean?" he asked.

We sat on that same sofa where, a year earlier, we had watched our colleague on CNN, and he'd heard Logan act like a maniac on my front lawn.

I tried to explain I wanted our relationship to deepen, for us to be closer, to have more intimacy. "I want more."

"Are you saying you want to get married?"

"No. Maybe to live together eventually, but I mean to see more of each other. To do more during the week than just talk on the phone. To share a life."

"I thought that's what we were doing."

Oh boy, this wasn't going the way I'd hoped. I was flummoxed.

After a long silence, he finally said, "This whole discussion is making me uncomfortable. I don't think I can give you what you need. Or what you want, whatever. I need some time to think about it." He got up and left, giving me a quick kiss on the way out.

A week later a letter arrived from Matthew. He'd realized he wasn't ready for the kind of commitment I wanted. He had only just extricated himself from his marriage, and he wasn't ready for another serious commitment yet.

"I'm sorry we ever got involved. I can see now it wasn't fair to you. I know breaking it off now will hurt you, for which I'm sorry, but ending the relationship would be best under the circumstances."

I never saw it coming.

I kept rereading the letter, too numb to even call Emily. Finally, it came to me. The universe was telling me, for whatever reason, that I was meant to be alone right now. It'd be fine. I had a place to live, a good job, friends. I could survive being alone. Maybe it wouldn't be forever. And maybe it would.

I met Emily the next evening for a drink at McSorley's Pub.

Before the waitress arrived, Emily said, "Sarah, how's it going with Matthew?"

"He dumped me."

"Oh, no. What? Shit! Why? Are you okay?" She reached across the table and put her hand on my arm.

"I'm fine. Long story. Bottom line though, I'm okay. Even though his divorce came through, he wasn't ready for another relationship. Bad timing."

We ordered drinks, and as the waitress left, Emily asked, "What're you going to do now? Match.com?"

"Nope, I'm planning my next vacation. Solo."

Tough as Nails

"I would urge you to get here as soon as possible, Mrs. Berg-strom," the hospital psychiatrist said. "How soon can you make it?" Even over the phone her voice sounded soothing, her words delivered in a way that made Elin understand she was used to conveying bad news.

It was already late morning. Should she fly or drive? Elin wondered. She'd never been to LA, with its legendary traffic. If she flew, she'd still need a car, right? Wouldn't it be better to have her own? Could she make that seven-hour drive by herself? My God, she was pushing seventy.

She assumed her older granddaughter, Chloe, was safe at college. Not lying in an LA hospital ICU after an overdose. God, she dreaded the next forty-eight hours.

And what about Lily, her sixteen-year-old granddaughter, and the animals? She'd need to make arrangements for them. It didn't make any sense to bring Tucker with her, much as she would have liked her pooch's company. But Lily? No, she'd have to stay home, too. She couldn't miss school.

Meanwhile, Dr. Choi waited on the other end of the phone. "Sorry, I've been trying to think about how quickly I can get there. There's no way it can be today. I have to pick

Chloe's sister up after school and make arrangements for our pets. But can I talk to her on the phone?"

"She's still pretty out of it right now, but by tomorrow we're hoping she'll wake up."

"Okay, I'll get there tomorrow, probably late afternoon. Will you be available then?"

"Yes. Have them page me when you arrive." The psychiatrist left details for how she could find Chloe's room at the City of the Angels Medical Center.

Another phone call that turned her life upside down. She cursed her husband Reed for the hundredth time for dying and leaving her with this nightmare to deal with. How was she, having never been a parent, despite her years of counseling people, supposed to deal with crises like these? Really, it just wasn't fair. Fair. Ha! Who said life was fair? Isn't that what her sister Kirsten always said?

Well, she could whine and mope, or she could get busy figuring out what she needed to do to get over to LA.

She drove to Lily's school and got into the long line of cars waiting to pick kids up. God forbid a high school sophomore take the school bus home in fancy schmantsy North Scottsdale. As she waited in the pokey line inching forward, she thought about what to tell Lily. How much could that poor kid be expected to deal with? As she approached the pick-up spot, she spied her granddaughter talking to a group of boys and girls. So cute in her skinny jeans and white tank top, her long auburn hair pulled back into a wavy ponytail.

When Elin arrived at the spot, she opened the passenger-side window and yelled, "Lily!"

"Gotta go," she heard her say, waving goodbye to the other kids. Was she finally making some friends?

"Hi, Grandma."

"Hey. How'd school go today?" Although it took all of her self-control not to blurt out the bad news about Chloe, she'd decided on small talk for the drive home, waiting until they were eating their snack to tell Lily about her sister.

"Okay, I guess. Same old, same old, really."

Why did adolescents have to be so difficult to talk to? "How was soccer practice?"

"Pretty good, actually. I scored two goals. It's hard in this heat. When does it cool off here?"

"Not till the end of the month." Lily had been in Scottsdale with her for four months. "Two goals are great. Are you enjoying soccer again?"

"Starting to. It's easier when you know the other girls, I guess. The group's hard to break into. They're pretty tight with each other."

"Yeah, it must be tough to join a group that's been together for a while." Lily's resentment about having to move in with Elin, away from all her friends and the life she'd had in Chevy Chase, Maryland, was finally receding.

"Did you get your hair done today? It looks nice."

"Thanks." Elin had made a trip to the salon earlier, to have her gray hair cut into a stylish bob. As a gift to herself after her husband Reed died a year and a half ago, she'd let it go gray. Her sister insisted it would make her look older, but so what? The least of her worries at the moment.

They arrived home and Elin pulled the Audi into the garage. As they walked into the house, she said, "After you put your stuff away, before you get started on your homework, let's have a snack. There's something I need to talk to you about."

"Okay."

Elin walked into the kitchen. What could they have as a snack? She should have something healthy, still struggling with her weight, but the phone call made her crave something carb-y and bad.

A few minutes later, Lily walked in and sat at the granite island in Elin's large, sun-filled kitchen.

"Our snack options are yogurt, fruit, guacamole and chips, cereal, a smoothie—"

"I vote for guac and chips."

"You got it." The closer she came to starting the conversation, the shakier she felt.

"So, Grandma, what's going on?"

Elin focused on opening the guacamole container and getting the chips out, buying time. "A little while ago, I got a call from a psychiatrist at a hospital in LA."

"About what?" Lily dipped a blue corn chip into the guac and popped it into her mouth. "Do we have any Diet Coke?"

"In the fridge."

Lily got up to get her drink. Elin grabbed a handful of chips and put them on a napkin. "She called to tell me Chloe is in the hospital—"

"What's wrong *this* time?"

"She's in the ICU . . . following a drug overdose." Elin dipped a chip into guacamole, waiting to see Lily's reaction.

"Shit, really?" She frowned. "Is she okay?"

"I'm actually not sure. From what Dr. Choi said, it sounds serious. I have to drive over there tomorrow. I'm not looking forward to it." Probably shouldn't have said that.

"Did you talk to Chloe?"

"I tried, but the doctor said she's in a coma—"

"A coma! Shit, she's really fucked herself up this time."

Elin gave her a warning look about her language. The girls' parents, Drew and Meredith, had been very permissive with the girls when it came to language. Both had potty mouths.

"Sorry, Grandma."

Something about her apology caused Elin's eyes to fill. Lily noticed right away.

"Grandma, I'm sorry about how I reacted. I am. But I'm tired of Chloe's antics and screw-ups. I lost both of my parents, too, you know. And you don't see me—"

"I know, sweetie. It's just . . . I'm really worried. Did you know she was using drugs?"

"Weed, of course. But not anything more than that. It was always her drinking that Mom and Dad were worried about."

Elin knew about the booze. At the end of freshman year, Chloe's drinking landed her in the emergency room, leading to a twenty-eight-day rehab. Andrew had told Reed about it, but she was pretty sure they never told Lily, wanting to protect her. Just one of the many secrets festering in that family. Apparently, rehab didn't take.

Lily slathered another corn chip with guacamole. "Did the doctor say which drug?"

"Fentanyl. Synthetic fentanyl."

"Oh. My. God. Are you kidding me? We just talked about that in our health class. That's crazy. It's supposed to be, like, a hundred times more powerful than heroin or something. Why the hell would she ever take something like that?"

Having read about it in the newspaper, Elin wondered the same thing. Even before her parents were killed, Chloe seemed to be teetering on a precipice. Elin had agreed to be guardian for her younger granddaughter, but Chloe was nineteen and legally didn't need a guardian. Elin would, however, oversee the finances for her older granddaughter, already a handful, out of the house and running wild since high school.

But Elin could never have envisioned something this scary.

"Here's the thing, Lily, I need to get over there, see what's going on, and I'll be gone at least a couple day—"

"No problem, Grandma. I'll be fine by myself."

Nothing doing.

"No, I don't think that would be a good idea."

Lily raised her eyebrows. "Are you saying you want me to come with you?"

"No!" Elin said, too sharply. "I mean we need to figure out where you can stay for a couple of nights." Even as she said it, she realized this would be a challenge.

"Is there anybody you can stay with for a couple nights, any friends at school?"

"Nobody. If I was at my old school . . ."

A sore point. When Reed's son and daughter-in-law, Andrew and Meredith, were killed in a terrorist attack outside of DC fifteen months ago, Lily moved to Arizona. Elin had just lost Reed to cancer seven months before that and was still grieving herself, as well as recovering from a year of heavy-duty caregiving. She reluctantly agreed to serve as guardian for her Lily but wasn't willing to move across country. So, Elin had forced her younger granddaughter—Lily made it clear it was coercion—to move to Arizona to finish high school. Change her whole life, really. The move had been brutal for both of them. Tears all around. Learning to live with a teenager wasn't exactly a picnic. Since then, they'd forged a fragile truce. But Elin saw Lily's loneliness. And anger.

And then there was Chloe.

"How about this?" Elin proposed. "How about if my friend Basia comes and stays here with you. You've met her. She's nice.

She'll leave you alone and just make sure everything's okay. She'll drive you to school. That way you can stay with Tucker and Sasha and Chessie." When Lily moved, she brought her cat Chessie—short for Chesapeake—with her. Chessie was a great comfort to Lily, sleeping with her every night.

She waited for Lily's reaction. "That would be a huge help to me," Elin added, to put a little pressure on her to agree. She really didn't have too many options here. And she still had to get Basia to agree.

She could see Lily's hesitation. Finally, her granddaughter said, "All right. If it'll make it easier for you."

"Thanks. Let me call Basia."

The drive to LA across I-8 was long, the desert desiccated and brown after a long hot summer. Elin couldn't help but think a woman her age shouldn't have to be doing things like this alone. And after the boring drive, she'd have to face LA traffic, unfamiliar roads, doctors, and a messed up nineteen-year-old who was angry and lost. What had happened to that adorable little girl she had loved to read books to? To play dolls with?

She had planned to talk on the phone to both Kirsten and Basia on the way there, bringing them up to speed and getting their input on how she should approach her first meeting with Chloe. She tried her sister Kirsten first and had to leave a message. Couldn't reach Basia either. Crap. In the meantime, to keep herself from obsessing too much, she turned on some upbeat bossa nova music.

An hour later, Kirsten called back. Elin related what had happened with Chloe and explained she was on her way to LA to see her in the hospital and talk with the psychiatrist.

Before she could even get her take on how to approach Chloe, Kirsten said, "I warned you not to take that on. I knew those girls would give you nothing but headaches. How come you never listen to me?" Kirsten, with no children or grandchildren, was the older of the two, still bossy and controlling.

"It's not as though I really had much choice," Elin said.

"Of course, you did. There's always a choice. You could have said no. Your husband just died, and you couldn't handle it. They're not even technically your granddaughters."

Elin wasn't going to bite. Of course, they were her granddaughters. The fact they weren't biologically related to her was immaterial. She had been in their lives since they'd been born. She'd held them when they weighed six pounds. Touched their silky skin. Changed their diapers. Sang them to sleep. Read them *Goodnight Moon*. Loved them. She was the only grandmother they'd ever known. "And who else would have done it?"

"It's not your problem their parents were killed and nobody younger was available to take over."

Kirsten could be heartless. Andrew was Reed's only son. Right after Andrew and Meredith were killed, Elin and the family lawyer had gone round and round to try to find other options for care of the two girls. There just weren't any. Kirsten wouldn't stop talking about how stupid it was for Elin to think she could take care of two teenagers. She even suggested calling the lawyer back—now!—to say she'd come to her senses and changed her mind. How Elin had aged ten years since taking on this responsibility. "You look seventy years old, for God's sake!"

She *was* almost seventy years old. What was she supposed to look like? Finally, she said, "Enough! This isn't helping. I made a commitment to take care of these girls. And that's what I'm going to do. If you can't at least be supportive, I don't want to speak to you." She hung up. Kirsten would be pissed, but too bad.

By the time she got off the phone, she felt even more rattled. Her stomach was doing flipflops. Why should she feel guilty for taking on the responsibility of caring for her grand-daughters? Of course, it wasn't ideal. In fact, it was the last thing she would have thought about doing after losing Reed, but there just weren't any other decent options. Those poor girls didn't ask to have their parents killed. They needed someone who loved them to be looking after them, not some stranger. As the traffic worsened, she switched to New Age music in the hopes of chilling out.

Basia finally called back.

"Hey. Thanks a million for agreeing to stay with Lily. I just got off the phone with my sister."

"How'd that go?"

"About as badly as you might expect. She thinks I'm a sucker for having agreed to be guardian to Lily and Chloe."

"Nonsense. I'm over at your house right now. Tucker says hello. We'll all be fine here. So, how're you doing?"

"I wouldn't say I'm a mess, but this is a pretty darn hard. I just don't think I'm cut out for all this drama. Maybe Kirsten's right . . . It's not a coincidence I never had kids, you know. I'm afraid I'm not any good at this kind of stuff. All I want at this point in my life is peace and serenity. I had enough drama with Reed's ups and downs. And then Drew and Meredith were killed . . ." Tears stung her eyes. "You know what? I *am* a mess, a total mess. I'm fighting to keep it together for Lily and this meeting with the psychiatrist, but I'm not doing a very good job."

"Yes, you are! Not completely falling apart with all that's happened in the past couple years is defined as a good job. A *very* good job. I wish I could do more. It pains me to hear the tears in your voice."

"Staying at the house with Lily and the critters is a huge help, really."

Elin explained as much as she knew of what happened with Chloe—not much—and the upcoming meeting with the psychiatrist.

"Have you thought yet about what you're going to say to Chloe?" asked Basia.

"Been obsessing about it. I'm so pissed off at her I could spit."

They talked a bit longer before the traffic became so heavy Elin finally said, "I'm gonna have to say goodbye. I need to pay attention to what I'm doing here. These California drivers are the take-no-prisoners type. I'll call tonight when I know more. Thanks again."

She got lost a couple of times but eventually found the medical center, grateful she knew how to navigate using Siri on her iPhone. She parked—twenty bucks!—found the nursing station on the eighth-floor ICU, and asked to have Dr. Choi paged.

While she waited, she tried to compose herself, wishing she'd brought a written list of questions. There was a lot going on around her, what with constant announcements paging doctors, and people in green scrubs rushing here and there, everyone in a hurry. That antiseptic smell took her right back to those anxiety-filled days of Reed's illness. She hated that medicinal odor. Her heart rate quickened the moment she walked in. She heard her therapist's voice in her head saying, "Close your eyes and take a few long, slow deep breaths." She closed her eyes.

"Are you Mrs. Bergstrom?" The voice startled her.

"Yes, sorry, I am. Elin. I was just trying to . . . uh . . . center myself. Are you Dr. Choi?"

"I am. Let's find a quiet place with some privacy."

Dr. Choi escorted her down a wide hallway to a small, windowless room that said *"Consultation"* on the door. A worn blue sofa and a single red, vinyl-covered chair comprised the furniture. "Have a seat."

"Before we get started," Elin said, "I have a question. Why a psychiatrist, rather than a doctor with a medical specialty?"

"When the EMTs brought Chloe to the emergency department, after they revived her, the only words she said indicated she was disappointed to be alive after her overdose. So, it appears the overdose may have been a suicide attempt—"

Elin's quick intake of breath stopped her.

"So, we have a lot of questions about Chloe we hope you can answer. We need to decide where she should go from here. Were you aware of her drug use?" Dr. Choi, whom Elin assumed was Korean, spoke almost unaccented English. She wore a white coat over a red dress. Her straight, jet-black hair was pulled back into a bun. Very put together and professional.

Her head bowed, Elin forced herself to take long, deep breaths. "I'm not sure where to begin. Chloe is my granddaughter. After both of her parents were killed in that terrorist attack in DC, I became her sister's guardian." It had been all over the news for weeks afterward, so Elin assumed Dr. Choi would be familiar with it. "But since Chloe is nineteen, I'm just responsible for her trust fund." She pulled a tissue out of her purse, buying time, deciding what to say next.

"Oh dear, that must have been very traumatic for her, especially with the constant news coverage in the aftermath."

"It was. Both girls—her fifteen-year-old sister Lily, who moved in with me—were pretty traumatized and both are very, very angry. Lily's a sophomore now, doing okay. I insisted on counseling, which she resisted, but she's still going." She blew her nose, fighting tears. "Chloe's another story. She was already at college, living away from home, and kind of out of control.

"I knew she had an alcohol problem—her parents had sent her to rehab at the end of her freshman year—but I wasn't aware of drugs, other than pot, which I assume they all use—"

"Actually, not everyone, but continue."

"I'm not sure what happened after the rehab. Her parents kept it very hush-hush. I'm afraid they assumed rehab solved the problem. She lived back at home that summer, but some things came out after her parents' deaths to suggest they were preoccupied with their own issues right before the attack and not paying much attention to the girls."

"Were you aware of any suicide attempts before this?" Dr. Choi asked.

"No. Of course, I'm shocked, but at the same time I'm not all that surprised, if that makes any sense."

"Can you explain?"

"So, you know what happened to her parents, and I've already mentioned the wildness—staying out all night, getting involved with unsavory boys and the like—and the drinking. And to top it off, not surprisingly, her grades were poor. She was always on academic probation." She stopped and sighed, twisting the tissue in her lap.

"So, this young lady was not in a good place."

"Not at all, and hasn't been for a while."

"Would you say she was depressed?"

"Probably, but she was so closed off it was hard to tell. Sullen all the time. Not once since her parents were killed have she and I had a serious conversation about what was going on with her. She's resisted all of my attempts to get close to her. She resents that I control the trust fund her parents left—thank God for that—and don't just turn the money over to her completely."

Dr. Choi looked at her watch. "Okay, that information helps. Now we need to decide what'll happen next when she's discharged from ICU—"

"We haven't talked about her medical status yet."

"She's stable right now, out of the coma. Her heart rate, blood pressure and breathing are almost normal, although she's still very sleepy. The good news is it doesn't appear she'll have any long-term effects of the overdose. It looks like she needs treatment for substance abuse, and we'll want to make sure that wherever she goes has excellent mental health treatment available as well. This young woman needs intensive evaluation and counseling. She may be suffering from posttraumatic stress disorder as well as depression."

Elin let out the breath she'd been holding. "In the past, she's been very resistant to acknowledging she has any issues. I'm concerned she won't be receptive to getting treatment."

"What I'd suggest at this point is talking with her, seeing where she's at and how open she is. After that, the three of us can meet and decide what the options are, maybe tomorrow afternoon."

Elin tried to remember if there had ever been a conversation she'd dreaded more than this next one.

Elin walked into Chloe's ICU room, where three other patients lay on beds hooked up to all kinds of machinery, just like Chloe. Lights of different colors blinked. She could hear faint beeping sounds. In the dimmed lighting, she could see Chloe propped up on pillows, her eyes closed, a clear narrow tube coming out of her nose. An IV was attached to her left hand. She'd dyed her black hair white blonde, but three inches of dark roots showed, and it looked greasy, dirty against her pale freckled skin. She appeared to have lost weight. Was she sleeping?

Elin pulled a chair up close to the bed, leaning her arms on the white, flannel blanket covering Chloe, and bowed her head. This seemed like a good moment for a prayer or a conversation with Reed. Ironically, being here made her feel close to him, his last days spent in an ICU much like this one. She begged her racing heart to slow down.

She lay her hand on Chloe's. The girl opened her eyes.

"Is that you, Grandma?"

"It is, Chloe. How're you feeling?"

"Very groggy. I'm sorry, Grandma."

"For what."

"You know what. For putting you through this."

Elin was not about to say, that's okay, because it wasn't. "The main thing is, we need to get you some help, Chloe, to figure out what put you in a place so dark you wanted to take fentanyl."

No response.

Elin struggled to understand what had preceded and maybe caused this fentanyl overdose and possible suicide attempt. "Chloe, you didn't come home this past summer, so what did you do instead?"

"Your house in Scottsdale is not my home. I don't *have* a home. I'm homeless, Grandma. I *lost* my home when I *lost* my parents, remember? Plus, I hate the desert."

Damn. This girl was still so angry.

"Okay. Bad choice of words. I s'pose my house isn't your home." When was she gonna get over this anger? "I'm sure it's hard not having a real home, but the question remains, how did you spend this past summer?"

"I'm an adult and that's, frankly, none of your business."

"Ha!" It slipped out before she could stop it. "An adult is someone who's responsible and makes good decisions and financially supports themselves. Last time I checked you were doing none of those things." She was tempted to remind her who wrote all the checks.

Chloe said nothing. Tears leaked from her eyes.

"I'm sorry," Elin said. "The last thing I said was below the belt. But here's the thing, Chloe. You're a mess. You need help, and my job, whether you like it or not, is to help you."

"I'm such a loser." The faucets really opened. "I couldn't even kill myself."

So, it definitely had been a suicide attempt. Elin got up and moved to the edge of the bed, carefully avoiding the tubes that seemed to come out of everywhere. Chloe scooted over to make room. Elin kept hold of her hand. "I'm so worried about you." She grabbed a tissue and dried Chloe's tears, kissing her on her forehead. It took all of her willpower not to dissolve into tears herself. "Sweetheart, I love you so much. The past couple years have been so, so hard for both of us. Don't forget I lost Grandpa, too. I know that's not the same thing as losing both your mom and dad, but he was the love of my life."

Without warning Chloe's sadness morphed back into anger again. "This whole thing completely sucks."

"It *does* completely suck. I couldn't agree with you more." She decided not to point out how much it sucked to have to take care of two traumatized teenagers, all by yourself, at her age. Instead she said, "We're stuck with each other. Can we try to make the best of it? We've got some decisions to make, and the first one for me right now is figuring out where I'm going to stay tonight. But the big one that we're going to make together is where you're going to go after ICU. So please give that some thought. I'll be back tomorrow."

She rushed to get out of there before her anger drove her to say something else she'd regret. As she closed the door to Chloe's room, a young man—boy really—approached her in the hall, tall and lanky, hunched over, with long, disheveled hair and a thin, straggly beard.

"Are you Chloe's grandmother?"

Taken aback, she answered, "I am."

Big smile. "Hi, I'm her friend, Jayden." He wore baggy bell-bottom blue jeans, frayed at the hem, and a faded, green T-shirt. Black flip-flops comprised his footwear.

"They wouldn't let me see her 'cause I'm not family. How's she doing?"

He looked so scruffy Elin wondered if this guy was her dealer and hesitated to share information with him.

Sensing her reluctance perhaps, he said, "She and I were students together at LA State."

Were?

"I told her not to take that crap, that it was poison. But she wouldn't listen. I'm the one who called 911."

Should she talk to this guy? "She's out of the coma now and doing better. We're hopeful there won't be any long-term damage."

A big grin overtook his face. "Awesome! I was so scared."

"Had Chloe been using fentanyl for long?"

He looked confused.

"Never, as far as I knew. Booze and weed, that's all we did. Well, maybe molly occasionally . . ."

So much for that rehab two years ago.

"Was this the first time she'd ever used it?"

"Yep. And I kept telling her not to! That stuff can kill you."

"Why did she take it, Jayden?"

He looked at her intently. "Is there someplace we can go for a cup of coffee?"

"Sure, good idea. I'm sure the hospital has a coffee shop."

At the nursing station they learned there was a Starbucks on the first floor.

They rode down in the elevator together, not saying a word. Elin's stomach was in knots anticipating what Jayden might have to say. At Starbucks, she bought Jayden's coffee and opted for green tea for herself. They found a quiet corner in the lobby.

"So, Jayden, what do you know about all of this?"

"Chloe, you know, she was really unhappy. She just couldn't accept her parents' death. Like, she was so, so pissed off. Kept saying she hated Muslims. The only time she was at all mellow was after she drank a six-pack and smoked some weed."

No real news there. "I was kind of aware of that. But had something happened recently that made her want to do something more extreme?"

"When she got kicked out of school, that was, like, the last straw."

She blew on her tea, trying to absorb that. Chloe never told her she'd flunked out of college. "When did that happen?"

"End of last semester. She kinda went, like, downhill after that."

What? Elin had sent a huge check for tuition and living expenses, thousands of dollars. What had happened to that money?

"What has she been doing since that time? Where has she been living?"

"We've been crashing with some friends of mine in Malibu."

She tried to keep her voice even. "Is there anything else I should know?"

"Not really. I don't think so. What's going to happen now?"

"I'm not sure. She needs a lot of help. We'll be talking with the psychiatrist tomorrow to figure that out." She had to get out of there and find a hotel. "Thanks for talking with me."

"Tell her I said hi, okay?"

"I will."

The next morning Elin returned to ICU, but no Chloe. A quick trip to the nursing station revealed she'd been transferred to a regular floor. She took the elevator down to four. At the nursing station, she asked them to page Dr. Choi to meet her in room 409, deciding to wait outside until the psychiatrist arrived so they could go in together.

Ten minutes later Dr. Choi arrived, and they walked into Chloe's new room together. She was sitting up when they walked in, looking at a magazine.

"Hi, Chloe. How're you feeling today?" Elin asked.

"Much better. Not so out of it."

"Glad to hear it." She sat at the end of Chloe's bed. "I met your friend Jayden yesterday. He's worried about you."

Chloe shot her a wary look.

"He said a couple of interesting things."

"Like what?" That sullen tone immediately returned.

"Let's see, where to start? First, he said he had warned you about using fentanyl, but you wouldn't listen. But most interesting was that you got kicked out of LA State at the end of last semester—"

"Grandma, I can explain."

"I'm not done yet. I found that interesting since I'd sent a huge check for tuition, fees, and monthly living expenses for you. Okay, now it's your turn."

Chloe's eyes flashed. "Okay, you're right, I should've told you those shits kicked me out. They refused to accept that having your parents killed was a good excuse for failing courses—"

Dr. Choi had been observing the interaction between Elin and Chloe and said, "Maybe that meant you shouldn't be in school until you'd dealt with that."

"And I wasn't in school!"

"Yes, but you never bothered to tell me, so I sent all the money," Elin said. Should she play hardball? She had powerful leverage, but did she have the balls to use it?

"Here's the thing Chloe. That money in your trust fund is for your education, and if you're no longer in school I can't financially support you—"

"Wait, what? That's my money!"

"Not until you reach thirty, it isn't."

If you reach thirty.

"What am I supposed to live on?"

"As I see it, there are a couple of options," Elin said, casting a quick glance at Dr. Choi's expressionless face. "Option number one is you go into a twenty-eight-day substance abuse program with good mental health services—"

"Who's going to pay for that?"

"There's plenty of money in your trust fund to cover that—"

"You said that was for my education."

"It is, but I have a good deal of discretion about how it's used. Unless you get sober and deal with your mental health problems, there'll be no education."

Chloe sat with her arms crossed, lips pursed. A scowl covered her face. Not thrilled with option one.

Elin continued. "Option number two is you come back to Scottsdale to live with me and your sister. And you enroll in intensive outpatient treatment. There's an extra bedroom for you, and you can even use Grandpa's old car. But if you're living under my roof, I will insist on random drug and alcohol testing." She stole a quick look at Dr. Choi who responded with a slight nod of agreement.

"That is so unfair. I can't believe you don't trust me."

"Chloe, I love you very much, and I want you to get better. But you're right. At the moment, I don't trust you. You have drug and alcohol and mental health issues. If you can stop drinking and using drugs and behave in a trustworthy manner, I'll start to trust you again. At that point, we can talk about community college or other options. But first, you're gonna have to clean up your act."

Still pouting, Chloe said not a word.

Meanwhile, Dr. Choi had a big smile on her face, which Elin hoped meant she had done well.

Hearing nothing more from Chloe, Elin got up. "If you want to talk, I'll be here for the rest of the day. You can let me know your decision. I'll stop in tomorrow morning before I get on the road." She walked over to Chloe's bed and leaned in to give her a quick kiss and hug. But Chloe turned away and rebuffed her. Annoyed, but not surprised, Elin turned on her heel and marched out of the room, Dr. Choi trailing behind her.

"Well done," Dr. Choi said. "If I didn't know better, I'd have thought you had training in tough love."

Elin fought tears and trembled. "That was so damn hard. I feel like an ogre, but I saw how that girl's parents mollycoddled her, and look where that got us." She wiped a tear from her left cheek. "But I meant every word of it."

"Good for you," Dr. Choi said. "Because if she comes to live with you, you're going to need to be tough as nails."

Oh boy. "What I'm most scared of is she won't go for option one or option two, and then what? Left to her own devices, she's lost."

"I think she knows that," Dr. Choi said. "I think she's going to go for option two."

Elin drove back to the Marriott. She needed a long walk. With advice from the concierge, she got back into the car and found a lovely park. While she walked, she phoned Basia to see how things were going in Scottsdale and gave her the update on Chloe's status. She found it reassuring to learn that everything back home—Lily, dog, and cats—was fine. And Basia approved of her strategy for dealing with Chloe, so that was affirming. She found a cute outdoor café and ate a nice halibut dinner. After she returned to the hotel, she watched a movie on her iPad and read before turning in for the night. Another big day tomorrow.

She rose on Saturday morning after a good night's sleep, checked out of the hotel, and drove back to the hospital. Would Chloe agree to go into treatment or agree to live with her in Scottsdale? What might happen to her if she rejected both options? Don't go down that road, Elin warned herself.

She rode the elevator to the fourth floor and walked down the hall to Chloe's room. With her hand on the door handle, she took a deep breath, then another, and opened the door.

The bed was empty, made up with new sheets and blanket all tucked in. Did she have the wrong room? She checked the number: 409. Nope, correct room. She walked down the hall to the nursing station and waited for the clerk to get off the phone. Why they had moved her granddaughter again?

"Whew," the young clerk said. "Some people." She looked up at Elin. "Can I help you?"

"Yes, I'm looking for Chloe Satterwhite. She was in room 409 yesterday. Has she been moved?"

"Hmm, let's see. Satterwhite. Here we go. She left at about seven-thirty this morning AMA."

"AMA?"

"Sorry, against medical advice. Meaning she left before the doctor officially discharged her."

Shit. Wasn't that just like Chloe? Now what? She stood there thinking about her next move. Finally, she decided to consult with the psychiatrist. "Can you page Dr. Choi?"

Ms. Flores, according to her name tag, consulted yet another binder and said, "Sorry, she's off today. Is this an emergency?"

"I'm not sure . . ."

"There's another psychiatrist on duty. Shall I page him?"

Elin thought about that. Would it make sense to talk to someone unfamiliar with Chloe's case, starting from scratch to explain what was going on? Nah, might just as well get on the road.

"No, thanks."

As she walked back to the car, she tried Chloe's cellphone number. Went straight to voicemail. No surprise there. When she tried to leave a message, she was told Chloe's voicemail was full. Finally, she left a text saying how worried she was and how much she loved Chloe.

Was there any point in trying to track her down? Other than Malibu, she had no clue where Chloe lived or where she might have gone. It appeared she had made her choice, not selecting option one or option two. Chloe chose option three, whatever that meant.

Elin limped into the house, sore from the long drive back. Basia and Lily sat in the kitchen, finishing a pizza. Witnessing this normal domestic scene after the craziness of the hospital was a blessing.

"Welcome back. How'd it go?" Basia asked. "You look exhausted."

"I am." Elin plopped down, uncertain how honest she should be in front of Lily. This family had had its fill of secrets though. No more. She heaved a big sigh. "Not so good."

"What d'you mean?" Lily said. "Is Chloe okay?"

Both looked at her expectantly. "I honestly don't know." She summarized what happened. "In the end, she left against medical advice. I told her I wasn't going to financially support her unless she took one of the two choices I gave her. It looks like she rejected both. I have no idea where she is or what she's going to do. She won't answer her phone, and you can't leave a message. I'm worried sick."

Elin peppered Lily with questions about what she thought Chloe might do. Bottom line: Lily had no idea. Never close to Chloe, she hadn't had much contact with her sister over the past year and was as much in the dark as Elin was about what she might be up to.

Elin grabbed a piece of cold pizza, but it tasted like cardboard in her mouth. She thanked Basia again for staying with Lily, hugged her goodbye, and turned in.

In her bedroom, with the door closed, Elin pulled out a family photo album. She started at the beginning, when they were babies, and studied various photos of the girls over the years. Baby pictures. Lily as a toddler, on her first day of pre-school. Chloe starting kindergarten, in a cute little red-plaid dress. Lily learning to ride a two-wheel bike, with skinned knees. Chloe and Lily with Cocoa, the family's chocolate lab. Chloe in front of the fireplace, on the way to her first prom, all dressed up with her boyfriend, both grinning madly. The whole family on a vacation in Hawaii.

Reed, she thought, how did we ever get to this point? What happened to this family? I'm afraid I blew it. Tough love didn't work. I don't know if Chloe will ever get better. She's not a bad kid, but she's so lost. I don't know what to do to help her, other than to leave the door open.

Kirsten's words echoed in her ears. "Elin, despite what you think, you can't save everyone."

November arrived with no word from Chloe. Both Elin and Lily tried Chloe's cellphone repeatedly, left text messages, to no avail. The police were no help—Chloe was not a minor. Elin had no idea where to turn. She spoke to the family's estate lawyer back in Maryland, but he had no suggestions. She made an appointment with her own therapist, who tried to assuage her guilt, pointing out Elin had done everything a reasonable person could. She counseled Elin to accept her powerlessness and to focus instead on taking care of herself and Lily. Elin considered hiring a private detective to search for Chloe and waited every day for a phone call that someone had found her dead.

At nine o'clock on a Saturday night in mid-November, the doorbell rang. Lily was out with some friends, and Elin was already in her nightgown getting ready to get into bed and read. Who could possibly be at the door at that hour? Instantly, she started to worry something had happened to Lily.

She rushed to the door, and there stood Chloe and Jayden, both looking bedraggled. A beat-up old Toyota sat in the driveway. Chloe looked emaciated, hip bones poking through her black leggings, even thinner than she'd looked at the hospital. Her hair hung in strings. She didn't say a word.

Oh, dear god, she looks terrible.

Jayden, dressed in the same bell bottoms and a black T-shirt, said, "Hi, Mrs. Bergstrom."

He remembered her last name? "Come on in, you two."

Still standing in the foyer, Jayden continued, "Chloe has something to say."

Elin waited, stunned, confusion covering her face.

"I need help, Grandma. I'm a total mess." Her eyes darted around the foyer. She looked terrified and started to cry.

Elin hugged Chloe's skeletal frame, and Jayden piped up with, "Chloe said you wouldn't mind if I stayed the night, 'cause that was a super long drive! Geez, you've got a really nice place here. I sure wouldn't mind living here."

Not gonna happen, Jayden.

Elin studied Chloe's pale face. "Sweetheart, it's so good to see you. I'm so glad you're okay." *Was she okay?* "Have you got more stuff in the car?"

Chloe nodded.

"Jayden, can you go get the rest of her stuff?" As Jayden returned to the car, Elin put her arm around Chloe. "Let's go into the kitchen. I'll bet you guys are starved."

Now the real work would begin.

About the Author

Bonnie E. Carlson was born and grew up in Central Connecticut. Before her junior year in high school, she had life-changing experience when she was selected to travel to Malaysia and live there with a family. Among other things, it gave her the experience of being in the minority, though white, and learning another language. This adventure led her to major in Asian Studies at the University of Michigan in Ann Arbor, providing an opportunity to learn about the Midwest.

After completing a master's degree in social work and a Ph.D. in Social Work and Developmental Psychology, also at the University of Michigan, she became a professor at the University at Albany, State University New York, where she remained for 28 years. There she taught graduate social work students and conducted research on domestic violence, child abuse, sibling sexual abuse, the impact of incarceration on families, and related topics. Toward the end of her tenure there, her focus shifted to studying factors affecting relapse in women trying to recover from drug and alcohol abuse.

After falling in love with the desert in Scottsdale and Phoenix, AZ, she took a faculty position at Arizona State University, where she stayed until she retired.

After retiring, she pivoted to writing fiction. Her short fiction has been published in literary magazines such as *The Normal School, Broadkill Review, Foliate Oak, Down in the Dirt, Across the Margin,* and *Blue Lake Review.* Now she lives with her husband, dog and too many cats in Scottsdale, AZ and writes fiction and hikes to her heart's content in the beautiful Sonoran desert.

Made in the USA
Middletown, DE
12 February 2021

33584173R00175